a

THE SPEED OF LIGHT

THE
SPEED
OF
LIGHT

A NOVEL

Elizabeth Rosner

BALLANTINE BOOKS
NEW YORK

A Ballantine Book
Published by The Ballantine Publishing Group

Copyright © 2001 Elizabeth Rosner

www.ballantinebooks.com

Library of Congress Cataloging-in-Publication Data
Rosner, Elizabeth.
The speed of light: a novel / Elizabeth Rosner.
p.   cm.
ISBN 0-345-44224-5
1. Brothers and sisters—Fiction. 2. Holocaust, Jewish (1939—1945)—Fiction. 3.
Americans—Hungary—Fiction. 4. Budapest (Hungary)—Fiction. 5. Fathers—Death—
Fiction. 6. Women singers—Fiction. 7. Housekeepers—Fiction. 8. Scientists—Fiction.
I. Title.
PS3618.O845 S64 2001
813.'6—dc21
2001035331

TEXT DESIGN BY C. LINDA DINGLER

Manufactured in the United States of America

First Edition: September 2001

10   9   8   7   6   5   4   3   2   1

In memory of my mother

ACKNOWLEDGMENTS

I am grateful beyond measure to the many Holocaust survivors who have generously shared their testimonies, both orally and through their writing. My thanks go also to the many children of survivors whose stories have both reflected and illuminated my own.

Many books assisted me in the research for this novel, including *The Concise Oxford Dictionary of Opera*, *The Penguin Dictionary of Science*, *Taking the Quantum Leap* by Fred Alan Wolf, *A Dictionary of Physics*, edited by John Daintith, and *Physical Thought from the Presocratics to the Quantum Physicists*, edited by Shmuel Sambursky. I am especially indebted to Mark Danner, author of *The Massacre at El Mozote*, for his inspiring and courageous reporting.

Boundless gratitude to my agent, Joelle Delbourgo, whose enthusiasm and expertise created miracles; to my editor, Dan Smetanka, for his wisdom, sensitivity, encouragement, and insight; and to Gina Centrello, for her passionate commitment.

Finally, my heartfelt thanks to the family members and friends whose love and support sustained me through the years of writing this book.

Hasidic teaching says there are three ways to mourn:
through tears, through silence,
and by turning sorrow into song.

ONE

THE CHANGES began on a Wednesday, *miércoles*, the day that sounds like miracles.

My younger and only sister, Paula, had gone away, leaving the apartment directly below mine to test the reach of her voice. I stayed behind, with my eleven televisions, waiting for her to come back.

I was teaching myself not to feel.

In the room with the televisions, there were no voices: I had silenced them all. Instead I heard: a clock that ticked like a snapping twig; the hum and push of cars passing on the street; a neighbor's dog barking at the arrival of mail; the refrigerator purring; my own breath, in and out. All the rhythms, in and out. And inside my head: a melody from before, when my sister trained her voice to soar, when I listened to the notes float and resonate. I believed sometimes that I could see them.

Paula was auditioning, sending her hopeful music into the arms of Copenhagen, Prague, Vienna—places I had never seen and never expected to. I lived in the safe embrace of my apartment, whose windows overlooked a park and a playground and a street.

I had collected broken televisions and fixed them, one by one, sometimes guessing at the way to put things back together. I had no manuals to follow, no map. I made good guesses, I had a feel for those things, a kind of blind instinct. In the end, they all worked, although the colors were never exactly right. Some were always a little too green, others a little too violet. It didn't matter. The scratchy growl of their voices didn't matter either, because I often kept them very quiet. I spent most of my time watching the images, letting them tell me stories. I let them distract me from every terrible truth until nothing touched me at all.

It was never a decision, never something I asked for. It simply belonged to me, like a second skin. No. Like my only skin. There was no choice, no letting go. And if there had been the chance to refuse?

If I'd been asked?

I would still say yes.

It was my father's grief. It was what he gave to me, his only son. He didn't mean to, but it came to me without his permission. He gave up his language and his homeland, everything he could leave behind. But he carried his sadness with him, under his skin like blood. It wasn't his fault. He would have taken it back if he could. But it was mine now, as if I had lived it all.

At times, even my dreams felt inherited, as if someone else had owned them first. There would be dogs barking, murderous voices in the distance, smoke filling the dark air.

His actual stories I never heard. My father held all the shards of glass inside, where the edges cut him to pieces. When he looked at me, it was not so much into my eyes as through them, as if I were a clear window to the past. I looked back at him, I listened to the wordless dark. What else could I do? I believed this was what I was here for, to be the receiver of that gaze, to swallow it completely. The broken glass? I swallowed that too.

Here is what I knew how to do: how to get away. How to save myself by taking flight, by vanishing. My voice was a ticket of escape, one way to anywhere but where I was. I tried to take my brother, Julian, with me, to help him escape too, but it was more weight than I could carry. Only one of us could make it out alive. I didn't choose myself, not exactly, but the truth was, I had a ticket and he didn't. I had to use it or die.

"I'M GOING away for a while," Paula had announced the previous Monday over lunch. For once she didn't try to prepare me for a shock. "I'm taking myself on a Grand Tour," she explained, her arms flourishing, "hoping some opera company will give me a chance. According to my agent, I'm going to become quite famous." She sighed a little, eager or worried, I couldn't be sure.

"When?" I asked.

She came over to my chair and wrapped her slender arms around herself wishing, I knew, that she could hug me with them but knowing I couldn't bear it.

"I'll miss you too," she whispered, not looking at me. Then, in another voice she added, "I leave this Wednesday, early in the morning." She struck a dramatic pose, one arm up and one to the side, her head thrown back to expose her ivory neck. "I'll write you postcards," she said.

I would place them beneath my pillow and memorize them in my sleep. I would dream in languages I'd never heard.

At the door of my apartment, leaving, Paula stopped with her hand on the doorknob. "What's it like, Julian? What's it like to live inside your body?" She leaned against the door frame, frowning a little, waiting for me to answer.

I aimed my gaze above her head, at the place where the wall met the ceiling. In two days she would be gone. "It's very quiet," I said.

"Quiet," she repeated softly. From the corner of my eye I could see her frown grow deeper. She didn't know what I was talking about.

"What's inside yours?" I asked her.

She shrugged and said, "Music."

I nodded. "Think of plants," I said. "They're breathing and growing, eating and drinking. We just can't hear them."

Paula looked at me, and I tried to look back, tried to stay right there with her. She was far enough away that I couldn't see the color of her eyes.

"No wonder you have to be so careful," she said. "They'd have you for breakfast out there."

"Who?" I asked, although I knew who.

"All of them," Paula said, shaking her head. "Every goddamn one."

Every goddamn one, I silently repeated. Then out loud I said, "I wonder what I'd taste like," and Paula flashed that wide-open smile of hers.

"Like sweet potatoes," she said.

"In bocca al lupo," I said to Julian before I left. Mouth of the wolf. It was backstage code from the Italians, their way of saying break a leg. I blew a kiss into the air, not aiming at his face but somewhere high, over his head, where he wouldn't be afraid of it.

"Forget the wolf," he said back to me the way he was supposed to, the signal for courage and faith. But Julian needed it more than I did. He must have thought I was always leaving him, as if it were easy for me. I opened doors and slammed them behind me, never letting myself check if anything had cracked from the blow.

O N T H E morning of Paula's flight to Europe, I stood by the window in the early light and watched a white taxicab pull up in front of our building. Paula stood beside the trunk while the driver loaded her luggage, and a breeze lifted the ends of her dark green scarf as she turned to look up at my window. Her lips were painted the color of raspberries. She waved and smiled, tucking the scarf into the collar of her coat. I put my hand flat against the smooth glass and held it there. Paula disappeared behind the opaque windows of the taxi, and then the taxi disappeared too. Below me, the ginkgo tree was full of green, fluttering its fan-shaped leaves.

I adjusted all the sets, fine-tuning their brightness and vertical hold, wiping the electric dust from their screens. I turned up the volume for a while, filling my room with too many voices, all of them and none of them talking to me. Inside, where I lived, it was still very quiet.

My earliest memory is the sound of crying—my father waking up from a nightmare. Or was it my brother? A nameless sobbing in the dark. Julian told me I cooed like a bird before I learned to

speak; I made my mouth into an *O* and I began, with no reason,
to sing.

When I was still very young, before my mother died, we kept a
pair of canaries in a cage by the kitchen window; at night, the cage
was covered with a towel. Such a simple script: In the daylight,
they sang, and at night, they slept. I used to wonder if they knew
that outside the window lay a world they could never reach.

A T E X A C T L Y one o'clock on that Wednesday of Paula's departure, a cola-skinned woman came to my door with a lunch tray. I had
been warned by my sister to expect her; Paula knew better than to surprise me twice in one week. Still, though I'd already unlatched the door
for her, I felt unprepared for her arrival, needing to back away and sit
again in my leather chair. I was holding my breath, waiting for her to
go away.

Standing in the doorway, before she entered the apartment, she took a
slow look around. I found out later that she was taking photographs in
her mind of where everything belonged, even me in my chair, even the
way the cords of the televisions snaked across the floor. She was taking
care of Paula's apartment for the month, and she was bringing me a sandwich for lunch. Paula had shown her just how much mustard to spread,
just how to place the pieces of cut bread on the plate, how to fold the
napkin. Without the design on the plate I couldn't eat, I couldn't even
take a bite.

He could drown in a glass of water, the woman thought.

It was what she told me much later, that this was her first thought
when she saw me. But what she said out loud was, "My name is Sola."

I guessed her to be close to Paula's age, maybe thirty, but I wasn't about
to study her face, even from safely across the room. Instead, I imagined
myself as she must have seen me: pale and elongated, my brown hair un-
evenly trimmed, my disheveled clothing, my sleeves too short, exposing
my bony wrists. On Paula, the related features were so photogenic: liquid
blue eyes and a full-smiling mouth, a heart-shaped face, brown hair that
fell in a sweet disorder of waves. In mirrors I had discovered that my own

version was blurrier, less coherent, stretched too far. Behind my glasses, I felt Sola watch me.

She offered the tray to me exactly the way Paula must have shown her. She didn't even try to look me in the eye when she introduced herself, and I was grateful. I thought Paula must have told her that too.

Did I need to say that my name was Julian? I decided it wasn't necessary, so I said nothing and began to eat my sandwich. Avocado and Swiss. Sola walked toward the kitchen to collect Paula's dishes from the week before. As always, I'd washed and dried and stacked them beside the sink, with the silverware wrapped in a paper towel on top of the pile. I heard Sola's footsteps pause, begin again, and then stop.

"Excuse me," she said, forcing me to turn around in my seat. I saw her eyebrows lifting on her forehead, her mouth stretched into an almost-smile. She was holding the pile of dishes out in front of her, her brown hands dark against the white ceramic. "You do not have to wash these," she said. "I can come back later and do them downstairs with my own washing up."

This was her first mistake, although I knew she meant well. I shook my head, my mouth full of sandwich. She had an accent I couldn't quite place. I chewed and swallowed, completing what I had begun, and turned back to take a gulp of water. Still turned away from her, I thought about how many words it would take to explain things.

"I like to," I told her.

I think she said "Oh," and then she did a surprising thing: She laughed. It was very quiet, but I heard the flutter in her throat. I thought a long time afterwards about that laugh. There was a song buried inside it, or a story. Maybe both.

At first I am at Paula's apartment once a week to clean, which is easy because even though she seems not to care about how she scatters her clothing and leaves piles of papers around the rooms, in fact there is a kind of order in her mess. Once I learn her system, once I memorize each room, I am able to clean around her things without disturbing them. When I am finished, it is like nothing is changed but looks like everything belongs exactly where it is.

She gives me my own key because most of the time when I come on Friday afternoons she is somewhere else, singing. The first time I see her brother, Julian, he is on the sidewalk in front of the building, staring for maybe half an hour at a tree twice as high as his head. I am cleaning Paula's living room, and I see him from the window.

It is the end of October, and the leaves on this tree are a beautiful shade of yellow, the color of an egg yolk. Julian stands in one place very close to the tree, close enough to touch it, but not touching it. The yellow seems to splash onto his face. He just stands there, not moving, for all the time it takes me to vacuum and dust. I see that the tree is starting to drop its leaves onto the ground, and there is a pool of yellow at the foot of the tree that Julian looks down at, like someone doing a study, like he is trying to make sense of something. He has his hands in his pockets, and he is wearing a black sweater and a pair of blue jeans, his hair is blowing from the breeze.

I take that picture of him in my mind and carry it around with me the rest of the time I am cleaning and part of the next day too, the yellow of the leaves, Julian's face covered with light. When I come back the following Friday, the beautiful pool of leaves is even bigger than before, and I am glad no one is sweeping them away but letting them keep drifting there as the tree gives itself up. And what I feel is that the tree is dying and alive at the same time.

Other times I hear him walking around upstairs in his apartment, with sudden bursts of noise that seem like a crowd of people coming from nowhere. At first I think it is the radio—he is looking for a certain kind of music and catching a hundred different waves of sound—but Paula tells me the first time we talk about her brother, that he has a collection of televisions up there, eleven of them, I think she says.

"He doesn't usually keep the sound on," she says, trying to make it seem like this is just a normal thing, to have eleven televisions in one apartment. The look on her face tells me something else, that she is worried about him.

I nod. Eleven televisions and one golden tree.

I STACKED the boxy televisions with precision: two rows of four and one row of three, as close to square as I could get them. Some had scratchy fake-wood casings, and a few were missing a knob or a dial. My chair faced them head-on, as if I were the conductor instead of the audience. Sometimes I kept all eleven sets tuned to the same station; games like soccer and basketball were tapestries of leaping bodies and balls arcing through the air. But on the Wednesday that Sola appeared, I had eleven different channels, a giant animated quilt that flickered and danced without any meaning.

After she left the apartment, I finished my sandwich and washed the dishes, briefly picturing Sola directly below me in Paula's kitchen, with her hands in the soapy water too, both of us dipping and rinsing, making things clean. Behind me, a wall of two-dimensional people were talking and gesturing and crying and fighting, there and not there, held back by glass. I turned my back and they didn't notice, didn't care.

Singing was the only gift I could offer to my father, who seemed to live so far from the rest of us, even though we shared the same rooms. I loved those rare moments I was able to make him smile, the way his face cracked into lines and his eyes squeezed almost closed with pleasure. Whatever had happened to him back there, during the war, was wrapped in silence. So I filled the house with music. I tried to give him joy.

Mostly, though, his joy was as hidden from us as his past, the childhood he must have had but never described to us. Something told me not to ask, not to wonder out loud, and eventually I stopped wondering altogether. I focused instead on my mother, imitating the way she danced to the music that poured from a radio on the kitchen counter, the way she sang to me her sleepy

wordless tunes at night. I learned the names of the notes from her;
I learned how to sing in the dark.

ON THURSDAY, as always, I did my errands, timing my steps
from corner to corner, relentlessly measuring my territory. There were
three homeless men to whom I gave a dollar each, and I gave two dollars
to the blind woman in front of the produce market who collected for
the free clinic. She sat with her cane leaning against the edge of her chair
and an open book in her broad lap; its pages were the color of supermarket bags and her fingers swept across the dots of Braille, barely
touching them. There was a battery-powered radio on the ground by
her feet playing classical music very quietly. When I stuffed my carefully folded bills into the slot of her battered metal collection box, she
kept her face tipped upward and her eyes sealed when she murmured
"Thank you."

Frank's Kosher Deli was the farthest point from my apartment. Although I had experimented with different times of day for my visits,
eventually I learned that Frank's was crowded all day long; it took all my
concentration to keep clear of the crush of other bodies and demands. I
waited for a number with a seven in it, then held my body perfectly still
against a far wall until it was my turn. Frank, behind the counter, always
greeted me as if I had just returned from a long trip.

"Mr. Perel!" he shouted above the din. A solid wall of people pressed
close to me, aiming for the display case's cold cuts and salads.

"What can we get for you today?" Frank asked. He must have been
in his late sixties but still had a full head of hair and a set of even white
teeth lined up in his mouth. He kept a number-two pencil tucked behind
one ear to take phone orders. A deep note in his voice made me imagine
he lifted weights or rode a bicycle, something like that.

"My usual," I said, and he repeated it back to me.

"Large soup and half a broiled chicken, am I right?"

"Right," I said.

"What kinda soup you want today?" he asked.

"Surprise me," I said. It was a joke between us that he had started, because there were no surprises in the soup. His wife made the same weekly menu: split pea on Monday and Friday, onion on Tuesday, beef noodle on Wednesday, vegetable on Thursday, lentil on Sunday. On Saturdays they were closed.

"Good appetite, Mr. Perel!" Frank said when he handed me my order, and then he turned to his next customer, calling out the number like it was a winner. I held the bag in my right hand and paid with my left, always watching to make sure my feet stayed inside the green tiles of the deli floor, never touching the black ones around the edges.

On Saturdays I picked up a to-go order from a Chinese restaurant two blocks from my building. I kept a copy of the menu at home, although I had long ago stopped pretending to explore the choices. A small, moon-faced woman at the cash register served me jasmine tea in a palm-sized ceramic cup while I waited for my mixed vegetables fried rice. At home, I had my own set of chopsticks that Paula had given me one year as a birthday present. On one side of my refrigerator, I taped a collection of my fortunes, a story of the lucky world.

When Paula tells me she is going away, my first thought is that I have to find another client to make up for the lost money. But then she surprises me by asking if I want to stay in her apartment for one month while she is gone.

"I know your studio must be small," she says.

"Yes," I say, "but it is enough room for me."

"And the neighborhood," she goes on. "Doesn't it frighten you to live there? The drugs and the gangs? . . ."

I lower my head. She has no idea what it is like to hear gunshots in the night. I am not in fear for my own life, I am only reliving the other time, again and again. It is the sound that is trying to kill me too.

"You don't have to decide right away," Paula says. "But I just want you to know that you'd be doing me a huge favor. And, helping my brother too . . ." Her cheeks turn the color of plums. "That's the other part of the story, you see. I'd need you to do a couple of things for him, things I do sometimes to help him out. . . ."

"Things?" I ask.

"Nothing difficult," she says quickly. "Just things like making him lunches from time to time and basically checking to make sure he's all right. He keeps so much to himself . . . and I worry about him. . . ."

"I see," I say, although I do not really see. All I know about him is that he is standing next to a golden tree without moving, and that he stays inside with eleven televisions for company.

"Will you think about it?" Paula asks me.

I tell her I can think. That night, cooking beans in my small kitchen and trying not to listen to the people fighting in the next-door apartment, I understand again how this building is not a good place for me. It smells of very old cigarette smoke and some kind of food that I know comes from the Asian market down the street; my neighbors never say hello to each other or even smile once in a while. Everything is dark and close together and unhappy.

When I go to clean houses I am relieved to get into the air and the light; when I come home at night all I want to do is get into my bed and sleep. For a long time Warren, the American doctor, is trying to find me a better place to live, but I can take no more help from him. Seeing his face causes me to remember the hospital, and the hospital makes me think of everything from before. I want to clean myself like the window of a house, make myself clear for things to pass through. Nothing but a smooth surface between one place and another place. Flat and quiet.

"But a window is an opening," the voice of my grandmother whispers to me in my dreams. "A window lets the world inside. Without windows you cannot breathe," says my grandmother. She spreads her arms.

"In this country, windows are made from glass," I tell her, trying to explain. "They stop the air. Sometimes they break."

My grandmother shakes her head but keeps her arms wide. She

smiles at the way I cannot understand. "You know," she says. "A true window is always open. It never breaks."

My grandmother often visits my dreams. She is the only one who comes to me from the land of the dead, and she speaks to me in the language I no longer speak. When my grandmother touches my hair in my sleep, I feel like a lost child. There is never enough of her to comfort me.

"I can stay in your place," I say to Paula's machine. "Tell me when I can come."

I hold the phone in my hand and wait for the recorder to gather my voice. Paula hears it later, when I am doing something else, when I am perhaps ready to change my mind. But the machine plays one note and turns off. It gives me nothing back.

S O L A   C A M E back again on Friday, even though she wasn't supposed to. Exactly at one, she climbed the stairs and knocked at my door, tray outstretched. I was caught completely unprepared this time, unable to say anything when I opened the door. I noticed how wide and flat her face was, how her cheekbones and dark brows seemed to follow the same curving lines. For some reason, I thought she had recently been crying.

"Excuse me," she said, just like the last time. "Is it not closed up in here? Perhaps there is not enough air." She walked into the apartment and put down the tray, while I retreated to my chair. I wondered again about her accent; when she spoke, her hands moved through the air like birds.

"It's Friday," I said to her. "*Viernes.*" But my words came out too quietly.

"A window?" she said, crossing toward the one nearest my chair. "I should open it?"

Before I had time to stop her, Sola had unlocked the window, heaved it open, and leaned out. "Yes!" she announced to the street and to me, "Much better!"

The breeze touched my face with a rush; the window hadn't been opened in years, and it was as if the room had been waiting for a chance to inhale. I smelled fresh-cut grass and something sweeter, a flower I couldn't name. Sola's black hair caught the light and gleamed like it was wet, like it was alive. I had never seen anything like it in my life.

I shivered, although it wasn't cold, and Sola said, "Now you can breathe in here a little." I heard her laughter again, the flutter in her throat. She spread her arms like wings, and I sneezed. Three times.

Sola turned toward me with a look of surprise. "You are allergic?" she asked.

I sneezed a fourth time but shook my head. My eyes were watering by now, and I pulled a handkerchief from my pocket. "I'm not used to it," I managed, blowing my nose and dabbing at my eyes. Sola's smile looked so benign I could almost believe that the gaping hole behind her was harmless, too, just a space where a windowpane had been, an opening to let in particles of air and light.

"Are you okay?" she asked, and when she made a move toward me, to touch me, I had to leap up from my chair. She pulled her hand back quickly, as if from a fire, and I stuffed the handkerchief back into my pocket.

"I'm sorry," I mumbled, looking at the floor. "It's Friday. I just can't . . ." The sentence couldn't be finished, there were too many ways to complete it.

I heard Sola pull the window closed, pressing out the air like a sigh. "Never mind," she said. The brief sounds and fragrances of the street were sealed once again behind the window, and Sola stood beside my chair, beckoning me back to it. I saw in the deep impressions that the dark brown leather had memorized the shape of my body.

Sola pointed to the seat. "Look, it is waiting for you!" she said, and took a step back, giving me room. "Your friend," she said quietly, and after retrieving the pile of clean dishes she headed out the door and back downstairs.

Learning a new language for the names of things in the world brings me back into my hands. I touch a table and say table, hold a piece of bread to my lips and say the word bread. It is the way to think of everything right now, like the world gets created over and over as I look at it and place my fingers on its surfaces. No names from yesterday or the years before this one, as if nothing is true except this moment. *Table. Bread. River.* Now I am sleeping and now I am awake, I wash the dishes and dry them with a blue towel. I cut my fingernails and brush my teeth, the sun pours circles of light onto the floor, a lemon sits in a white bowl, water boils on the stove. I drink coffee from a mug the color of the ocean, the kitchen faucet drips three times and stops, Julian's footsteps move across the ceiling over my head.

Today is Wednesday. The sky is wearing a gray dress. Rain leans against the window. I am climbing the stairs of the river, one at a time, one at a time.

T H E   D A Y after Sola came on the wrong day, my apartment felt too big. I pulled my chair closer to the televisions, immediately felt all wrong in my space. Like the map was folded against the crease. I put the chair back, exactly in its carpet dents, my feet in their original shadows. I adjusted the blinds a fraction of an inch, changed the angles of light, changed them back. My molecules were jumpy and disturbed, excited electrons in high orbit. I drank two glasses of water standing at the sink, washed the glass, dried and replaced it. I straightened all the stacks of dishes in the cabinet, four white dinner plates, four salad plates, four bowls. I counted the spoons in the drawer, brushed invisible crumbs from the counter. Threw away a sponge.

The more confined an atom, the more the subatomic particles are set into motion.

I tried to imagine Paula's voice, the waves of it coming through my heating vents. I leaned against the refrigerator to feel it vibrate against my shoulder, the cold white creature humming in my dreams. She was so far away, and singing to strangers. I read my fortunes for company, reminding myself there was luck in the world in spite of everything. Prizes and good news were on their way to me, friends were thinking about me, I would resolve a conflict very soon. The refrigerator played a low note, but I couldn't name its frequency.

At infinity, even parallel lines touch.

Physics floated in my head. Tendencies to exist. Tendencies to occur. "In the zone of middle dimensions," I wrote in an imaginary letter to Paula, "in the realm of our daily experience, Newtonian physics is still a useful theory. We are solid material bodies occupying empty space. It comforts us to believe this."

TWO

EVERY MORNING I drank one cup of green tea, strong with the taste of leaves. I couldn't tolerate coffee; it made me jumpy and gave my body a stutter. My movements would get stuck in a twitch of jerky motion, no forward progress until I backed up and started over. And coffee made me sleepy too, made me want to collapse into bed in the middle of the day or pass out in my chair or even drop onto my forehead at my desk in the midst of a sentence.

Something about Sola's arrival triggered a restlessness in me, like a hundred cups of coffee. Or was it Paula's departure? Hard to tell because they coincided. But it was a disturbing sensation, to be unable to remain in my chair watching the wall of televisions, or at my desk for anything longer than half an hour, or at the window gazing out toward the street.

Suddenly I felt I had to be in some kind of motion, and even a walk couldn't be enough because I needed a purpose, a direction. Aimless strolling was impossible, I felt everyone could tell I had nowhere to go. It was in my gait or the way my hands stayed in my pockets, the tilt of my head. I had to invent reasons for myself, tasks that required my feet to travel from Point A to Point Q and back again. I tried constructing a new dictionary of errands, L for laundry and T for tea and B for bank and G for groceries. W for waiting, U for uncertainty, C for confusion, catastrophe, collisions. I had collided with an open doorway, space where there had always been a solid wall. *Now what,* I kept asking myself, *What now?*

gegenschein: counter glow; a faint elliptical patch of light
in the sky that may be observed at night directly opposite
the Sun, caused by a reflection of sunlight by meteoric particles in space

THE UNIVERSITY Press was paying me to update their *Dictionary of Science.* I had a two-year contract and a stipend to keep me going;
they made direct deposits to my bank account every month, twice the
amount of my rent. It was what my dissertation supervisor arranged for
me when I left the Ph.D. program.

"I didn't want to hear that you'd gone to work at Burger World,"
Dr. Jonas said, adjusting her glasses and tapping a pencil against her
wristbone. The week before, she had reluctantly accepted my resigna-
tion from the program in Extreme Ultraviolet Astrophysics.

"I'm just not interested in going any farther," I wrote in a very brief
letter. "There is no clear way to explain, except to say that the research
has lost my attention. I'm sorry."

On a wide oak table next to the kitchen, I kept my laptop and the four
piles of books I was using as sources for the dictionary. It wasn't always
easy to translate what I knew into language other people could understand. I worked late at night and early in the morning, just before and
just after sleep. The profusion of definitions and diagrams made safe
boundaries for my dreams.

Every four months, I was supposed to confer with the editor assigned
to me, tell him how far along I was in the trajectory from *ab* to *zymotic.*
He didn't have to know I wasn't following the course of the alphabet,
that I was traveling at random, following some inner logic beneath the
surface that guided me. I simply trusted it, like gravity.

Dearest Jules:
Two auditions the day after tomorrow, and hours of practicing today. My hotel room looks out over the harbor and at night I can hear
a foghorn in the distance (E flat). It helps me sing myself to sleep.

Love to you, P.

UNTIL PAULA was born, when I was four, I didn't speak to anyone. I had been collecting words and phrases in my head for a long time,
constructing sentences and more, but there never seemed any point in
saying things out loud. I listened carefully to what was said all around
me, I studied the way people talked to one another, but my own words
stayed inside. I drew pictures a great deal, I told myself silent stories
about the creatures I'd imagined. My mother read to me every night in
bed; I turned the pages of the books and followed her pointing finger as
she traced the words. Late at night I heard my parents discussing me on
the other side of my bedroom wall, convincing each other I had already
learned how to read even though I never spoke a word.

When my mother returned from the hospital carrying a small white
bundle that turned out to be my newborn sister, she held her out for me
to examine. Her face was tiny, her hands at the edge of the blanket reminded me of starfish I'd seen in a coloring book. She was asleep.

I offered my first sentence to the world: "It's going to rain today."

By the time I was nine, many people believed I was a genius. I was
borrowed from my fourth grade class and taken to the school psycholo-
gist's office where I was tested over and over to be certain. I arranged
puzzles, performed calculations, explained what I saw in a series of black-
and-white drawings. When the results were final, my parents were
more worried than pleased. "He'll be unhappy or crazy, at the very least
an outcast," my mother lamented to my father one night when they
thought I was asleep.

None of it seemed important to me. My IQ only partly explained
what it felt like to be in rooms full of children my own age with whom I
was sure I had nothing in common. There was no way to describe how
far away I was from all of them. When the testing was over, I returned to
class, still unable to pretend I was like anyone else.

Even as a child, Paula made everything look so easy. She surrounded
herself with friends, entered the world as eagerly as I retreated from it.
She performed in school plays, attended birthday parties, walked with
the neighbor's dog. I watched her with her friends, sometimes, amazed at
the way they talked to one another so earnestly, laughed with such ease.

It seemed impossible to me that anything could be understood that way, through words.

> **statics:** the mathematical and physical study of the behavior of matter under the action of forces, dealing with cases where no motion is produced

PAULA BEGAN singing before she had fully mastered speech. I remember my parents' amazement when they realized she was able to perfectly reproduce a song she had heard on the radio—at first just the melody with her own invented syllables, but gradually she got the words right too, even mimicking accents and nuances in the singers' voices.

When Paula was six, a music teacher told my parents that their daughter had perfect pitch and recommended private lessons. She practiced in the basement, her pure sounds echoing against the cement floor. Sometimes I would sit on the steps and watch, stunned by the way she trusted her voice so completely that she could send it out into the world, using all her air and muscle and faith to make it carry.

When adolescence broke my voice in two, I became virtually speechless again. It happened the same year my mother died, and for a while I thought maybe that had been the cause, maybe her death broke my voice. Her absence silencing me the way it silenced my father.

But one day he roused himself enough to hear me speaking in that odd two-toned pitch. "You sound like a man before you really are one," was all he said.

It added yet another dimension to my discomfort in my body: never to know which would issue forth when I spoke, my new voice or my old one. For an entire summer I stammered, using my first sound the way a musician tunes an instrument: playing one note over and over until it's the right one.

Sometimes it felt as though my mother and I led a separate life from the one that Julian and my father shared. When the two of

them climbed the long pine-shaded hill to the neighborhood synagogue on Saturday mornings, she and I went elsewhere—to the
store or the park or to my music lessons. There had been only one
argument on the subject, as far as I knew.

"It's bad enough that you don't go yourself to services, now you
want her to be a heathen too?" my father said. Both he and my
mother were in the hallway, one at either end, and I sat in the
kitchen with my spoon hovering above a bowl of cereal. Julian was
with me too, making no noise at all.

"Heathen," my mother repeated. "What about happy?" I couldn't
see either of them, but I imagined she had her hands on her hips,
her mouth set in a thin line.

"What does happiness have to do with anything?" my father
wanted to know.

"Everything," my mother sighed.

There was a brief silence, and my mother whispered something I couldn't make out. It was foggy that morning and cool
outside; the kitchen felt dim and abandoned. Julian studied the
wallpaper, its tireless repetition of flowers and stars, the faintly
visible texture of woven fabric, the distant edges where a corner
had begun to pull itself away from the wall. A door slammed. My
father told Julian it was time to go, and I remained where I was.
Released.

He is inside. I can hear the mixed-up noises of his televisions, not
loud but like a crowd of people in the street one block away, or a
party from another building. I know he is there, but he is not opening
the door. I think it must be how he tells me to go away, he is busy, or
afraid, or some other feeling I do not understand yet. So I say
through the door, "Your lunch is here, on the tray outside," and I go
back downstairs and dress myself for work. Later, leaving, I see the
tray is still there, not touched, and I say in my head to his sister,
Paula: What do I do now?

"THE TABLE is in a different place," Sola said when she came back on the second Wednesday. I had heard her on Monday, but didn't answer her knock, pretended I was away. But on Wednesday I confused myself by looking forward to her footsteps, listening for them at a minute before one. And I was hungry. Because of the table, she had to put the tray down a bit farther away from me. Her black hair caught the light as she leaned down.

"I did move it," I said, surprised she had noticed.

"I have a good memory," she said.

"Photographic?" I asked her.

She thought for a moment, as if translating something in her head, and then nodded. "My mother and my grandmother and the mother of my grandmother, all of us have it. We memorize just with looking." She paused, looking off somewhere. "In my language it is called 'painting on the inside of my eyes.'"

I wondered where she had just traveled to inside that pause, and then she spoke again.

"It is going to rain today," she said, gazing toward the window. In the echo of my own sentence from long before, I was overcome by a memory of the first time I saw rain coming, the way it enclosed me in its wet arms.

"You can feel it," she continued. "The air so heavy."

I stared at her hands as she spoke; it seemed the words were coming from her fingertips.

"When it finally rains, there is a sigh in the world because it is such a relief, to finally break open. The earth spreads its arms to welcome the water from heaven. And the laughter of the angels."

"I thought it was tears," I said, not meaning to speak out loud.

Sola looked at me as if she'd forgotten I was there. "Laughter," she said.

"What's the word for *angel* in your language?" I asked.

She shook her head. "I cannot say it." And then she left the apartment, forgetting to collect the dishes, forgetting to close the door. There was thunder when she left, and I heard the first drops of rain burst against the window.

I bring one suitcase and one small plant with me when I move to the apartment. Paula pays me enough to cover the rent for my empty place and to have something left over; I tell her it is too much, but she will not listen.

"You're doing me such a favor," she says, the day we talk it over. We stand in her bright kitchen and she writes me a check. There is a vase of white roses on one counter.

"It is no problem for me," I tell her, thinking about the smells in my old hallway, the closed faces of my neighbors.

"I'm so grateful," she says, giving me the check and touching me on the shoulder. Her hands are so small. She smiles at me.

"One month," I say, folding the check into my purse. "It is a good idea for both of us." Already I know I am going to breathe better here, and Paula's brother gets to have some company. I have a timer from Warren, so in my old place, the lights can go on and off by themselves. The ghost of me keeps living there, and my neighbors will not even notice I am gone.

"Julian might seem strange to you at first," Paula tells me. I feel her waiting for me to ask her questions, but I do not have any. Not then.

She reaches over to the vase of roses, touching one of the buds with a fingertip. "He's very sensitive, to the smallest things, to things most people wouldn't even notice. . . ."

Julian has the dust of the past beneath his fingernails. I know how to recognize this, because I have the taste of that same dust in my mouth.

"I remember seeing him," I tell her. She turns toward me with a hopeful look. "Outside, near that tree in the front." When I get close enough to touch its leaves, I see they hang like small fans upside down. They seem to wave even when there is no wind.

Paula nods. "He planted it himself," she says. "Four years ago, it must have been, when we first moved in. It's a ginkgo tree."

"Ginkgo," I repeat softly, feeling the word click in my throat. "He takes good care," I say.

"When we bought it he told me it was for me to look at from my window. He said it would be a tree of golden light."

I do not say how it is strange to think they are brother and sister, with the same parents. Paula is always smiling, moving, gulping everything. And Julian is like a dream, always ready to disappear. Some people might say she can awaken him from this long sleep. But I know better. No one can bring another person back to the world, not even with the love of a thousand sisters.

T H E   D A Y I met Sola, I saw a program called "The Nature of Sex." For an hour and a half, I watched swans, red-winged blackbirds, macaques, horseshoe crabs, green turtles, all of them. Spring: the chain reaction. I tried to understand why, but all the narrator told me about was how and when.

The cycle of the cicada: seventeen years in a chamber, waiting for the internal alarm. Nymphs, climbing in a relentless upward journey, the adult holding on to the bark long enough for its wings to dry so it can mate.

Afterwards, the image I kept seeing all night in my half-sleep was the baby macaques' hands and feet, so small and naked and tentative.

Tuning my instrument meant focusing relentlessly on my body: the art of breathing, the straightness of my spine, the shape of my mouth before the sound emerged. I learned to listen through my bones, feel for the vibration in my mask.

When I was offered a place at the academy to continue my vocal training, the school found me an apartment in San Francisco, but I insisted on living in Berkeley. "I want more green," I told them. The place I found had two vacancies, one unit down and one up, perfect for me and Julian. He was in the Ph.D. program then. I pretended I was the one who needed him to live near me, to watch out for me.

Julian wanted me to choose which of the two apartments I preferred. The downstairs had a claw-foot tub in the bathroom, while upstairs there was just a stall shower. I wanted the tub, and so it was settled: my brother and his menagerie of televisions would live over my head like a chorus of angels drifting down to my room at all hours.

I always worried about him. It was like he was doing some kind of lifelong experiment on himself, trying to see how long he could go without touching anyone. It never made sense to me. I couldn't imagine what it must be like to be closed up so tight. Even thinking about it made me feel suffocated. Sometimes after visiting his apartment I wanted to take extra-deep breaths just to fill my lungs with air again. I didn't breathe enough in his place; it was like I was trying not to take up any extra air from him, air that he needed to survive.

MY APARTMENT faced south. The playground across the street had a swing set, seesaw, jungle gym, monkey bars, all of them with feet sunk deep into tea-colored sand. Every day I saw dozens of mothers and children there; occasionally a father would arrive, self-consciously pushing his child on a swing or standing guard as she climbed the metal bars of the jungle gym. I stood at my window, designing entries for the dictionary in my head as I watched.

A child waved. Dropped a plastic truck, dug in the sand with his bare hands, threw some into the cold air. His father shook his head.

A child sat on the seesaw, waiting. The childless end pointed into the air.

A child on a swing pushed off, gathered speed, soared and returned, soared and returned. Laughing.

For a time, there was a baby living next door to the house I grew up in. Late at night, when the baby woke up crying, I awoke too, feeling as if the sound of that baby came from inside of me. I lay there in the dark and waited for someone to bring the child the comfort it needed.

How could anyone bear it? I often wondered. How could anyone even attempt to bridge the gap between oneself and the world? All I knew how to do was live deep inside my body, far from the dangerous surface.

> **molecule:** the smallest portion of a substance capable of existing independently and retaining the properties of the original substance

MY FATHER had no capacity for joy: it was squeezed out of him long before I entered the world. Perhaps the years of being with my mother saved him for a little while, but even she realized it was impossible to resurrect someone standing so close to his own grave. Somehow she gave up trying to rescue him and turned her efforts outside, reinventing herself as an advice columnist for the local paper. She dispensed wisdom day after day, helping strangers make polite sense of their lives.

Then she died, surprising everyone. A routine operation killed her by accident, miscalculations in the anesthesia, a brief hospital visit that turned into a permanent disappearance. Paula was eight and I was twelve; our father collapsed inside himself like an empty paper bag. It was supposed to be the year of my bar mitzvah, but everything stopped as if the Ice Age had returned. Paula managed to sing her way out, break free of the frozen water. I got caught in the ice.

Twenty years later, when my father died of his prolonged sorrow, I inherited his clothes. The housekeeper said she didn't know how to sort through his personal things and asked me to look over all of it or give it away: shoes, suits, underwear, socks.

I left the boxes unopened for a year before I felt ready to examine their contents, inhaling the sour scent of him. The thin cotton undershirts and the bone-white boxers that he had worn every day I set aside for the

Salvation Army, to rest against someone else's skin. The shoes were still polished, though slightly flattened from storage; the suits needed to air. But when I tried them on, they were a perfect fit.

At my first recital, when I was seven, my father sat weeping in the audience, a handkerchief wadded in his fist. I was singing something very cheerful and bright, nothing in a minor key, and yet he looked absolutely heartbroken, almost sad enough to make me think I was doing something wrong. But then he leaped to his feet for the applause, smiling through his tears.

"You sang like a magic bird," he said to me, crouching down to kiss me on both cheeks. "Just like a magic bird."

Julian was still sitting in his seat; I could see him over my father's shoulder. I waited for him to catch my eye, but he wasn't looking at me, or at anything as far as I could tell. The rest of the audience was in motion, people headed in every direction, my mother a blur of smiles as she accepted everyone's praises of me. And Julian sat like a sculpture in his folding chair.

IT SEEMED as though Paula was always on the way somewhere else, always reaching upward for the next step. Within two years of our mother's death, my sister went to live with her voice teacher, a sharp-boned woman who claimed that Paula needed to be around someone for whom music was more important than air. At the dinner table one night it was agreed that Paula would spend a year with Madame le Fleur, as a trial.

"And then we'll see," my father said.

"See what?" Paula asked him.

My father held up a forkful of food and looked at her across the table for a long, silent moment. "See if music is really more important than air," he said.

When my mother died, my father acted like a wounded animal, someone who might, if left alone, starve to death or self-destruct in some other way. Julian and I tried to take care of him; I learned very early about taking care of myself, asking for nothing. At dinner, when it was just the three of us, we were a kind of silent film: my father descending into his usual trance of inhaling whatever he'd brought home from the store, Julian absorbed in the ritual of eating his precise geometry of food, and me: trying to make my plate look as if I'd eaten something.

The past can be like poison if you swallow too much of it. Julian had no defenses, no way of saying no to what was being given to him. I knew that there were things I could not, should not accept, things that did not belong to me. I had my own plans, my own direction, the sound of my own voice told me where to go. When Madame le Fleur told my father I was gifted and that she, Madame, could help me turn my instrument into something extraordinary, he had to believe her, he had to say yes to her. And yes to my life.

FOR THIRTY years, my father taught high school chemistry. Although he washed his hands at least a dozen times a day, he always smelled like the crystallized residue at the bottom of a test tube, like the sulfurous echo of a Bunsen burner. He left the house every morning at seven and returned, sighing, at exactly four-thirty, his face sagging and his tie loose.

One day when I was in third grade, he came home early; I remember seeing his car in the driveway when I got off the school bus with my empty lunch box in one hand and in the other an art project I'd recently finished. When I got inside the house, I heard my parents talking, but they lowered their voices to a whisper when they heard the door close.

"Is that you, Julian?" my mother called.

"It's me," I said. She came to the kitchen doorway wiping at her eyes with a paper towel.

"Dad's home?" I asked her.

"That's right," I heard him say from the kitchen.

"What's the matter?" I asked them both, sidestepping past my mother to get a look at my father. He had his head in his hands, and his fingers were digging trenches through his thinning hair. I noticed dark half-moons of sweat under his arms.

"Your father's had a hard day," my mother said. She went to the refrigerator to get me a glass of milk. My father kept his head down. I saw his gold wristwatch gleaming in the kitchen light, and I sat down to drink my milk.

"Foolish crazy woman," my father muttered, still not looking up. "Who ever heard of such a thing?"

"She meant well," my mother said. It was the kind of thing she said about everyone, and I think she believed it. People had good intentions, even when their actions turned out badly. She put a kettle on the stove for tea, and then disappeared behind the door of the fridge again, pulling open drawers and sliding things around.

I watched my father's face emerge from behind his palms. His forehead had a set of red prints where his fingers had been pressing. "Here's a science lesson," he said to me, his mouth twisting to one side. "Never go looking for a gas leak with a lit match, got that?"

I looked over at my mother for an explanation. She was at the sink now, washing vegetables. "You don't need to upset him," she said softly, without turning around.

But for once my father wanted to tell me everything. "This crazy student teacher," he said, shaking his head. "Burned her whole face and right arm, not to mention all the eyelashes on the kid helping her. They're both in emergency." He rubbed his eyes and even brushed his fingers across his own lashes, as if to reassure himself they were still there.

I felt my skin get hot and prickly for a moment, imagining the explosion of fire, hearing in my mind the teacher screaming for help.

"Would you please get that kettle," my father said to my mother through clenched teeth. The arrow of steam was aiming for the ceiling. "You know how I hate that sound."

I jumped up and got to it before my mother did, twisting the knob to stop the flame. She smiled wistfully at me, her hands full of vegetables.

We heard Paula waking up from her nap. The piercing whistle faded to nothing.

I try to make myself so exhausted during the day that at night it is easy to fall into sleep like a stone into a well. No thinking or waiting for dreams, no conscious letting go of the muscles I use all day in my work, no room for remembering sorrows. I pull back the blankets and climb inside like I am already entering the world of the sleeping, the pillow is my doorway. I close my eyes and close myself away from everything.

It takes a few days before I realize that the nightsounds at Paula's apartment are different from the ones at my own place. There is a softer whisper of cars passing farther away, a feeling that the walls and doors are thicker, muffling the noises. I keep thinking I am going to hear someone fighting next door or doors slamming in the late late darkness, but the only thing I hear is a ticking clock from the living room and an occasional murmur of voices from someone walking on the street. It keeps me from forgetting I am somewhere else, living inside a borrowed life.

AFTER THAT gas disaster at his school my father was never quite the same, as if he'd retracted inside his turtle shell even farther than before. I remember my mother being more gentle toward him, more careful, and when a glass shattered in the kitchen I saw him flinch like someone touching an electric wire.

He didn't go to work for a week after the accident, staying in bed with symptoms of a flu that came on as suddenly as they disappeared a week later. My mother said not to disturb him, he needed to rest, and once or twice in the nights I heard him crying out what sounded like the word *ferbrent* over and over, then a shushing sound that had to be my mother's voice, calming him back down into what I hoped was a deeper and dreamless sleep. Paula crept downstairs to my basement room to ask me what I thought was wrong with him, and I told her I had no idea, even though I did.

"But what are we going to do?" she asked.

"Nothing we can do," I said.

She shook her head. "I'm scared."

"I know. He's got some things that are scaring him too, nightmares."

She nodded, all wise with comprehension. "Okay," she said. "They'll go away then, won't they? In the morning."

"Sure," I lied. His nightmares lived in daylight too, I knew that somehow without anyone ever telling me. A certain kind of barking dog, a backfiring car, an explosion of fire in a chemistry lab. Reality came too close sometimes, reaching through skin and bone.

"Can I sit on your bed, just until I get sleepy again?" Paula looked so fragile, her hands like some small white plant blooming in the dark.

"Okay," I said, and she climbed up, leaning against me through my pillows until I felt her begin to tip more heavily toward sleep a few minutes later. "Bedtime for you now," I whispered, and I even let her lean against me as we walked back upstairs to her room.

"G'night," she mumbled, and I went back down to my own room, stopping once to listen for the nightsounds of the house, my father snoring now and back in all the places where we couldn't reach him.

"Sweet dreams," I said into the dark.

Madame le Fleur insisted I wear scarves anytime I went outdoors.

"Your throat is like a baby," she said, her fingers lightly touching the skin of her own neck. "It's so easy to catch a chill, to stiffen the muscles. We must always strive to keep the passageways open, so the sound can be purely moving through." She stroked the air with her empty hands, bracelets jangling, and I imagined gold and silver notes floating like invisible particles of dust.

I wore scarves everywhere, just as Madame told me to, and I kept my throat safe and warm, wrapped in silks of every color. At night I massaged the skin of my face and neck with expensive creams and lotions sent by Madame's friends in Europe. I stayed out of the sun and refused whenever possible to sit near windows.

"The old ones said you could get sick from a cold wind,"

Madame said. She and I were drinking hot water with lemon out of celadon teacups.

"They were right," she went on. "Maybe not because the wind is full of illness, but because it can make you vulnerable."

"I'm never sick," I told her. It was true. I couldn't remember ever having to stay home from school or take any medicine, while Julian did both, always needed to see the doctor for one symptom or another. So often he had a fever and was sitting up in bed with a book and a thermometer when I went off to catch the school bus in the morning.

"Please give this note to his teacher," my mother would say to me in a whisper, closing the door of Julian's bedroom behind her and sighing. The teacher would invariably ask me to bring Julian his homework, which he always managed to do while reading or eating his soup or daydreaming. I only partly envied him for that, wondering where the rest of his mind was when his hand was filling in the blanks of his assignment sheets. I understood that his teachers could offer him nothing. His own mind was world enough, or so it seemed.

I H A D learned Spanish from television, first from *Sesame Street*, which taught me numbers to ten, some simple phrases, and the names of the days of the week.

Miércoles. The day that sounds like miracles.

I discovered a Spanish soap opera channel and watched it an hour a day, muttering with the actors in my tentative echo. I liked the way the rounded words felt in my mouth, even when I didn't understand them. Whenever I could, I watched Spanish movies with English subtitles, braiding together the languages in my mind. When Sola came back on the second Wednesday, I asked her right away if she spoke Spanish. I had been waiting for two days to ask, and by the time she appeared at my door the question was already flung into the air. She looked surprised at first, then suspicious.

"Why do you want to know?" she asked.

A wall went up as she said this, palpable as stone.

"Never mind," I mumbled, hoping she would let it go.

"I do speak Spanish," she said gently, perhaps to make me feel better. "It is my *official* language." When she said this word, her eyebrows nearly touched each other. "But my own language is very different. Older, much more beautiful. Like the sounds the earth makes. I cannot tell you how beautiful it is."

"*¿Por qué?*" I asked her.

She shook her head, and her hair gleamed as it moved. "It is buried now," she said, and that was all.

Madame was like a strange mother bear, nurturing me in one moment and baring her fangs in the next, teaching me not to be afraid of anyone or anything. She told me she had been raped as a young woman, although she wouldn't tell me any details.

"Just learn this," she said. "Never let anyone take your power away." I caught a glimpse of the flame that burned inside her.

When I sang with her, it was as if our voices were giving each other strength, soaring together toward the open windows of her living room. Slowly I began to hear my own voice surpassing hers, lifting beyond it and distilling its own purer essence. At the end of a lesson like that I would see tears wet on her cheekbones, and she would dab at them with the backs of her hands.

She gave me instruction in how to breathe, how to walk, how to stand still, how to place my hands while I sang. Sometimes she kept a cool finger on the bone of my shoulder to remind me to keep my neck extended and my throat open, just that one finger reminding me of so much.

THE YEAR Paula went to live with Madame le Fleur was the year I began to watch more and more television. I had found a broken set on the sidewalk in front of a neighbor's house with a sign that said FREE, and I fixed it one weekend by guessing my way through. When Paula visited on the weekends, she came down to my basement room and watched late movies; I sat on a pillow on the floor so she could lie down on the bed.

After a while, I began to keep the set on all the time, even when I went to sleep. If my father came in to turn it off in the middle of the night, I woke up immediately; I needed its low voice and flickering lights to soothe my dreams. Eventually, my father stopped trying to turn it off, and my days took on a predictable and comforting rhythm.

In the afternoons, as soon as I got home from school, I closed the door and spread out my work across the bed; class by class I did what I'd been assigned, never fully paying attention as I filled in study questions and calculated answers. After helping wash the dishes from dinner, I went back down to my room and sat in the gathering darkness, watching whatever was on.

Upstairs in the dining room, I could hear my father's typewriter clicking its steady messages of scientific reassurance. Sometimes he retreated to his small library, arranging and rearranging the shelves. He had a collection of books about the war, about Hitler, about the Nazi secrets, about the inner workings of the Third Reich. I never saw him read any of them, but they stood on his shelves in their black-and-red covers, shiny with their stories of destruction. His chemistry books spread below them in pastel rows, worn at the edges from so much handling. Upstairs was the room Paula and I once shared; the door remained shut, sealing in the scents of her, waiting for her return.

After the second year of living with her, Madame le Fleur held a recital for me in her living room and invited my family as well as some of her friends who were also singers and musicians. I remember worrying that Julian would be afraid and uncomfortable around so many strangers, but he found a chair in the corner of the room and sat so still everyone probably forgot he was there. The program I'd prepared included one piece in German that Madame had performed when she was a young woman in Paris. It came from a poem about the stillness in nature.

I noticed my father wouldn't look at me when I sang that piece;

he kept his head turned away, toward Madame's perfectly aligned back as she played my accompaniment. It was such an old poem, so peaceful. I tried not to watch him not watching me; I kept my gaze high, my throat open.

"Was something wrong?" I asked afterwards, when he kissed me on the cheek.

"What do you mean?" he said.

"With the Schiller," I said.

He frowned, patted my shoulder, looked across the room for Madame. "Never mind," he said. "Anyway, it's her fault. You don't know better, but she should." His voice trailed off when Madame joined us. I imagined my father sizing her up: the simple green dress, her silver hair pulled into a tight bun, glasses on a chain around her neck, a pair of pearl earrings her only jewelry. Glittering brown eyes, a thin smiling mouth. No rings on her strong, slender fingers.

"They're saying she could become a great spinto," she said. "A very special type of soprano." She stroked my hand, smoothed one of my stray hairs back into place. "Yes, your Paula is coming along very well, don't you think so?"

"No more German for my daughter," my father said, by way of an answer, and at first I thought Madame didn't hear him. There was a long silence; Madame placed both her hands on my shoulders.

"It is a language of the classical world," she said. "Part of her training, with Italian and French. All of them, you see? You can't choose."

My father looked at her as if she were a child, misinformed about the world. "I'm choosing," he said.

I felt her fingers press harder into my shoulders, felt something harden inside my stomach. We would continue in secret, I thought, and Madame would pretend to comply with his wishes. "As you wish," she said, ice in her voice. "I am merely the teacher, not the parent."

My guess was right. I sang in German without his permission, the lieder hidden in my repertoire like coded messages designed only to fool one person. I was learning how to fly away.

> **persistence of vision:** the sensation of light, as interpreted by the brain, persists for a brief interval after the actual light stimulus is removed; successive images, if they follow one another sufficiently rapidly, produce a continuous impression

M Y F A T H E R died so many times before he died. Some mornings before he shaved and left for work, his face looked so ashen and destroyed it was as though he had pulled himself out of the grave. He looked at me and I knew he didn't see me; he walked through the house like a ghost.

"Jacob," my mother would say, trying to bring him back. "Jacob, it's all right." When she gave him a glass of orange juice, he stared at it without recognition; then he took it in his hands and tasted one small sip.

"Drink it," she told him. "It's good."

One of the storytellers passing through our house had told me about what they drank in the camps; he called it a *brew* made of the liquid from peels and garbage, who knew what. "Bread mattered more than God, there," the man said, "and the bread was from sawdust, nothing you could live on. By the end, I was ninety pounds," he told me, patting his now-round belly. "But you can't imagine such a thing."

I could imagine it. When I looked down at my own narrow wrists, I saw my father's fragile bones; in my eyes I saw his haunted look. At night I heard him sometimes whimpering in his sleep and instead of my mattress I felt hard wooden planks. His dreams were woven into mine, his unspoken memories twisted in my mind and in my blood.

Dearest J.:

This is what the Little Mermaid looks like when she's caught in the ice. (Remember when you read that story to me?) But now it's midsummer in Copenhagen and the sunlight goes on forever. No news from my auditions yet, and there is terrifying competition. I don't know what I'd do without this wolf-skin for courage.

Love from P.

WHEN I was still in high school, I had strong reactions to what I saw on television, reactions the way someone allergic to bee stings will develop huge swollen hands and feet, maybe even come close to dying. Watching the news, I'd feel like weeping because some camera had pointed at a bulldozer tearing apart the side of a mountain, or there was a seabird collapsing from the weight of its oil-covered feathers.

Worst, of course, was some child with flies crawling at the edges of eyes and mouth, a child just minutes from death. The emaciated mother was sitting a little distance away, not quite sane probably, and yet just conscious enough to know that her baby was dying and she could do nothing about it. Starvation images hurt me the most; I could feel the gleaming knives of hunger stabbing, but I couldn't look away. I had to keep watching for as long as the images remained on the screen.

Gradually, though, the numbing began. I'd stare at the screen and get very still, almost frozen. My breathing grew very shallow and quiet and I didn't even need to blink my eyes. The images seemed to be entering some part of me that didn't think or feel but just absorbed, finally passing through me and back into the air again, leaving no trace. This was how I learned it could be done: I could go past the pain into the calm, two-dimensional blankness.

One of the first nights in our new place together, I stayed out late with a friend and came home to find Julian seated in a pool of light on the stairs inside our building.

"I guess I don't make much of a guardian angel," he said.

"You need an angel more than I do," I said. He looked paler than a moth, the skin around his eyes almost blue with fatigue. "Shouldn't you go to bed sometimes?"

"I'm all right," he said, and stood up, his head almost bumping against the suspended hallway light. I could hear his televisions, murmuring in the darkness, and remembered the way we used to listen for our father when he snored like a train. I wanted to touch Julian's hand, but I knew he would flinch and suffer if I did. When he turned to go upstairs, I could see the wings of his shoulder blades beneath his shirt.

I T W A S the housekeeper who sent me my father's clothes, packed neatly into boxes labeled with my name and a set of abbreviations to describe the contents. I didn't want them, but nobody asked me. Paula had mother's old dresses, so maybe it made sense for me to hang my father's dark suits in my closet, an equivalency of ghosts. His books went into the basement at first, a task beyond my reach. Paula said she only wanted the photographs, nothing else.

I had the housekeeper ship me his leather chair, the one that he sat in when he read his newspapers, the one he disappeared into so many times when it was just the two of us in a room thick with silence. Even if the television was on, he didn't speak a word to me but kept turning the pages of the paper, information coming from all directions, the newsprint held up like a deflecting shield against the broadcasters, their words hitting him sideways.

Paula was away, my mother was gone, there were so many things we couldn't speak about. I imagined Paula pouring notes into the air like letters of the alphabet, like words lifting from a page; I pictured my mother dissolving to dust. My father and I listened to each other breathing, distant and vast as galaxies.

> **time reflection symmetry:** the proposition that any physical situation should be reversible in time; according to this principle, if time could be reversed (i.e., run backwards) the time reflection of a particular physical situation would correspond to what one would normally see by reflecting the situation in a space mirror, except that all particles would be replaced by their antiparticles

TIME NEVER made sense to me the way it seemed to make sense to other people. Paula was always planning things in her diary, turning the pages of her calendar like tea leaves in a cup, reading her own future. The more she aimed toward being famous, the farther in advance she wanted to plan things. She began carrying around a small black notebook, making lists of European cities that had opera companies to join. The names made a map of the world.

My days were boxed into the programmed hours of the television. The shows kept me aware of where each day began and ended, how the days broke down into parts. The morning shows were different from the afternoon shows; early, people held coffee cups and talked about what the day would be like, while later there was a sense of the day being reviewed, gone over to reveal its hidden messages. In the end, everyone seemed to agree that they were willing to try it all again in the morning, take their chances one more time. Someone could be trusted to keep constant score of every game and stock movement and temperature. Now I counted the days of Paula's itinerary, listening in the news for a mention of the city she was in, marveling that time was not the same everywhere. She was sleeping while I was awake, and singing as I dreamed.

Keeping my focus was the main thing, figuring out how to keep Paula's absence off to the side somewhere, concealed from view, so it wouldn't distract me to uselessness. I chose a different hour each day to play one of her recordings, to retain some piece of her voice in my ear, pretend she was still here. The postcards helped too, even though they confirmed the truth of the distance between us. I didn't allow myself to think about her goals, about the possibility of her trip resulting in a longer departure, something more permanent and severing. Only when my early-morning or late-night worries wrenched me away from my dictionary did I get caught in the terror of her leaving for good.

All I could think to do was keep the TVs on louder, refuse any alterations to my routine, maybe even refuse to answer or unlock the door when I heard Sola's footsteps ascending toward me. I knew how to prevent the rest of the world from entering, I had practice reinforcing the boundaries of my skin. I could lock her out, entry denied; she didn't know the password. No one did. Except Paula, and she was on the other side of the world.

Dear Jules:
There is something otherworldly about these warm evenings and the color of the light. I'm beginning to wonder if my voice is different here, changed by the latitude. Is that possible?
I send you more love, P.

"I DO NOT watch the television," Sola said. "I have things to do."

I could tell by the way she said *things to do* that she meant an almost infinite supply of them, there would always be a list she had to choose from. But I noticed how her hands moved when she spoke, how she always touched things. Was she trying to keep remembering where she was in the world? Each time she delivered my lunch, she stood in the doorway a little bit longer before leaving. I ate my lunch slower and slower, testing my limits.

"Where did you live before this?" I asked her one day.

"In someone else's house," she said.

"And before that?"

"Someone else's house," she said. "I am living in this country because of a certain man, a doctor, who lives there." She put down the dishes on a table and sat at the edge of a low wooden chair near the door. "He is very kind to me." She drew small, caressing circles around one of her elbows. I saw the muscles move in her jaw like she was practicing words inside her mouth.

"It feels like a dream sometimes, everything from before today," she said. "Even right now, how do I know what is real?"

"I don't know," I said, even though I wasn't sure the question was directed at me. I thought of the days I spoke to no one and no one spoke to me, the faces of the television full of images coming from what seemed like distant planets. Even the rhythms of traffic outside my window, street sounds that had to be human voices, none of it meant anything.

"There is no way to shake off the dead," Sola said, "even if you are very gentle."

I held my breath. The televisions whispered to each other, and I felt on the verge of a terrible panic, waiting for her to continue.

"There is only waiting," she said, "until they lift off into the air, and float."

I begin, slowly, to recognize some kind of broken place in Julian, like a bone never properly healed, and so the muscles and skin are growing all around to pretend they can make up for the splinters inside. At first, when it is too familiar to me, I try to ignore him, I try to keep to myself and continue to live with my hands out in front of me, touching things to keep myself awake. But the more I notice him, the more it comes back to me, I cannot help remembering the way I feel at the beginning of the time After. In the hospital, there are so many days when I am staring up into the white emptiness, staring because I am blind and frozen and there is no such thing as time.

It is only after the American doctor comes that I begin to get up and walk around the ward. I find a window that looks out across an empty field, and I begin to stare at that too, knowing that the empty, colorless field outside is how I feel on the inside. It is just at the end of winter, and I sit in a small metal chair by the window for weeks. Warren begins talking to me, his voice like a song I can almost but not quite remember, until slowly, slowly, there begins to appear some green outside that window. One of the nuns is working in a garden, planting seeds in the ground.

And somehow I begin feeling my own skin and the warmth of the sun through the window, my eyes begin to look for signs of more color, more spring. I get up from my chair next to the window when there are more flowers than I can count, and I know that I have to move on from there before the flowers fade and drop to the earth. It is inside of me always, the dead field, but also the picture of the living field is holding there too. I come to America with one change of clothes and a turquoise bead from my grandmother's wedding dress. This is how I begin again.

THREE

SUNRISE WALKING, keeping track of the changing time of light, best in the summer when most people were still asleep or barely beginning to be awake, the empty sidewalks and streets, the occasional car with its bleary driver, headlights for solace against the recent dark. I had a one-mile loop that took me fifteen minutes to complete, a better way than tea sometimes to snap my cells into alertness so I could open the books on my desk and feel surprised, eager, as close to happy as I knew how to be. The world made sense when I worked in my alphabet, the particulars of the dictionary organized my day and its meaning. At my back, the colors of the televised morning gleamed improbably, brightly. Only my desk promised the truth.

I missed the sound of Paula testing her voice in the morning, a sound as reliable as the sunrise. She must have done it in the bathroom, standing in front of the mirror, because I felt the way the tiles caught her vibrations and sent them flying up to me on their way into space. *It's still here*, I imagined her thinking, maybe even reassuring herself. *The voice is still inside me.*

Now she was waking up in another language, testing her voice in a landscape of strangers, making sure she could still find people to listen. The scales were vowels, maybe always the same ones even in Denmark or Austria, the same reasons to shape her mouth and pour music into the air.

astatic coils: two identical coils connected together in series
and suspended on the same axis; when a current passes
through them, any external magnetic field will result in the
same turning force on each, but in opposite directions; thus,
neither the Earth's magnetic field, nor any other external
magnetic disturbance, will affect the rotation of the axis

The first time I come to clean Paula's apartment, I think it is something
impossible, there is too much disorder, I cannot get underneath to
where the surfaces are dirty. In the bedroom there are clothes piled
on chairs and on the dressing table and even on the bed, towels
here and there, shoes in all directions, jewelry spilled across one side
of a table, five coffee cups all dried up and crusty, magazines open
and upside down on the rug.

Inside I am shaking my head, but when I keep looking around, I
see there is nothing truly dirty here. So maybe it is possible to do
something.

I start by gathering the coffee cups and taking the towels into
the bathroom, hanging up clothes and finding the shoes that belong
together, moving some of the piles to a chair so I can make up
the bed with clean sheets, opening windows and shaking pillows.
The disorder does not completely disappear, it just gets moved
around a little, because I do not want to put things where Paula
cannot find them, I know that people like her sometimes know
exactly where everything fits.

The closet is wide. There is a place for shoes to hang, lots of
different shapes of black ones. I mix and match, find places for each
pair. And the room comes back together, until the next time.

After a few visits, I know her patterns, the way the place is in
some ways always the same underneath the surfaces. And
when Paula asks me to live there for a while, I have to imagine
myself living around and among the things that are all around like a
circus, and I have to see if I can picture myself in the middle,
sleeping there and drinking my juice in the morning. And it is not my

way, but I know it is clean, because I am the one cleaning every week, and so I say yes.

"I know it's a mess," Paula says. She moves her shoulders up and down, and smiles like a child.

When I see Julian's apartment, I am surprised at the difference. His rooms are so tight with order it looks like he keeps things attached to their positions with glue. Nothing out of its place, ever. The dishes clean and stacked up in a pile, the sponge in the same corner by the sink, the chairs exactly pushed against the table. Even his papers on the desk are in neat piles, edges lined up like rulers. And I wonder how it is on the inside, if a life this straight and square has any places for surprise or not knowing. I memorize the room, the chair where he sits, the shape his hands make on his lap where the fingers twist around each other. He is afraid, and I do not know why.

WHENEVER I started spinning through my anxiety wheel, one worry after another (what if Paula dies, what if Paula gets a job in Europe and never comes home, what if there's an earthquake, what if there's a blackout, what if I get a brain tumor, what if Paula gets a brain tumor, what if someone tries to break into the building while I'm sleeping, what if there's a fire, what if one of the other tenants goes crazy, what if a stranger knocks on my door, what if there's a car crash on the street in front of my window), I tried inventing a chant for myself, a litany of promises. *I will not be afraid of voices, questions thrust at me by strangers, comments on current events and sports heroes and weather. I will not be afraid of a door held open, the obligation of saying thank you. I will not be afraid of poison in my food, a fortune warning of doom, spilling hot soup on my hands. I will not be afraid of Paula dying, my world ending in catastrophic darkness. I will not be afraid of mirrors, my reflected face in an expression of panic or despair, my body an unfamiliar blur of limbs covered in blue. I will not be afraid of my father's ghosts, the chemistry lab on fire, the acrid smell of burning flesh, a family transformed into smoke and ashes.*

But the only remedy that really worked was to turn up the volume of the televisions and attach my gaze with as much concentration as I could gather, to an image or a story or a series of facts; a series of meaningless details about somewhere or someone or something, anything to peel me out of my own skin and the terror I could generate from the inside.

The year after my mother died was the year my father sent me to live with Madame le Fleur. First there was a period of paralysis, then chaos, followed by a series of housekeepers, all of them eventually leaving in frustration at the size of the task my father kept setting before them. We didn't know how to help one another, we could barely speak when we passed in the hallways. Madame le Fleur made her offer to my father three different times before he finally accepted, after the fifth housekeeper had given him her notice. I packed two suitcases and agreed to visit every Sunday afternoon; we would try this arrangement for one year and then decide.

Suddenly it seemed better for him not to listen to my singing, although at the time I had no idea why my voice had become something hard to endure. I only knew that he seemed to prefer silence, as did Julian. I was ten and Julian was fourteen. This was the beginning of the rest of my life.

She had gone to the hospital for a hysterectomy, a routine procedure that veered without warning into catastrophe. Something involving the anesthesiologist, a reaction to the drug, leaving my mother in a coma from which she never awoke. One day she was making me lunch and the next day she was gone.

It was Julian who told me when I came home from school. My father was still at the hospital, unable to face us. I had just been selected to star in the school play; in the pocket of my dress I had a note from the teacher addressed to my mother, and I didn't know who to give it to now, who would sign on the line that had my mother's name.

Julian said, "After a while, everything will be okay."

I don't remember if he cried along with me, and I know I never saw my father's tears, if he shed any. Maybe at the hospital, next to her bed, he wept himself dry. She didn't even have any gray hair yet, at least none that I ever saw. I thought, for a time, that maybe I was supposed to stop singing, that it was wrong to sing when your mother was dead. At first, no one spoke to me about it, about what to do with my voice, and I didn't ask any questions. But then Madame le Fleur came to visit, bringing a vegetable casserole and a card for my father. She said I could come over anytime I wanted, she would play the piano for me and I could sing for her.

"Perhaps it will give you comfort," she said. And it did.

I WILL not be afraid of falling down in public, I will not be afraid of the roots of trees buckling the sidewalk and rising to meet my legs as I walk, I will not be afraid of the branches of trees parting the air in front of my face, I will not be afraid of people's eyes, the holes of their pupils, the way they make me feel I might lose my balance. I will not be afraid of breaking if someone touches me by mistake, I will not be afraid of shopping carts in the supermarket, their shiny aggression, I will not be afraid of children who run without looking, I will not be afraid of trucks leaping onto the sidewalk when their steering fails or the driver has a seizure, I will not be afraid of getting lost if I turn left instead of right on the way home from the laundry, I will not be afraid of other people touching my clothes by mistake in the laundry. I will not be afraid of getting the wrong food at the deli, I will not be afraid of the smell of grilling meat, I will not be afraid of Paula never coming home, I will not be afraid of a plane crashing into my living room, I will not be afraid of a ringing phone, I will not be afraid of a neighbor knocking on my door, I will not be afraid of the sound of the wheelchair tipping over, I will not be afraid of laughter.

It was because of Isaac Goldman, the conductor, that I was in Europe to sing. What drew me to him at first was also what sent me away in the end. Isn't that always how it goes? I fell in love with the power of his hands, with the idea that he could tell everyone what to do, when to begin to play, when to take the breath before the first sound. That was the most exquisite moment, how he

got the musicians—and me—to find that place, that instant, before the music.

"It's the great mystery," he said once, "and the great gift. How
to fill the silence with expectation. How to make everyone—the
orchestra, the audience, even the instruments and the air—ready
for the very first perfect note. Everything else, everything that
comes afterwards, is inevitable."

He had been around the world at least twice by the time I met
him, guest-conducting in Europe's most prestigous concert halls,
fought over by several orchestras who wanted him for their own. "I
can't belong to any one city," he said every time he declined an offer of a permanent position. "For myself I prefer the idea of four
homes in four different countries," he told me, "four seasons, four
movements, four corners of the world. It's not that no place is like
home, it's that no place *is* home. Home is in music, for me, not
places."

He had plucked me from an apprenticeship in the San Francisco Opera, after listening to me audition to be an understudy for
a role in *Don Giovanni.* I was twenty and terrified of him, as if his
gaze could turn me to stone. He insisted I be given the understudy
part, then kept finding opportunities for me to sing a line here or
there. When he glared at me across the stage, I had no idea he was
falling in love with me, and it was a long time before I realized his
hands could be the hands of a lover.

T H E R E   W E R E more survivors than I could count who came to our
house, passing through on a journey of remembering. One woman who
came to visit showed us a collection of drawings, portraits of her lost
family. Their faces were all dark wide eyes and unsmiling lips, women's
hair in braids or wrapped tightly around their heads. Children younger
than I was. She told my father that the ghosts came to her every night for
years, holding out their hands and beckoning, pleading, trying to make
her understand.

"Finally I couldn't stand it anymore," she said, her voice cracking open. "I began to draw them, every line and curl and shadow just like they were sitting and posing for me. In three weeks I drew all of them, one after another."

So these were the faces of the dead, held inside her all this time. She took the handkerchief offered by my father and blew her nose with two sharp blasts. "Do you know what? Last night for the first time they spoke to me, for once I could hear and understand them, and they were saying thank you. Good-bye and thank you. I'll never see them again."

My father didn't say anything.

"You believe me, Jacob, don't you?" she said to him. "I knew you would."

They were from the same small town in Hungary, Debrecen, although they hadn't known each other before the war. My mother served coffee and cake, then disappeared with Paula for another music lesson. I stood mesmerized in the doorway while the woman and my father sat in the dining room and spoke in a language I'd never heard him use. He became someone else for a few hours, someone this stranger could speak to as if they had a shared secret. She had a tattoo like my father's, blurry and indigo against her skin.

More than once Isaac said that I could easily be mistaken for a *shiksa*, that I was "blessed with a small nose and light eyes." He told me I was lucky, as he studied his own dark features in my dressing room mirror and ran his thick fingers through a head of voluptuous curls the color of steel. "I, on the other hand, have the kind of Jewish face that ends up in cartoons."

He told me that he always kept a bag packed, "in case of emergency. No place is one hundred percent safe," Isaac said. "You're on your own, when it comes to life and death."

All I could think about was music, the way singing gave shape to my life. I didn't know anything about fear, about safety. That was my brother's universe, not mine. I lived in the air, buoyant with sound.

I C A M E back from my walks to the deli or to the bank, realizing when I released my breath as I entered my apartment that I hadn't quite been breathing since I left, something tight in my chest stayed with me all the way to the store and back again. It was only here, in the perfect familiarity of these rooms that I felt safe enough to fill my lungs and release them. That chair, that wall of televisions, that table spread with papers and books. The closed window, looking out.

At the age of twenty-one, when I began to see Isaac, to work with him, Madame le Fleur dropped me, said a voice could not serve so many masters, and if I was choosing him I could not stay with her.

"I'm not trying to put myself inside you," Madame said, "the way he is, the way men are. I'm only trying to help you emerge for yourself, to be fully grown. There's a big difference. Maybe at your age you can't see it yet, but believe me, you'll see. I suppose they can't help themselves, it's what they do, without even choosing it or asking why. But he will push at you in a way that's different from my pushing. He wants something for himself, to take something, to make you give to him. I'm not so pure as to say I have no goal for myself too—of course I do, I want to make you excellent, a diva, it makes me proud to be your teacher, I have a gain from that too. But it's not to say you belong to me, I am owning you, no. Only to say I helped to create your voice, I helped you to give birth to yourself."

She made a wiping gesture with her hands to wash clean of me, she would not look back. And she would not give me her blessing either.

She only said, "Go. Sing."

T H R O U G H O U T M Y childhood, my father's ghosts came into my room like a nightmare, invading my sleep with what he didn't tell me. I dreamed about being chased by German shepherds, the heat of their breath on my back and the thud of their paws as they attacked me. I touched imaginary scars in the dark, feeling the textures of his past on my skin. Other people's stories blended in too, a shifting collage. The gallows where the bodies of attempted escapees hung, their Medusa faces blue and bloated. The child kicked to death by a guard, the sound of shattering bones and breaking teeth. From my sleepless bedroom I could hear the survivors' voices droning for hours in the dining room, rising and falling. I didn't know how to do anything except listen, and memorize it all. But my father's silence haunted me more.

Isaac had a ferocious sexual appetite, I felt as though I couldn't satisfy him even if we stayed up all night making love, and often it seemed to me that he was using my body as a kind of passageway to another world; by entering me he could get to the other side of his life. But lying beside his sweating and spent body, I could feel his disappointment in me, because I had once again failed to provide him the perfect release he sought.

Still, he added to my faith; he showed me how to believe in my desirability, my promise. "You must know it in your smallest bones," Isaac said. "Know that there is a god living inside your voice, a god who can whisper the secrets of the universe."

When he conducted me, I believed.

OTHER PEOPLE'S stories lived inside me like bacteria. Sundays were the worst because the camp prisoners had to take cold showers outdoors even in the middle of winter, had to stand naked and dry themselves in the wind while they waited for their uniforms to be returned to them from the disinfectants. Even dressed again in their wet clothing, the air froze some of them to death. "These days were worse than the workdays," someone said. Sundays.

Prisoners murdered each other for food. Stole food to save a life. Shared and didn't share. The ovens never stopped burning. The hair piled into mountains; the woman from Hungary saw it through the window of the building where it was stored. Suitcases outnumbered the dead, their contents spilled out and explored for treasure. "Everything was useful except your soul," she said.

When the talk shows were on, I forgot the stories for a little while, they disappeared inside the flow of other voices, men talking about why they enjoyed wearing diapers and why they felt compelled to sleep with their wives' sisters, children who adored their drug-addicted mothers, women who sold sex over the phone. Nothing made any sense, but it kept me from thinking about gas chambers and burning bodies and the tattooed number I could never remember.

> **potential energy:** the energy that a body possesses by virtue of its position; for example, a coiled spring, or a vehicle at the top of a hill, possesses potential energy

I WAS not the strangest person on my block. There was a woman who never left her house without wearing a surgical mask, a huge hat and gloves, all her surfaces protected from the dangers of the air. She walked with her head down, watching the ground for cracks or garbage or rodents, who knows. I was always amazed she didn't crash into things: street signs or people out walking their dogs. She could have been twenty or seventy, anything in between. Once I saw a city bus roar by while she was on the sidewalk, and I swear I saw her totter, as if the fumes had pushed her.

Another woman walked up and down the street like someone in search of a grave to lie down in; she was so thin she looked invisible inside her clothing, like empty pants walking along. Seeing her was almost more than I could take. Her hair was the color of bleached trees dead in a forest.

Someone nearby owned a battered gray Pinto that was always parked on the same corner and filled with what looked like thousands and thousands of plastic bags. They filled the car completely, up to the ceiling and against every window, a few even squeezing out of the seams between the doors. The driver's seat was perfectly empty, I saw one day when I got close enough to look inside. Someone must have moved the car on street-sweeping days, but I had never seen anyone driving it, I almost believed the car moved itself, driven by a ghost. Once it occurred to me that the bags were photo-degradable, that this was a giant experiment to try to dissolve the car from the inside out, let the sun cook the bags and break the whole thing down into particles small enough for the earth to reabsorb. It would take a long time, longer than my own time on the planet. The slow-motion death of plastic and metal and glass.

There was a discount movie theater less than a mile from my apartment, but I couldn't go to the movies at all. The images were too enormous, much bigger than life and filled with a volume I couldn't adjust. I was at someone else's mercy, some invisible person in a booth behind my head, and the screens made everything so vast and overwhelming, so hugely scaled-up. I remember as a child how it felt to be shrinking into nothing in the scratchy fake-velvet seats, how I wanted to hide from the color and sound of giant-sized life. On my televisions, here at home, everything was small enough, as quiet or loud as I chose.

> **triple point:** the only point at which the gas, solid, and liquid phases of a substance can coexist in equilibrium; for a given substance, the triple point occurs at a unique set of values of the temperature, pressure, and volume

"What does ginkgo mean?" I ask Julian one day. I have his lunch tray in my hands; he is standing at the window and looking down at the tree, which is not gold now but the color of new grass.

He does not turn around but stays with his hand on the frame of the window. "It means silver apricot," he says. "Gin-kyo."

I repeat the syllables twice, like I am chanting something. I picture apricots shining like beads in the branches.

"The ginkgo is one of the oldest trees in the world," he says. "Some people call it a living fossil."

I tell him I do not know what a fossil is, and he says, "The remains of an organism embedded in the surface of the earth's crust. Usually only the hard parts are preserved, like shells and bones."

Suddenly I think this beautiful tree is like a skeleton of the past, another memory of the dead. But it does not make sense to me. Sometimes nothing makes sense to me, but I do not say that to Julian.

"That sounds strange, doesn't it?" he says. "To talk about trees like they're the same as shells or bones." He turns from the window for a moment, and we look at each other for a moment before Julian turns away again. I feel so much like I want to touch his face, to make sure he is real and to make sure I am real too. But I know I cannot.

E A C H   T I M E I looked at Sola's face, I tried to hold her gaze a little bit longer, tried to give myself permission to notice more than before. When I said certain words, like *bones*, for instance, I saw her flinch; I saw the color of her face fade very slightly, as if the light had changed in the room.

The only woman's face I knew at all was my sister's; I'd known it all my life. Everything about Sola was so much more confusing. Was she beautiful because of her sadness, or was her sadness something separate? The day I told her about the ginkgo, I saw for the first time two very small scars beside one of her eyes; they looked like scratch marks. And they made her appear to be crying a little, even when she smiled.

> **deliquescent:** having the property of picking up moisture from the air to such an extent as to dissolve in it; becoming liquid on exposure to air

T H E R E   W E R E two more apartments on the back of our building, one inhabited by a young couple and the other by a graduate student who never left his room without his bicycle and an enormous backpack bulging with the geometric spines of books. He reminded me of when I used to study at a carrel in the university library, surrounded by so many books no one there knew what I looked like. Paula told me about the couple one afternoon not long after we had moved in.

"Gary was in a terrible motorcycle crash," Paula said. "This was just before they were about to get married, and he was paralyzed from the waist down. The most amazing thing is that Elaine, who could have easily walked out, kept her promise and stayed with him, arranged her life alongside his." Paula shook her head in disbelief. "He's got a beautiful face," she said, looking out the window. The landlord had built a ramp for the wheelchair that wrapped around the back of the building and down to the sidewalk. To me, the rhythmic rocking and groaning of the boards as the chair rolled along was an oddly soothing sound.

"They're trying to have a child," Paula said after a while, and looked at me for a reaction. "Can you imagine it?"

"Imagine what?" I said.

"Growing up with a father in a wheelchair," she said, almost whispering.

I didn't say anything.

Just then Gary wheeled into view on the sidewalk below us. He had a bag of groceries in his lap and a baseball cap on backwards. To me he looked pretty happy, like his life was more or less working out all right. Elaine, who had one hand on the back of the chair, smiled and said something to him. They both laughed.

"Amazing," Paula said.

The difficulty, Isaac explained to me, was the limited size of my voice. "It's pure and lyrical and full of nuance," he said. "But you're just not suited for the cavernous opera houses of the world." He was stroking my throat as he told me this, tenderly, the way one would touch a captured bird. I shuddered, letting the information pass through me in one electric jolt, and then I surrendered to it. It was the beginning of something I had to understand about the truth and how to use it.

Herman Roth, my manager, agreed with Isaac, claiming it was essential that we understood the reaches of my territory. "I hate to say it but there's marketing involved here." I didn't believe he hated to say it; he was a manager, wasn't he? Marketing was the idea.

"I'm talking strategy," Herman went on, tapping his gold pen on a blank pad of paper. "Where to aim ourselves."

I thought *ourselves* was an interesting choice of words.

"That's why I hired you," I said to him. "I sing and you market."

"Sure," Herman said, beginning to doodle. He traced a zigzagging line down one side of the page and then repeated the line in parallel. The gold pen gleamed and winked as it moved. "Listen," he said, still adding lines to the page. "Your voice is spectacular, we all agree about that. But how far do you want to go here? What are you shooting for?"

The obvious answer was "As far as I can," but clearly Herman wanted something more specific. I told him I wanted to be listened to, but even to myself I sounded abstract, a little too polite.

"How famous do you want to be?" Herman said. "I'm talking very bluntly now."

"No kidding," I said. I felt color spread on my face like sunburn. "Famous," I said. It sounded hesitant, even though I knew in my heart that I wanted this more than anything, more than love. "Very famous," I said, more forcefully than before. "Bigger than life."

Herman smiled like he'd won a big prize. "I thought so," he said, lifting his pen from the drawing for the first time since he began it. "I had a feeling all along, but I wanted to hear you say it out loud." He tore the sheet off his pad and crushed it into a ball with his left hand while his right hand began setting up columns.

What both of them helped me see was the importance of choosing a particular direction, selecting my target. I needed to know where the air was too thin for me to breathe, and where I could flourish. I was subject to cycles, I knew that already: there were seasons for music and seasons for training, seasons for performing and seasons for retreating.

Once I was given a part in a small opera company in Northern Ontario, and it wasn't until I'd been there for two days that I realized what was wrong: it was too far north for me, I had flown into the cold and the dark of winter. The sun was dangerously far away from me, or I was dangerously far from the sun. I understood I needed to avoid cold winters after that, it was bad for my vocal cords. But I didn't explain to Isaac about the feeling that if I'd been a bird, I wouldn't have flown there.

I did tell Julian about it and he understood me completely. That was why I told him. It was true ever since we were children, that there were certain ways I could talk with Julian that weren't true with anyone else. He had a relationship to the world that I couldn't quite fathom, and sometimes what he said to me made no clear sense, but he made me feel understood.

"You *are* a bird," he said to me when I explained to him about Ontario. "And you weren't supposed to be heading north in the middle of winter."

"So does that mean I can only sing in Florida in December, or what?" I almost laughed at the expression I would see on Isaac's face when I told him about this.

"It means you have a habitat," Julian said without laughing. "I think everyone probably has one."

"Okay," I said, "then what's yours?"

He thought for moment, chewing on his lower lip.

"Indoors," he said.

I T W A S the first Tuesday of the month, my day to go to the bank. Standing in line, I was transfixed by an albino teller, a man in his early twenties with hair the color of toothpaste and skin that seemed practically transparent. I never saw him smile, although he was extremely polite to customers, patiently waiting for them to sign their deposit slips and tuck the crisp bills into their wallets. Several times I noticed that when he counted money in large amounts, the tip of his tongue protruded very slightly from one corner of his mouth. It hurt to look at him, as if I were seeing more than I was supposed to see, as if he had nowhere to hide. But when it was my turn, and I saw him up close, what really struck me were his eyelashes, how white they were too. Albinos must have thinner skin than the rest of us, I decided, thinking suddenly about the fading blue tattoo on my father's forearm.

I could not remember my father's number, no matter how many times I looked at it and tried to memorize it. I could picture the way the tattoo looked, the numbers wavy and imperfect, colored like old blue jeans. His skin was very pale and very smooth in that spot, as if the reddish hairs that flourished on the rest of his arm had departed to make room for this strange jewelry, this private message of pain. He used to hold that arm closer to his body than the other one, as if protecting it from the unkind glances of strangers, and when his arms were bare the tattoo was always the first thing I noticed. That number, embedded in his skin like a vein. It was none of my business and the story of my life, but I never touched it, not even once.

I needed mirrors for reassurance, convinced my instrument needed to be lean and straight, a hollow tube. Watching my father eat with so much ferocity made me lose my appetite. Either I ate by myself, before the rest of them, or I sat and pretended to eat, pushing the food around on my plate to make the piles look smaller. I wanted to see my collarbone and my jawline, I wanted to make my body a tight drum for sound.

It was only with Madame le Fleur that I gave myself permission to eat a full meal; she made onion soup and toast, a casserole with vegetables and potatoes and cheese, served me butter cookies with tea. I felt my throat opening to my belly, felt food as a nourishing thing. If I could stretch like this, stretch my mouth and my body, maybe I could stretch my repertoire too, stretch without breaking.

When I began to work with Isaac, he said I needed to gain weight.

"Your voice could be more powerful if you had more physical strength behind it. You don't have enough solid weight to drive the sound. You need sonic muscles underneath all that grace."

I was standing in my slip in front of the mirror, doing my breathing exercises. He patted his own wide chest, and it made a sound like a bass drum. Then he pointed to my rib cage and laughed.

"How can such a small instrument produce a large sound?" he said to me. "You need to get bigger, I don't know why I didn't realize it a long time ago."

I didn't know what to think. I had a sudden fear of disappearing inside a layer of animal fat, becoming one of those enormous Wagnerian divas whose massive bodies and heaving breasts shook the stage. But I thought he might be right. I worried that my voice really was too small and that my body had no power. I began to believe that I could enlarge everything about myself, simply by eating.

All the years of playing with food on my plate, nibbling: now I had to force things down. I stuffed myself with creamy foods and large portions, I ate two of everything and sometimes three if I could manage not to make myself sick. Isaac cooked for me: he seemed thrilled every time I outgrew a piece of clothing or pinched a new centimeter of flesh around my waist. At times he fed me with his own hands, as if I were an animal he had recently tamed. My breasts grew fuller and rounder, my belly began to curve outward, my arms and thighs took on the plumpness of a healthy infant.

But when I sang, my voice sounded the same to me. Isaac swore it was getting stronger, he promised that the results wouldn't appear immediately but that already my sound had become more full, more resonant.

"I can't hear the difference," I told him.

"Since when can you be your own best judge?" he said. "You can't recognize how much better you sound, but I can. Trust me."

I studied myself in the mirror, watching myself from every angle, and I began to get frightened. Secretly, I consulted with other singers. They were surprised to see how much I had changed. "What has happened to the ingenue?" they asked. And then they warned me to remember the trouser roles. I would lose the chance to play those boys whose voices hadn't yet changed. "Just make sure you know what you're doing."

Panicked, I rushed home to Isaac and told him he was trying to destroy me, burying me alive inside my own skin. He raged back at me that I was crazy, that he was the only one who knew what was best for me.

"What can other singers tell you? They don't know anything. They're just jealous."

"I wanted another opinion," I said to him.

"When you asked me, I gave you the right answer. Who needs another opinion?"

"I gathered information. I'm making up my own mind."

"Making up your own mind?" he was shouting now, a vein pulsing in his forehead. We glared at each other like murderers. I saw something crack inside him.

"You're nothing without me," he said darkly, and that was the moment we left each other—so that he could prove he was right, and I could prove he was wrong.

MY FATHER'S world lived inside me, but my mother's world was the one in which I lived. She tried to teach me what I needed: how to introduce myself to strangers, how to wash my clothes, how to say thank you for a gift. Clearly in her mind these were essential survival tools, strategies for participating in the social fabric that wrapped around her, and by extension, around all of us. Her instructions hovered in the air above our dinner table, my father occasionally glancing at the way he held his own fork and knife to see if he conformed to her method (he didn't). Paula learned faster than I did, even imitating the way my mother patted the corners of her mouth during the meal.

Sometimes my father ate with such intensity my mother had to leave the table. He kept his head down, swallowing as if he had no time to chew, jaws working so hard his ears moved. The pale red hairs on the

backs of his fingers gleamed. My mother fried eggs and potatoes, pouring the entire pan onto his plate, a mountain of pleasure. Except it never
looked like pleasure, more like labor, like medicine. Like air to someone
drowning. To fill what could never be filled: the memory of hunger.

Paula looked away, and I sliced my meat into smaller and smaller
pieces, arranging geometric designs. I could see that my mother wanted
to say something, get him to stop, but maybe she understood his need
was more important than her manners. So she went to sit on the couch.
I could hear her turning the pages of a magazine, like someone in a
waiting room, listening for the sound of her name. Waiting to be called
away.

I remember once asking Julian to help me with my homework, a
math assignment in algebra. He was in his room and working on a
puzzle that absorbed him so completely it took me an entire
minute of knocking before he answered me.

"What?" he said at last.

"I'm having trouble with this math," I said to him through
the door.

"Math," he repeated, opening the door just wide enough for us
to see each other's faces. "What kind of math?" he asked.

"Let me show you," I said, trying to push open the door. His
foot was in the way. "Can't I come in?" I said.

"No," he said, then bit his lower lip. "Okay." He stepped to the
side a little.

I sat on the bed with my book and my pencil, waiting for him to
tell me what to do.

"Tell me," he said.

"Tell you what?"

"The problem," he said.

I read him the sentences from my book and looked up when I
was finished. "See what I mean?" I said. It was about gasoline prices
and inflation. I had no clue.

"Close your eyes," he said.

"Why."

"Just close them."

I did. He took the pencil from my hand and started writing in the margin of my book. When he let me open my eyes and look, I saw a picture that resembled the cave paintings I'd been reading about in my history class.

"What is that," I said.

"It's your math problem," he said. And he explained it to me: the arrows, the shapes that grew larger and smaller, the circles inside circles. It was like nothing I'd ever heard before, but it made sense. That was my brother.

I HAD a theory that my father gave up his language because it belonged to the killers; he could not live with the sounds of their voices inside his own. In his new language, everything could be precise and unambiguous, he could speak in the vocabulary of science and never reveal his heart.

I embraced it too, the premise that everything had a reason, an explanation. Logic ruled the universe. Even the unknown could be described by theories, equations; a solution always existed, somewhere. You just had to be persistent and organized, you had to think.

> **mechanistic theory:** the view that all biological phenomena may be explained in mechanical, physical, and chemical terms

> **vitalistic theory:** the view that life and all consequent biological phenomena are due to a "vital force"

ONE AFTERNOON I saw Sola on the sidewalk talking to Brian, the graduate student; he was straddling his bike as he spoke with her, and he kept rocking the front wheel back and forth, toward and away from her. It looked like a serious conversation; I tried to imagine what he must have been telling her. I saw her shake her head a few times and he shrugged his shoulders, climbed on the bike, and rode away, probably heading back to the library.

Sola immediately turned around without watching to see where he was headed. When she looked up at my window, I was so surprised I forgot to move away.

"That Brian," she said to me the next day. "He is not as smart as he thinks he is." She wasn't being unkind about it, just matter of fact. "Some people think everything on paper, in books, is what is best to fill up your head. Big words are better than small ones, like that." She shook her head at the absurdity of this. "He is telling me about the weather, about moving pressure fronts, relative humidity. Charts, graphs, computers. He is surprised I do not find it so very interesting, all of the science about the weather."

Sola smiled and held up her hands. She stroked the insides of her palms with her fingertips. "I could tell him I know all about weather from my bones, from the way there is something electric in my skin and hair when I wake up in the morning. And animals know it too, without books or computers." Sola looked at me and raised one eyebrow. "So who is smarter, Brian or animals?"

Actually, I thought there was something very beaverlike about Brian, the way he pedaled on his bicycle and gathered the materials to build huge structures in his mind. I imagined he left a current behind him in the air, swimming through clouds and dust, slapping the world with his tail. But I liked the idea of Sola outsmarting him, knowing as much in her skin as he could from a library or computer.

"I've learned mostly from books myself," I admitted. I tried to feel what she was describing, the electricity in her skin and hair. All I could picture was my goose-pimply flesh on a cold morning and the way my hair stood straight up on the back of my head. These didn't seem to be readable clues to the weather so much as leftovers from a long night of sleep.

"You know more than you think," she said.

I imagine telling my grandmother about this man on the sidewalk who starts talking to me about relative humidity. I do not know why he wants to, what makes him feel the need to teach me what he knows about the earth, wind, water, sky—all of it pouring out of him and into me. Why?

"He wants to show you something," my grandmother would say. "He wants you to see the inside of his head."

"But air pressure," I say. "Movements, rising and falling temperatures. What can I say?"

My grandmother smiles in my dreams. "He just needs your face. He wants to hold on to your ears so he will not fall down."

"But no one can be so steady for someone else. What if I walk away?"

"He knows you will not. That is why he picks you. Out of everyone."

Maybe it is true. I do not know how to walk away from people, it is something I need to learn if I am going to survive in this city. Too many times someone comes up to me, leaning in too close and whispering in my ear something about trading massages or making a donation to a youth group organization or saving the rain forest. I feel like a child with no protection, an unlocked building with no sign telling people to keep out. I cannot remember in my village seeing people walking around so damaged, so much in need of help. Sometimes, like the woman in the red jacket and broken eyeglasses who always sits in the café down the street, it is just a need for someone to talk to, someone who seems to be listening. The woman in the red jacket has a soft, blurry face and a childish voice; she always wants to know what time it is, but when I tell her the time, it never seems to matter to her, she just wants to hear an answer to one of her questions.

In a way, it is not so strange to see that Julian does not like to go out of the apartment; there is a lot to be afraid about. There is the man who walks with a radio held to his mouth so he can walk down the street talking to people from outer space. I see him hold the radio in the air, high above his head, collecting messages no one else can catch, and I have to cross the street to keep clear of him. Something about the look on his face and the way his arms reach over his head remind me of a soldier with his weapon, and I have to turn away before any more memories catch me by surprise.

FOUR

The voice begins in the mind—and it can end there too. I saw singers think their way into such fear they couldn't climb out again. Isaac told me fear is my greatest enemy, but when I asked him *Fear of what?* he only said *Fear of fear.* So I stopped asking.

"You have a shimmer at the top," he said once. "It makes up for your medium size. Your almost invisible vibrato. But that shimmer is quite marvelous."

I held my hands together, locked my fingers against each other. Marvelous shimmer. Medium size.

"Listen through your bones," he said. "And sing from there."

> **excitation:** the addition of energy to a nucleus, an atom, or a molecule, transferring it from its ground state to a higher energy level. The *excitation energy* is the difference in energy between the ground state and the excited state

MY ALPHABET was still growing, pages adding themselves as if produced in my sleep. I forgot sometimes for whom I was writing it, wondering whether I would surround myself with a fortress of paper until they found me, dead in my chair, composing the definition of gravity.

I heard the wheelchair on the ramp downstairs, a conversation too muffled to hear beneath the bump and crack of the boards. I heard Sola's door open and went to stand just near the window where I could see her talking with the couple from the back, all three of them nodding and smiling. She waited politely while the chair was hydraulically lifted into the van, waved them off like the person remaining on shore at the launch of a cruise. But then I watched her get into her own car and pull away, saw the way her hair moved across her shoulder when she buckled her seat belt. I kept my hands in my pockets, waveless, went back to my alphabet and its steady pulse of science filling the room.

The first time I talk with the man in the wheelchair I do not know where to look. At his face? Does that make me someone who is pretending not to see his body, the arms and legs that sit so collapsed they seem made only of cloth like a doll? If I am looking at his legs, does he think I am disgusted or sad, giving pity with my eyes?

I look at the girlfriend, her shiny open face, I look at his mouth as he talks to her, talks to me. They are both so friendly and pleasant I am a little confused. I find I want to touch him on the shoulder, feel if there is still the same kind of bone that I have, but of course I do not touch him, I do not touch her either. We smile across the sidewalk spaces.

"You're staying in Paula's place?" they ask me, both at the same time, so they laugh at each other. "Buy me a Coke," he says, nodding his head.

"Just for a while," I say. "Because she is away."

"In Europe," the man says. He tells me his name is Gary and she says her name too. Elaine. I shake her hand and he nods at me because there is nothing to shake. They get busy with lifting the chair into the van, and I am glad they do not ask me any more questions. I offer to help but the woman says they do this all the time, it is no problem. I wave them good-bye, watching the way the van seems to take up so much room on the road. I think about his body in the chair, shrinking inside his clothes, disappearing, and then I want to get to work, make my hands busy with making things clean.

INVISIBILITY FOR me was not a choice so much as a necessity. I wanted to watch, not be watched, I wanted to keep an eye on the edges of things, the distances between myself and everyone else. I knew I had to be careful, that strangeness can draw attention to itself, which is exactly what I had to avoid.

The woman who seemed empty inside her clothing, the man talking to his radio, they were more revealed than they realized, but they probably couldn't help it. I wanted to hide inside my skin, inside my bones, use the televisions to bring me news of the world so I didn't have to reach for it with my hands.

At first, when Paula began singing, I feared that the attention she received would splash onto me, that the whole family would become a performance. But the spotlight was a narrow beam focused on one child. In relief, I kept watch on her from my chair in the dark.

What did my father want? I sometimes asked myself that question, picturing him in his chemistry classes and reading his newspapers, glasses settled for balance on his bony nose. He appeared so solid to me, dense with life and appetite, yet I sensed he had cracks so deep they could never be sealed up, fissures separating his heart from the rest of his body. Or maybe it was me, the crack between us, the impossible distance from my silence to his.

Sometimes I felt I could have been one of his students, calling him Mr. Perel, asking for help with an experiment. Even at home, he made me think of the obsidian surface of laboratory tables, the safety goggles, the asbestos gloves. I thought he wanted simply to make it all the way through each day without breaking into pieces.

On his twenty-fifth birthday I brought Julian on a bus ride to the edge of the bay, a curving piece of green that cupped the water and offered sanctuary to birds. It was also a place where people let their dogs run wild and swim after thrown sticks and generally greet one another the way dogs like to. I wanted to see if I could spread the edges of his map. I guided Julian onto the bus as if he were blind, and narrated the route as he kept his face close to the window.

"That's the library and those are the BART tracks, there's an elementary school and two gas stations. Police department and fire department ..." I watched the ghosts of his breath appearing and disappearing on the glass in front of him, and hoped that my voice was a reassuring hum in his ear. When the bus stopped at Point Isabel's parking lot, Julian and I were the only ones left. The blue-gray water stretched itself toward us and broke against the rocks piled along the edges of the park. San Francisco was a foggy blur across the water.

We saw two black dogs barking at a man holding two tennis balls and a racket; when he smacked the balls into the air, the dogs exploded after them like heat-seeking missiles. The man laughed and waited for them to come back so he could launch them all again.

"Come on, Jules," I said. "Let's start walking."

I think he pretended that he was my dog, that he was following me because he belonged to me. The bus pulled away in a chorus of engine roar and smoke, reminding us that we were marooned here for the next hour. Julian and I watched the black dogs return the balls again.

"People call this place the dog park," I said. I was wearing a black beret and a leather jacket, which Julian said made me look like a movie star. "I like that dalmatian over there," I said, and pointed in the direction of a black-and-white blur. When the owner whistled, the blur stopped in its tracks and a second dalmatian appeared as if out of nowhere.

"Matched set," Julian said.

Julian's legs were longer than mine, but I noticed him measuring his steps carefully, planting his feet in an approximation of mine. I let my arms swing, and from time to time a dog would approach to explore one of my outstretched hands. Julian kept his in his pockets, but some of the dogs approached him too, pressing curiously against the fabric of his jeans. I said "Sweet dog" to each one, as if we were old friends.

When we circled back toward the bus stop, I noticed a ginger-colored dog that seemed to be keeping its distance from all the other dogs, not growling or mean, but with fur rising in a ridge along its back like a flag of warning.

That's Julian, I thought.

In my own apartment I clean things with vinegar, with lemon juice. All day I breathe chemicals, vapors that sting my eyes and make me dizzy. The owners leave the house, encourage me to open windows so the air is clean again when they return. After a while I begin to change my tools, tell them I will not use the poison ones anymore, I am sorry. If they are not happy they can find someone else.

It is Julian who shows me the green liquids, the soaps for people who get sick from chemicals. Environmentally sensitive, he says, then calls himself a canary in a coal mine. Cold mind is what I think he says at first, so I ask him what it means. Coal mine, he says, and explains about the lack of oxygen, the gases killing the birds as a warning to the men underground. And, of course, I think of Eduardo, his body being crushed by the collapsing rock walls. No warnings where he is at work, no birds.

I T   A M A Z E D me to think that some people didn't live with demons sitting so heavily on their shoulders, that it was possible to go through entire days without sieges of paralyzing anxiety. I watched them coming and going, even Gary in his wheelchair, and it seemed to me that he moved more freely than I did, his wheels rolled without pausing to consider where or why or how. But I stood in my doorway so hesitant and felt myself trapped in the amber of indecision, suspended in timeless time until I could take the rest of the steps to the next door, and then beyond the door to the street.

I had to give myself a destination and a route, mapped in my head so I wouldn't have to stop again and choose whether to go straight or take this shortcut, whether or not to take the sunny sidewalk, whether to walk quickly or slowly, whether to check my watch at the start of the journey or at the end or halfway between the two. And then there were all the terrors of possible encounters, strangers who might try to make eye contact or worse, say hello, and then what would I do?

There was a man who lived somewhere nearby and whatever the weather, year-round, he wore a jacket with a hood, its shape just close enough to his face to prevent me or anyone from seeing much of it. I understood him, or I felt as though I did: that was the kind of protection I wanted for myself, but I didn't have the courage to take measures that extreme, to make such a visible statement of my own hibernation. I wanted to appear to be like other people, imitate their surfaces so that no one would try to guess my inside story, the way I believed the hooded man inspired people to guess and wonder and talk. I wanted to seem so much like anyone else that I'd be invisible, and could disappear inside my quiet, private world.

> **ether:** the hypothetical medium that was supposed to fill all
> space: postulated as a medium to support the propagation of
> electromagnetic radiations; once the subject of controversy,
> now regarded as an unnecessary assumption

T H E   W O R L D moved so very fast, and I could not keep up. The meanings of everything seemed to change from day to day: objects, words, facial expressions. Often I did not recognize anyone I passed on the street, and if I didn't get a glimpse of Paula on her way somewhere, or if it wasn't a day to visit the deli or the Chinese restaurant, I felt as if I might have been transported into another dimension without knowing it.

There was a language everyone knew how to speak except me. The world was too big. I didn't know the territory or how to orient myself. All around me, people seemed to know what to do. They climbed into their cars with absolute certainty, while traffic lights systematically guided the flow of life, signs casually explained themselves, even dogs walked purposefully toward their destinations, sniffing, barking. I was the only one who hadn't been told where to go, how to get there, who to be.

Once I heard a teenager in the neighborhood say about Julian, "There goes Boo Radley." I knew what that meant, I had seen *To Kill a Mockingbird* and remembered the ghostly face of Robert Duvall when he leaned against the wall of Scout's bedroom in a closing scene of the movie. I knew all the kids were afraid of him, but eventually everyone figured out he was gentle and harmless, only monstrous in their imaginations. Julian and I watched the movie together, a long time ago, but I never knew if he saw himself there, that pale sweet shadow.

When I give up my language it is because all the words belong to the dead. In English, I can make everything poetic and impersonal. I can say *house of fire* instead of *fire station*, I can make things up. None of it reminds me of what my mother whispers to me in the middle of the night or what my brothers are saying every day as they go off to work in the fields after breakfast. But at first, all I do is echo and repeat: the words sit in my mouth like stones from another planet.

"W H A T   D O you call it when the mud is like a waterfall?" Sola asked me. She told me she was trying to learn five new words every day.

I saw the image, mud falling in waves. "Mud slide," I said. It sounded so plain. We were standing on the front step of the building, watching the street sweeper move awkwardly along the edges of the sidewalk. Small flurries of dust rose in its wake.

"What about the bird who kisses flowers?"

"Hummingbird," I said, preferring her versions.

She closed her eyes and wrote my faded words on some page in her mind. Then she spoke with her eyes still closed. "We have a name for the moment that is the darkest time of the night, the moment before it begins to become morning. It also means hope. That is the sound of your name, in my language." She turned toward me and for a very brief moment I looked into her open eyes; they were all pupil, dark pools of space that could absorb everything, pulling me in too. I had to look away before I disappeared.

> **angle of reentry:** critical to a spacecraft because of the enormous quantity of heat generated as it enters the atmosphere; too sharp an angle would cause the spacecraft to burn up, too oblique an angle would cause it to bounce off the atmosphere

I N   T H E neighborhood where I grew up, there were new houses under construction less than a block away. On weekends, when the sites were abandoned, I wandered through the skeletons of the unfinished houses, naming the invisible rooms for the life that would soon be invited inside. I tried to imagine the walls that one day would no longer be transparent but real and thick and unreadable. And later, when the houses were finished and inhabited by strangers, it was hard to believe that I had stood among their bones, and that the bones were still there, hiding.

When I thought about my father and his wordless history, I felt that both places couldn't be real at the same time: the world that held the source of his nightmares couldn't hold the fact of this other place, where we lived now. One had to be a dream, or a lie.

> **heat death of the Universe:** It has been held that the Universe is a thermodynamically closed system, and if this were true it would mean that a time must finally come when the Universe "unwinds" itself, no energy being available for use. It is by no means certain, however, that the Universe can be considered as a closed system in this sense

I   W A S not a good sleeper. At least one or sometimes two nights a week, I lay awake for hours trying and failing to turn off my mind. Listening too hard to my own breathing and the sounds of the streets and the ticking of the heater, the hum of the fridge, remembering what it was like to be awake like this in the middle of the night when I was young and listening the same way for the sounds of Paula breathing across the room from me, her breath fast and shallow and full of little sighs that were almost whimpers. I wondered what she was dreaming about and if I would ever go to sleep and have dreams of my own or if I might just stay awake all through the dark night until the windows began to glow with the suggestion of morning.

My insomnia began when I was about eight years old. I never told anyone about it because I didn't know it wasn't normal. When I started falling asleep in school, one of the teachers asked me whether I was feeling all right because I had some dark shadows under my eyes. She wanted to know, *Didn't your mother notice anything strange?* I had to shake my head because both my parents had dark shadows under their eyes too, and I thought that this was what happened to people as they began to grow up.

Paula was still in a sort of crib in those days because my parents worried she would roll out of bed in her sleep. They told me I used to do that and land with a thump in the middle of the night. They would come running in to see if I was okay and I'd still be asleep on the rug next to my bed as if nothing at all had happened.

I believed what the experts said about sleep deprivation, that it was bad for the memory, bad for the emotions, bad for the body. But now I felt a weird comfort in my insomnia; it reminded me I was still the same person I had been as a child, still staring up at a dark ceiling and watching for signs of morning. And I believed that if I ever fell out of bed for some reason, Paula would come running upstairs to see what was happening because her bedroom was just below mine and surely a thump as loud as I'd make would wake her out of sleep no matter what she was dreaming about.

I knew so much about ornamentation and technique, a mastery of sound. But sometimes I was afraid I didn't know how to sing the truth, the colors of pain and joy, the palette of life inside the words.

Isaac told me I wasn't ready for auditioning, my voice was still adolescent. "You're growing every day," he said. "I can hear it. But the world is large, and you have only one chance to show yourself for the first time. After that, you're either returning in triumph or begging for a second attempt."

I listened to Callas, I studied her voice as if it were a museum filled with paintings. I heard the places where she allowed herself to sacrifice beauty for truth, perfection for expression. Sometimes the rawness of her sound astonished me, I couldn't believe it was still compatible with greatness.

"Don't pay attention to Callas," Isaac said. "You'll get ideas."

"Meaning what?"

"Theatrics," he said. "It's not the passion that creates the music. It's the other way around."

"Maybe you're biased," I said. "She was a great actress."

He looked at me from underneath his heavy eyebrows, that condescending gaze that made me want to leave the room. "Biased? Are you making a statement or asking a question?"

I shrugged, knowing we'd begun another battle, wondering if I could retreat before any more weapons were loaded. He was trimming his beard, regarding himself in the mirror and the smaller reflection of me behind him. I watched the fine ash of gray clippings float into the sink.

"Everyone knows Callas was an actress, that's not some brilliant revelation," he said. "But you're too naive to understand her relationship to pain, the suffering inside the music. Maybe you'll never understand it."

I felt my face heating up, the flush of anger rising. "Don't say *never* to me," I said. "Don't make predictions."

"So prove me wrong," he said, laughing like the edge of a knife. "Go ahead."

So many times Isaac interrupted me, correcting my first note, filling me with doubt. "I'm probably the best teacher you could have," he said. "I stop the bad habits before they deepen, knit into your sound. If the first moment is wrong, you can be caught there forever."

No gimmicks, that's what he said, and he was right. I wanted to find the natural voice, the natural sound. He said he had to undo what Madame had taught me, unravel the outer skin. To find the music in my bones, the cavities of skull and chest. The places of infinite inner space.

I KNEW Paula had no idea what her leaving really did to me, how it threatened to unravel my world again, the way it happened before when she went to live with her music teacher, after our mother died. Alive, my mother had held the family in place, kept us connected in some invisible way, because my father lived so much in his head, so far from us. When Paula's voice teacher finally managed to convince my bereaved father that she could be a better caretaker than he could, that meant I was left alone with him, the two of us adrift together but not together at all. That was the year I began to collect the televisions, to find company in their flickering blue light.

And now that I'd learned to live in my own orbit, with Paula hovering close enough to keep me from being afraid, I had to watch her spin off again into the distance, no molecules to hold us in contact. I couldn't tell her, couldn't ask her to stay, that was clear. She had a voice to send into the air, and I had to stay here, in my leather chair, waiting for her to come back. She was my only link to the world of other people. Until Sola came.

What I hated were the endless testimonies, people who came through our house as if we were living inside a permanent funeral, all these visitors relentlessly mourning their own miraculous survival, telling the stories of the ones who had been lost. There was so much crying. I used to make excuses to leave the table, the plates of uneaten food and piles of wadded-up tissue.

When my mother and I climbed into the hush of the car and drove to my lessons, I felt like I was being saved from drowning.

ON THE public television channel I saw a story about a man who had trained a flock of geese to follow him in a self-propelled glider. The program's narrator said he called himself Father Goose. There was some footage he had taken from a handheld camera that showed the geese flapping steadily beside him, so close we could see them breathing.

All I could think was that it was a miracle, their bodies held up in the air like that. Somehow this father could teach something he didn't really know, in his own bones, how to do. His false wings could teach their true wings to bear them up, to carve themselves around the air.

Dear Jules:

It's surprisingly hard to sleep at night with so much light in the sky. I could pull velvet curtains across the windows, but I keep waiting for the stars, which never come out.

> I hope all is well there, and
> send love from your P.

IN HIGH school my history teacher convinced my father to send me to a psychiatrist. This time it wasn't to measure my IQ but to find out why, in Mr. Bagdasarian's words, I seemed so "unhappy." I was also suffering from such intense headaches that I had to stay home from school at least once a month.

There was a battery of tests with names like the Death Anxiety Scale or the Alienation Inventory. They wanted to measure things, I could understand that. It was a territory people wanted to make sense out of, because we all knew it made no sense. How could anyone believe there was a useful scale of meaning that included "experiencing the murder of one's own children"? When they asked me about my father's life during the war, I shook my head.

"He stayed alive," I said. "That's all I know."

The psychiatrist smelled of antiseptic and wore a white coat with a name tag that read DR. G. MALONE in bold white stencil against a navy blue background. I decided the G. stood for Gerard. My father insisted I be permitted to sit in on their conference about me.

When Gerard concluded I was "pervasively saddened," my father said, "So who isn't?"

The doctor adjusted his glasses and went on to describe my "chronic state of anxious, bland depression" and "psychic closing-off."

"You're talking about how much time he spends in his room?" my father asked. "If you ask me, it's a good thing to know how to be alone in this world."

I sat next to him on the client-side of the doctor's wide oak desk. My father's hands twisted a small white handkerchief into knots as the doctor discussed his report. I could feel his teeth grinding in his tight mouth, even without looking at his face. After a while, I tried not to look at either of them, but counted the vertical blinds behind Malone's head, waiting for it to be time to go home.

That same year of going to the psychiatrist, I had a recurring dream about a rock in my closet. It seemed much bigger than the closet itself, and yet it remained inside. I could see it through the open doorway, granite-colored and smooth. In some of the dreams, I was the rock, or I was aware of being inside it somehow, contained within it and inseparable from it; and in other dreams I stood beside it, touching its skin like an animal I wanted to get to know. There was no menace in it, nothing about being crushed or rolled over, just the solid and immobile mass of it, filling every pocket of space.

Although I went to Dr. Malone's office once a week for three months, I never told him about the rock dream. I felt certain that it was just the kind of information he would have transformed into his own cryptic notes and taken away from me for good. Keeping the rock to myself seemed important, like proving I could keep a secret even under torture.

When I spoke to him at all, I called the doctor Gerard, even though most of my sessions with him were virtually uninterrupted silence; he never confirmed or denied the truth about his first name. I lay on his beige leather couch, a soft matching pillow beneath my head, and I counted my breaths; Gerard sat on a chair behind me, waiting, I guess, for me to say something intriguing.

Sometimes I felt certain that he was sketching his childhood home from memory or making a list of items he needed to pick up on the way home from the office; maybe he was analyzing his own dreams to stay on top of things or maybe he even dozed from time to time. At exactly ten minutes before the hour, Gerard roused himself enough to say "That's all for today, Julian," and I slowly reentered the vertical world, briefly dizzy from the new rush of blood that carried me out of the office.

> **reversible process:** (in thermodynamics) a hypothetical process that can be performed in the reverse direction, the whole series of changes constituting the process being exactly reversed; a reversible process can take place only in infinitesimal steps about equilibrium states of the system; in practice, all real processes are irreversible

ON FRIDAY nights while my mother was still alive, we had our sabbath meal in the dining room: white tablecloth and lit candles, challah, grace after meals. There was one line my father never wanted to read aloud: "I have been young, now I am old, yet never have I seen the righteous forsaken, or their offspring begging for bread." He skipped it every time, enclosed it in silence.

For years, we were all vegetarians because of my father. He couldn't stand the taste of meat, even the smell of it made him a little sick, he said. We all ate the same meals, nothing cut from the body of a warm-blooded animal.

Around the age of eleven, I began to get too skinny. Like my father, I ate a lot yet I never felt full. One day, my mother brought home a kosher chicken and after placing it on the counter, she covered it with a kitchen towel so my father wouldn't see.

"Jacob, I can't help it," she said to him, casting a glance toward me. "I feed him everything I can think of, but he needs something more. Protein. Do you understand?"

My father sighed, thought for a moment, nodded his head. "Do what's right," he said. "So the kids shouldn't starve in their own house."

"Nobody's starving," Paula said, although she was thinner than I was. "It's just Julian. He thinks so much it uses up extra energy."

My father smiled. I felt my face go red. "Vegetables are good for the brain too," he said to me. "Don't you know?"

Paula went to sit in his lap. He bounced her up and down for a minute, with a serious expression, and she leaned against his chest, laughing. I couldn't remember if he ever did that with me.

irreversible process: any process, except one that is a completely reversible process

F O R M O S T of my childhood, I thought my father's birthday was November 4. That was when we celebrated it, although *celebration* wasn't exactly the right word for what we did, which was to give him presents he never needed or particularly enjoyed, and to take him out to dinner, which was an ordeal for all of us.

He didn't like being the center of attention, or maybe he didn't like being reminded of his own mortality. Paula and my mother made jokes and giggled; my father and I ate our meals too fast, ready to leave long before the check came. "By the time he was my age, my own father was already dead," he would say, illogically. It was an odd notion to imagine the dead aging like the rest of us, still counting birthdays from the grave.

When I was nineteen and my father was turning fifty-five, he made a bizarre announcement.

"Today isn't really my birthday," he said, with an ironic grin.

The three of us were sitting at the kitchen table for Sunday breakfast; Paula was making French toast, and my father had already opened his gifts: a set of monogrammed handkerchiefs from Paula, and a Swiss Army knife from me. "My real birthday is the opposite of this," he continued, waving his fork in the air.

Paula said, "What do you mean, the opposite?" and turned away from the stove.

"April eleventh," I said.

"Exactly!" my father said. He stabbed the fork in my direction. "Smart."

"What?" Paula said again. Behind her a piece of bread sent up threatening wreaths of smoke.

"The toast," my father said.

"What's April eleventh," she demanded, turning back to rescue the pan.

"At Ellis Island I wrote down my birthday for them the way I always wrote, eleven then four then twenty-five. In Europe we always do the day first, then the month after. So they figured I was talking about November fourth, 1925."

Paula started laughing and dropped the burned piece of bread into the sink. "And you kept it a secret all this time?" she asked. "Did Mom even know?"

He shook his head and swallowed a mouthful of orange juice. "What's the big deal?" he said. "A birthday is just a day. No difference between calling it one day and calling it something else."

"Amazing," Paula said. "So why tell us now?" She dipped more bread into the batter.

My father smiled and mopped his face with a napkin. He always perspired when he ate. "I figured it was time already. I want you to get it right on my gravestone." There was a silence. The smell of burned toast and cinnamon floated everywhere.

Dearest J.:

Budapest is a mere leap from here, a float down the Danube. It's too tempting to miss—and easy to add to the itinerary. One more language in my ear. I'll be asking Sola to stay a bit longer, but I promise I'll be home before too long.

Much love, P.

AN EARTHQUAKE struck Kobe, Japan. I watched the scenes of destruction for hours, remembering the times I had been shaken by smaller quakes in my own city. But this was so much more vast: a giant hand grabbing your world and rattling the bones of every building you could see, tearing them like paper. One reporter said it looked like Godzilla had stomped through the city, randomly punching and kicking.

I understood the physics but not the meaning. I watched the shock and disbelief on the faces of the old women huddled in their blankets, a hundred screens of dull amazement. The Japanese signs and subtitles made everything look like a foreign movie, imitating disaster in a make-believe world. The number of the dead kept rising, and none of it seemed real to me at all.

cohesion: (in physics) the mutual attraction by which the elements of a body are held together

Dear Paula:

Some people don't know that the universe makes music. The earth plays the radio all day and all night, we just don't know how to listen, how to catch the frequency. They gave a Nobel Prize to the pair of scientists who captured the sound made by the Big Bang. The first cosmic aria, noise of creation. I would have liked to hear that with them for the first time.

I want to be able to hear like a dog, those low notes and high notes our ears can't read. When the TVs are silently running, I strain for their secret sound, voices pitched below my range. They're there, I can see their lips moving and their openmouthed laughter, but it's like all the history before I was born, invisible and inaudible but every-where present, palpable as temperature, molecules of the past that float around me and inside me, cells in my cells.

Matter can be neither created nor destroyed? No. Matter is constantly being created and destroyed, the eternal motion of the cos-mos. From the center of stars to the edges of my skin, to the chambers of my heart and the bones in my ear, singing your name.

I NEVER signed my letters to Paula. I never knew where to send them.

buoyancy: the tendency of an object to float; the term is
sometimes used for the upward force (upthrust) on a body
(see also ARCHIMEDES' PRINCIPLE: if the upthrust on an object is equal to the object's weight, the object will float)

One day when I am putting a lost shoe into Paula's closet, I notice a
clear plastic bag full of hanging dresses, styles like the ones in old
movies. I recognize one the mother is wearing in a framed family
photograph: sky-blue silk with small buttons all the way down the
front. It makes me think of the turquoise bead I have from my
grandmother's wedding dress. Unzipping the bag to reach inside, I
feel one of the sleeves, which is soft as the skin of a baby. I know
without anyone telling me that Paula has no mother for a long time.
And the father is gone too.

The clothes hang empty, but they are full of ghosts. I imagine my
grandmother's open baskets, how they are waiting for something to
fill them up, and I see how Julian and Paula are orphans like I am.
We are dangling like leaves on the ginkgo tree, letting go and
holding on at the same time.

T H E R E   W A S   a heat wave. It began to build on Thursday; in the
deli there were fans on every counter and Frank mopped his forehead
and neck with a dark blue handkerchief. People stood complaining to
one another about the temperature. By early Friday morning, hot air
pulsed through the closed windows of my apartment, even, it seemed,
through the pores of the plaster walls. I stood leaning my face into the
open refrigerator, my clothes wetly pressing against my skin, the air at
my back still furiously baking, and I took three cold showers between
breakfast and lunch. Even the playground outside my building was
abandoned; the jungle gym was probably too hot to touch. Every
weather report said the temperatures would climb even higher.

"Don't exert yourself if you can avoid it," the meteorologist on Channel 4 gravely advised. "This heat is a killer."

I put a thick towel down on my chair and when it was soaked I re-placed it; the leather felt as though it might be melting. I imagined the tar on the streets turning to viscous black soup, trapping footprints and in-sects like a nightmare. There were reports of babies and animals dying in parked cars with closed windows; there were remedies offered for heatstroke. I sat in my chair, panting like a dog, trying to decide if plung-ing my face into a bucket of ice would be a good idea or a shock to my system.

Sola gasped when she came to the door, and I heard the dishes rattle on the tray as if she almost dropped it. "Your apartment is on fire," she said to me. "I could feel it even on the stairs." She walked over to my chair and looked me straight in the eye. "Come with me," she said firmly, not asking. "Downstairs."

I noticed a film of sweat beginning to appear on her upper lip and her forehead, wisps of hair attaching themselves to the side of her face. My mind was liquid, and I couldn't find the strength to say *no*. I followed her to the door and then hesitated at the threshold, trying to think.

She smiled at me. "Come down." She beckoned with the tray at the top of the stairs.

Heat rises, I thought slowly, and turned to look back at my apartment.

"They are all off," Sola said.

It was true, though I didn't know if she turned them off or I did. The eleven televisions were empty shadows, a wall of dark silence. I thought I saw a heat shimmer rising from my chair. So I turned around again, and stepped across the threshold.

The lighting on the staircase was dim; I watched my feet plant themselves in the center of each step without quite trusting them to hold my weight. Sola's back descended ahead of me, guiding me toward the cooler air of Paula's apartment. I tried to summon a memory of the last time I'd been down here but couldn't find one; the heat had emptied me out.

"It is cooler here, is it not?" Sola said, and set the tray on Paula's coffee table. "Do you still want your lunch?"

I looked around the room and realized there were no televisions here for company, nothing to wrap myself in. I imagined that Paula was just about to return from a brief outing and wished I could see her face, even for a moment. The tray on the table sat waiting.

"What about you?" I asked Sola, wondering for the first time what she ate and when.

"I am not hungry," she said. "But I can sit with you."

She sat in one of Paula's rattan chairs and reached for some water from a nearby table, the glass sweating in her hands. I saw a slice of lemon floating on top of the ice cubes, I saw how her long fingers laced around the glass.

"You need water too," she said. "The heat can dry you up."

Like a plant, I thought.

"I can get some more," she said, and got up. Her light blue dress was made of some very thin material; it floated against her bare legs when she walked. From the kitchen I heard ice cubes tumble into a glass and a knife descend against a cutting board. It was so very odd to be sitting there without Paula, without televisions. I took a bite of my sandwich and studied the backs of my hands, feeling I had never seen them before.

Back in the rattan chair, Sola smiled and watched me swallow. I noticed that her teeth looked as white as the whites of her eyes. She touched everything with her fingertips or with the smooth surface of her palms: her dress, the glass, the arms of the chair, her own face. Then she began to talk breathlessly, weaving together her sentences as if they were part of a long story she added to every day.

"This apartment, these pictures on the walls and the colors of everything, I feel like I know your sister a little, you know what I mean? It is like the way a person walks around on the street and you can tell what they are like on the inside, maybe not their feelings so much, but what kind of heart they have, whether they are kind."

I nodded.

"You know mostly I am living with other people, families, friends, sometimes too many of us crowded into a small space. It is very different to fill up several rooms with just one person's life, and to have empty rooms all around, I am not used to it yet." Her hands danced, illustrating the story. "When I go to clean the houses I see how they live with so much empty spaces around them, and it is like the forest has no trees, no sound of life. For me it is very strange."

"You clean houses?"

"The pay is not bad," she said, slightly frowning. "I know some special tricks like combing the fringes of the rugs to make them perfect, sweeping curves into the design of the carpet. People with money seem to like the special touches. And I always know to put things back in the right place, I can remember everything just so."

"Painting on the inside of your eyes," I murmured. I had finished my sandwich and my glass of water, the lemon still curled around what was left of the ice. I was beginning to feel drowsy, listening to the soothing melody of Sola's voice.

"Go ahead and rest," Sola said. "It is all right."

I was too hot to be afraid. I leaned my head back against the soft cushions of Paula's couch and blinked up at the ceiling. Above me somewhere were my leather chair and my televisions, invisibly baking in the silent heat of the afternoon. I closed my eyes, knowing I could never sleep in a room with someone else, and thought about whether the sounds of my footsteps could be heard from down here, whether the sounds floated down as well as up. I caught a few more words of Sola's, something about the afternoon siestas she took as a young child when the sun was at the hottest place in the sky; then I drifted away completely.

> **hydrogen bonding:** unusually strong dipole-dipole attractions that occur among molecules in which hydrogen is bonded to a highly electronegative atom

"JULIAN," SOLA said. My eyes were closed but I could tell she was standing near me, close enough so I could smell her skin; it smelled like lemons, maybe some cinnamon too. "Are you awake?"

I'd been half-dreaming about a river, gliding past trees whose branches dipped into the green water. "Yes," I said, opening my eyes. Through the diagonal blinds, I saw that the playground was at my level now, the empty swings still waiting.

"What time is it?" I asked her.

"Three," she said. "I have to go now. Okay?"

"Go?"

"I have to work," she said. "Mrs. Barrett-Jones."

"Of course," I said. She had changed from her blue dress into a T-shirt and shorts, and her hair was pulled back from her face and tied some-how, maybe braided, I couldn't tell.

"It is still so hot," she said, touching her forehead with the back of one hand. "But the air is conditioned at Mrs. Barrett-Jones's house." She laughed a little. "I forget what the air is like outside when I am cleaning there. It is a surprise when I go back out, a jungle!" She pulled a large canvas bag onto her shoulder. "I am late."

"Thank you," I said, somewhat stupidly. She didn't ask what for. "Good-bye," I said.

She smiled at me before leaving, and at the door she said, "You can stay here, of course. Maybe I can see you later."

I didn't say anything. It was still too hot to think. As soon as she left, I wanted my chair back; I missed the way it supported my arms and the way the springs creaked beneath my familiar weight. Paula's apartment was too bright, the glare of everything hurt my eyes.

I went into the kitchen and drank two glasses of water without ice; the lemon had been put away and the cutting board leaned against the wall behind the sink. The counters gleamed and I could almost make out my reflection in the faucet. Paula was here somewhere, in the cobalt blue bottles on the windowsill, the eggplant magnets on the refrigerator. But she was not here; I couldn't remember exactly what she looked like, and the sound of her voice hadn't been here in weeks. I had a sudden dread of never seeing her again, losing her face and her singing forever.

I went back upstairs and closed my door, then opened it to listen for the sound of Sola coming back from work.

inertia: (in physics) the tendency of a body to preserve its
state of rest or uniform motion in a straight line

A S T H E light faded and the sky took on the color of a bruised peach,
I heard Sola's key in the outer door downstairs. I thought she paused for
a moment, maybe listening for sounds of me, and then she went inside. I
tried to imagine where she walked in the apartment, heard the opening
of a tap for water; she was running a bath. I even considered knocking
on the floor to see if she might answer.

The sky darkened to ashes, and the streetlights came on. Eventually I
heard what must have been the draining of the tub and the silence of
Sola drying herself off. Without meaning to, I imagined her dark skin
against the towel, the drops of water gleaming like stars. All the televisions flickered into my dark apartment. I finally stood up to turn on the
light and heard the creak of her footsteps on the stairs.

"Are you there?" I heard her ask from the stairs. "Julian?"

"Yes," I said, and then louder, "Yes."

She came to the door wearing the dress I'd seen earlier; her hair was
combed back and hanging straight down her back.

"Come in?" I said, hearing my own question.

"It is still so hot," she said as she stepped inside.

I nodded.

"It is cooler downstairs," she said from the doorway. "Do you want to
come back again?" She leaned one hip against the doorjamb and waited
for my answer.

"You must be tired," I said, pushing my hands into my pockets. I felt
suddenly ashamed of my white hands and feet, the way they must have
looked to her. "You've had a long day."

She ran one hand across the top of her head, feeling all the way back
to the ends of her hair. "I am waking up again," she said. "The night is
when I am the most awake. I see very well in the dark, you know." She
smiled and touched the collar of her dress, fingered a button there that
was too small for me to see.

"I have some vegetables," she said suddenly, clapping her hands and making an echo in the stairwell. "I can make a soup, a cold one. Gazpacho."

"Gazpacho," I repeated. It never showed up in Frank's kosher deli, I knew that much.

"It is delicious," she said.

I pulled my hands out of my pockets without knowing what I would do with them next, thinking I could give myself permission to taste. But I left the televisions on. The light I had just turned on I turned off again, and my pale skin glowed blue from the wall of colored light.

Sola said, "They keep their own company."

In Paula's kitchen, I sat on a chair and watched Sola prepare the soup. She told me not to help.

"I love to make it a certain way," she said. She peeled three cloves of garlic and diced them with deft, relaxed motions of the knife. She named the fragrances as they filled the room: lemons, tomatoes, onions, peppers, cilantro. *Limónes, tomates, cebollas, pimientas, cilantro.*

"It is good in your nose even before your mouth tastes it," she said. "Just breathe."

I saw the insides of Sola's wrists by mistake. She was cutting a mango for dessert after the gazpacho, slicing along both sides of the fat seed, cupping half the fruit in one hand and scoring the gleaming flesh with a knife held in the other hand. She made a design of diamonds. As her hands moved, I saw raised lines on her skin that looked as if they'd been drawn with ink, dark lines alongside the veins. She saw me notice.

"Razors make perfect cuts," she said, still slicing the mango. Then she put the knife down on the counter and turned the fruit inside out; the diamonds popped up like illustrations in a children's book. "For you," she said, holding the mango out to me.

I kept my eyes on the mango, but I couldn't help seeing how the juice had begun to run down her fingers and onto her wrists. I took the fruit and breathed its nectar.

"Make a mess," she said. She brought her wrist up to her lips to catch the juice that had pooled there; I saw her tongue touch the edges of the scars. "It is a very long time ago," she said.

I didn't ask any questions, but she went on, her words forming slowly. "I am in a hospital, but I will not eat and I will not speak to anyone. The nurses try everything to get me to eat, talk, but day after day I stay in my bed staring up at the blank ceiling, waiting for death. I know it will find me if I keep very still. I am prepared to wait for a long time."

I watched the side of Sola's wide brown face as she spoke; I recognized the silences. She said that one day an American doctor arrived on the ward, placing a wooden chair beside her bed. He began talking to her about his own life, about the weather outside the hospital windows, about a bird's nest he had discovered beneath the staircase.

"But I do not know a word of English," Sola said. "He is just talking. Anything he wants to say, he says it." She smiled a little and shook her head. "I do not know why, but he knows I am listening, even though I cannot understand. I cannot help it. Something in his voice is like music."

I thought about Paula, how no matter what she was saying it sounded like a song. Sola told me the rest of the story without looking at me, instead gazing up and to her left, as if on a high closet shelf she stored certain pieces of her history. After two months, the doctor convinced the directors of the hospital to let him take her with him to America.

"He wants to heal me at home, he says. He thinks he can bring me back to life." Sola lowered her eyes for a moment and then lifted them again, finding the place where she had left off.

"No one can give another person a reason to live," Sola said. After one and a half years she couldn't stay with him anymore. "I learn enough English to manage, and I learn a little bit about living in comfort. But I cannot stand how much he is trying to give me."

She took the other half of the mango and scored it like the first, curving it into a juicy arch. "I think sometimes I am dead, that this is what it is like to be dead, this nothing inside me. I have to cut myself open a little bit to see if I am living or not."

Watching her mouth to see how, I ate the sweet bites of fruit one by one, astonished by the way the juice flooded my mouth. Her words and the flavors of the mango blended in my throat.

"What can be more vivid than the sight of your own blood?" Sola said. "Do you understand? Such a brilliant thing, the way it pushes out of you." She took a bite of mango and swallowed with her eyes closed. "The voice of my blood says, 'You are still alive.' "

I am named by my mother in honor of her own mother, Sola Luz, and in honor of the light she feels covering her at the moment of my birth. She believes I am touched by an angel, that I come into the world with open eyes and an open heart; she tells me that I do not cry at first but make a sound that is like laughter. Even the midwife who helps to deliver me says afterwards she cannot believe there is anything like it.

Later, after everyone I love is dead, my name feels like a curse, a reminder that I am the only one surviving, remembering everything for the ones who are not even born yet, listening into the future. I have to carry with me the sounds of my own mother's voice as they kill her, and all of the cries of my brothers and my father and my cousins, every one of the children of my village as their necks are sliced open one by one. Now that blood is singing, it is still crying out, and in my dreams it haunts me, the terrible chorus of all the dead. I crouch in the bushes and hear it all, my fist stuffed into my mouth so I will not add my own cries to theirs.

And afterwards, when the silence of the night is at its deepest and the murderers sleep with their hands caressing their guns and knives, the blood drying on their skin, I dig a hole in the ground just big enough for my face, and I am screaming into the breast of my silent mother, screaming into the earth until I have nothing left, not even tears.

THAT NIGHT was one of the sleepless ones for me. Usually I stayed in bed and drifted through the sea of darkness for hours, performing calculations or counting my heartbeats or trying to recall word by word an item from the evening news, thinking about anything but the elusive cradle of sleep. I knew by this time that sleep had a will of its own, and there was no use attempting to summon it by force or by trickery. I was simply awake and not minding it.

But that night there was a sound that separated itself from the other familiar ones. At first I was sure it came from across the street, a neighborhood cat or even a child wailing for love, some kind of distress signal sent into the black distance.

Then I realized that the sound came from inside my building, it was wafting up through my heating vents and it was coming from downstairs, from Paula's apartment, from Sola.

She was crying.

More than that, she was sobbing, great wrenching sounds that were somehow muffled and indistinct, howled, I realized, into a yielding pillow or blanket. It reminded me at first of the cry of a child I'd seen one day fall hard from the jungle gym, erupting from silent shock with a lungful of angry air, screaming with the pain of having lost his grip and being hurled to the unforgiving earth. But this was a hundred times more powerful, an inconsolable cry, a surrender.

I had known this sound my whole life. This was mourning.

I didn't think about what to do; somehow I simply followed my body. Moonlight from the window made my hands luminous as I reached for my bathrobe, and I watched myself turn the doorknob of my apartment. The smooth facets of the crystal felt almost icy against my palm. I listened to the steps that creaked, then the silent ones; my bare feet felt the scratch of the wool carpet on the stairs and the cool wood on the landing. I shivered once, from cold or fear or both. The pain in Sola's cries pulled at my bones like gravity.

When I pushed Paula's unlocked door, I whispered "Sola, it's Julian," so she would know for certain it was me. I stood in the hallway outside the bedroom, and although the sobbing stopped, she was still breathing through tears. I could hear them catch in her throat.

"Julian," she said back to me, her voice thick with grief, longing, things I recognized.

"Yes," I said, and moved into the doorway where I stood, waiting for I didn't know what. There was a glow from the streetlamp far beyond the bedroom window; it revealed Sola's shape curled on the bed, her dark hair spilled across the pillow, her hands covering her face.

"I am keeping you awake," she said behind her hands. "I am sorry."

"No," I said quickly. "Don't be sorry. I was awake, I heard you, I wanted to see if you were all right, if there was something . . ." I raised my empty hands into the shadows of the room. The floor was smooth against my feet. "What can I do?"

Slowly, slowly, she pulled her hands away from her face. It was too dark for me to make out the expression there, but in the silence I felt the sound of tears still spilling from the corners of her eyes.

"It is all right," she said softly, as if she were the one offering comfort. "It is all right to cry sometimes like this." I heard her sigh. "When so many tears build up inside they need to come out, like a river pushing against, what is it? The thing that tries to block the flow of the water?"

"A dam," I said. It sounded like what it was, a stopping place, a solid limit.

"Dam," she said. "The river has to break the dam."

A car passed on the street and cast a brief shadow across the window. Sola turned over, so that she was facing away from me, and I thought that maybe she was telling me to leave. I stood for a moment in the doorway, still looking for a clue.

"Julian?" she said. Her black hair streaked the pillow like a painting.

"Yes?"

"Will you stay until I am sleeping?"

I took two deep breaths, my arms wrapped around myself for courage.

"There is space here for you, if you want," she said.

I astonished myself. I lay down beside her.

FIVE

When Julian lies down next to me, I am able to fall asleep, and the nightmares disappear for a while into the darkness. I do not dream at all, at least I do not remember anything, not even the soothing voice of my grandmother who often comes to me on nights when I am crying. I am not sure if Julian is asleep too, all I know is that he stays beside me long enough for me to forget everything.

At dawn, I see he is gone, leaving before it is even light, without any sound. I listen for him upstairs, for his footsteps or the voices of the televisions or running water. I imagine I can still feel a little of the warmth in my back from him lying next to me during the night. But from upstairs I hear nothing.

AT FIRST I must have been holding my breath or in any case trying to breathe very quietly so that Sola would be able to fall back to sleep. I listened to the cadence of her inhaling and exhaling and I counted the beats between breaths too; I was waiting for the rhythm that would mean she was no longer awake. Her black hair was like the dense feathers of some wild creature and her shoulder curved exactly as high as her hip. She was on her side facing the wall and I was on my side facing her back, my body following the curve of hers. Between us was a sheet and a thin blanket and air that was radiant with her heat and her smell of cinnamon and lemons and some indescribable kind of scent, almost like baked corn but not quite that either. What did I smell like? I wondered, but I couldn't smell myself at all. The dark room was full of her breathing and once, just once, she gave up a deep sigh that seemed to come from very far away.

I didn't sleep at all. I waited until Sola's breathing had been steady for one hundred repetitions, and then in my smallest and quietest movements, I lifted myself away from her back and her bed and her room. On my way back upstairs I felt like a ghost, replaying the scenes of myself going down to her room in response to the call of her grieving. It had happened, and I believed it, but it didn't seem true.

It is a long day for me: I have two houses, one after the other, and only half an hour of space to rest in the middle. And at the end of the day I am visiting my apartment for the plants and for seeing that the windows are not broken.

Some days I think this cleaning in the middle of other people's lives makes me feel too tired or too small in the world, but then I watch my hands moving through soap and water, I feel the soft cloth of rags and see the way the surfaces of wood and glass and granite shine. I learn again about breathing, about touching and moving, making beauty in a space. I tell myself it is good when the work is only in my hands and not pulling too hard from the inside. I do not look for my own future, only the shape of each day that is right in front of me.

Paula is returning soon, and that means I go back to my sad apartment again, that place where I am pretending to live in time. In Paula's apartment I get to feel what it is like living among rooms filled with color and light and beautiful objects to hold in my fingers; I begin spreading myself wider into this open space. But I remember this is not my life, only something borrowed for a little while.

Before I leave for my long day, I write a small note on a piece of paper and leave it folded next to Julian's door, thanking him for holding back the shadows.

A L L M O R N I N G I watched the playground from my window, the televisions silently broadcasting behind me, eleven versions of overly cheerful faces, ads in every false color of the rainbow. The heat had sucked in the fog and now the sky was full of gray mist, hovering so low it seemed touchable.

Sola's note was folded into a triangle, and her handwriting reminded me of ivy, the way it trailed across the white page. I folded it back into its shape and kept it in my pocket.

For a while, I turned up the volume on just one of the sets. I saw a program about children who were saved from drowning and then died when they were given too much oxygen too quickly. The problem was that their brains had been in a kind of hibernation, and needed more time to be brought back to life. There was something too about cellular freezing and something about slowly thawing, charts and graphs that showed how temperatures rising too rapidly produced shock and death.

I thought about the experiments in the camp that measured how long the body could withstand immersion in freezing water, how many times a person could be resurrected. I remembered a voice at our dinner table, saying, "They called themselves doctors. But they were not even human beings."

On a program about carcinogens, an environmentalist said that in public policy there was a "health risk assessment": the rating to measure how many people per million will die of cancer from exposure to an air pollutant. "Ten is acceptable," he said, "although the general factor out in the 'open air' is four hundred per million." I wanted to know who got to decide any of this. I heard about the people who believed that power lines too close to where they lived were causing cancer. I heard about bacteria in tap water that were infecting tens of thousands, no one even knew how many deaths were likely. Someone was suing a Dieters Tea company for the death of his wife. Every time someone mentioned the phrase *ethnic cleansing*, I thought I might vomit. There was too much horror and it was all too familiar. We were all canaries in a coal mine, and there was not enough oxygen to go around.

I was auditioning in New York City when my father died, and Julian called in the middle of the night with a strange hoarse voice to tell me the news. "Massive heart attack," he said, and it sounded like the word *heartache* to me at first.

When I thought of my mother, wishing she were still alive to comfort us, I realized that now Julian and I were alone in the world with one another. And how would my brother cope? Alive, my father had claimed him absolutely, filling his head with science-talk, making Julian a perpetual recording device. What would Julian do with all the silences now?

I made it home just in time for the funeral. My father's casket was a plain pine box; inside, where we could no longer see him, he was wrapped in a shroud of muslin. Julian and I each poured three handfuls of dirt into the grave. I felt at times like I was watching everything happen on a stage; I only knew I had been crying when I happened to touch my own wet cheeks with my fingertips. My face felt numb, everything was dreamy and blurred. Somehow I was dimly aware of the melody of the Mourner's Kaddish embedding itself in my memory. Julian stayed at the graveside until all the dirt had been shoveled back in and patted down into a small brown mound by the gravediggers.

It was a weirdly beautiful day, and a gentle breeze moved through the leaves of the trees surrounding the cemetery. Nobody spoke all the way back to the house, where some women from the synagogue were serving coffee and cake to the dozen or so mourners. I could still feel my father's presence, even smell him a little, especially when I sat for a while in his library among his books and his piles of papers. I wondered if he would always be there, floating invisibly above all of our heads, whispering into Julian's ear, listening to me sing.

That was the first time I imagined I could reach toward the dead with my voice. Maybe all this time my mother had been listening to me too.

> **squaring the circle:** the problem of constructing a square
>   exactly equal in area to a given circle; the exact area of a cir-
>   cle cannot be determined, except in terms of π, which cannot
>   be expressed as an exact fraction or decimal; the problem,
>   therefore, appears to be impossible of solution

B A C K   A T my desk with my dictionary, I kept thinking about Sola's
gazpacho and the mango I tasted for the first time in my life, about the
scars on her wrists and what she had said about the voice of her blood,
about wanting to see if she was alive inside. Paula was going to stay
away a little longer, and I didn't yet know if Sola was going to stay here.
Suddenly I could not imagine her leaving, I could only picture the
movements of her hands and her shimmering black hair. In my chest I
felt a restless stirring, as if there were some animal inside me that was cir-
cling, looking for something.

I got up to stand at the living room window and caught a glimpse of
my own face; beyond it, the playground was empty. Sola was cleaning a
house somewhere, perhaps combing the fringes of an elaborate Oriental
carpet with her smooth brown fingers. I went back to my wall of televisions and turned up their volumes one set at a time, hoping to see how it
was done: laughing, driving a car, baking a cake, brushing teeth, feeding
a child. Taking a woman in your arms and touching her cheek with your
cheek, holding her there in your steady arms.

At the hospital there is one nun who is always nearby when I open
my eyes in the early morning. Sometimes she is sitting in a chair
against the wall beside my bed and saying her rosary, rocking a little
as she prays. Sometimes she is walking up and down beside the row
of hospital beds, her thick dark shoes on the wooden floor. She looks
younger than I am, and when she talks with the other nuns, she
speaks Spanish with an accent from somewhere else. She has a soft
voice that matches her pale skin. They call her Sister Isabella. In the
first days I am there, when I am still too shocked to do anything but

stare up at the ceiling, she brings a small washbasin to my bed and gently takes my hands one at a time. With a small brush she scrubs beneath my fingernails, taking away the dirt that I am stealing from the earth. I do not tell Sister Isabella about the killing, I do not tell her or anyone about what I see and hear. I let her hold my fingertips in the warm water, and I think about the river.

After I am living in America for more than one year, I decide I want to write her a letter, or send her something to say thank you, but I do not know what to do at first. Then I think I can send some money to the hospital, something they can use for helping other people, children maybe, or they can use it to buy medicine or blankets or instruments for the doctors. I just need to give something. I find out there is a way to send a money order from the post office, and I mail it to Sister Isabella, with a note saying only that I send her blessings. I look at my fingernails when I write to her, I think about the dirt she is washing away. She never writes me back.

I WATCHED Sola leave in her cleaning clothes, gave her a fifteen-minute head start and a chance to remember something she might have left behind, then I went downstairs to the apartment. The stairs announced my descent but no one was listening, and Paula's key turned in the lock as if it were my own door opening to me.

In the kitchen I drank a glass of water, washed the glass and replaced it in the cabinet. I counted Paula's white plates and wondered how many of them I'd used for lunch. I put the bottom plate on the top of the pile, just in case I'd never seen that one. The kitchen gleamed; Sola was keeping everything as clean as if she were working there. I stood at the door of the bedroom but didn't go inside, just looked at the pillows and Sola's blue dress folded over the back of a chair. I wanted to touch it but I didn't.

The rooms smelled faintly like lemons. I couldn't hear myself walking on the carpets, I couldn't hear myself breathing. Paula's voice was caught somewhere in the corners of the high ceiling. I could almost hear her singing to me, to the ginkgo tree outside.

I finish cleaning the first house by noon, and for lunch I eat some black beans and rice on a bench beneath an oak tree. I often sit there, because it gives me a view of the bay and the flecks of white sails on the water, and this picture always brings me a sense of peace. I think about the day I am out there, on one of those boats with Warren; his friend takes us out on a windy clear day a few months after my arrival. The feeling of the sea spray against my skin and the wide stretch of blue water and blue sky lifts me out of myself for a few hours, and everyone smiles at each other all day. We drink white wine and eat cheese and olives and bread, but every so often I remember that this is not really my life, that I do not really belong in this picture.

"Are you happy today?" Warren asks me, and I tell him I am, because I know that is what he needs to hear. And it is true, for a few hours of being washed by the air and held against all of that blue. Warren is wearing a white shirt and gray shorts, and I am also wearing something white, so together I imagine that we look like people that belong together, on this boat on this perfect day. But inside I know better, and I can tell by the way his friends talk to me so carefully and kindly that they have no idea who I really am. The fact that I am new at their language is only a small piece of my strangeness to them and an even smaller piece of my strangeness to myself.

After my lunch, I go to my second house for cleaning that day. On the kitchen table Mrs. Bergman leaves me a pitcher of iced tea and a note asking me to please pay special attention to her daughter's bedroom, as Stephanie is coming home for a visit the next day. Her handwriting is graceful and flowery, just like the house, which has pale silk-covered furniture and glass cabinets filled with crystal and silver objects that seem to hold light inside their curving shapes. Certain rooms of the house appear to me as if they are never entered except by me with my dust rags and my polish.

I do not know the daughter, Stephanie, but her photographs line one wall of the study; she is the mother of a new baby girl, and pictures of the mother and child are spread out across the desk, waiting to take their place on the wall. I cannot help glancing at the pictures, and feel the familiar stab in my heart when I see something in the baby's eyes that reminds me of my own little girl, even though they look nothing alike. This baby is pink and blond, with a mouth shaped like a heart and very round cheeks. My Camucha has dark hair and dark eyes, which are always wide open, swallowing everything they see. Even though she is lost to me, I think that she holds the memorized world inside her bones, painting with her eyes the same way that I and my mother and grandmother do it. I never know for certain if she has this gift too, but I feel in my heart that she does. For the thousandth time, I tell myself that wherever she is, she remembers me, even now.

Upstairs I can hear Mr. Bergman coughing in his sickroom, a room I never enter. He has a nurse who lives in the house and takes care of him all day and all night, and that room is under her complete control. She does not like me, I can feel this from the way she never meets my eyes whenever we are in the same room. She has extremely short gray hair and large eyeglasses, which make her head seem too large for her body. I always ask how Mr. Bergman is doing, and she always makes her answers very short, as if it is not my business asking.

"He's as well as can be expected" is the kind of thing the nurse often says, which never makes much sense to me. Other times she says, "He's stable," which I find out means that his condition isn't getting better or worse. That is when I feel the most pity for Mrs. Bergman, because she is living with this situation of things not changing and not going away either.

This day, like so many other days, she comes home before I am finished cleaning, and once again her arms are filled with large shopping bags from stores whose names are elegantly printed on the sides. She pours herself a glass of iced tea and sits at the kitchen table as she sorts through the mail. On the surface, she looks perfect:

every hair in its place and earrings just so and lipstick that is like she puts it on every few minutes. Yet I can tell from the way she turns her head so carefully that inside, she is almost falling into pieces.

On the other side of town, Julian is sitting with his eleven televisions, waiting for his sister. And maybe Paula is longing for her home too, feeling far from everyone who can speak her language. The world is so big, and people become so stretched apart from each other. Even living in the same house, I know, people can be strangers, people who do not know how to talk to each other. When I am living with Warren, there are days I have no words at all, nothing to help him understand me. He tries so hard to listen, but on the day he finds me with my arms covered with blood he knows not to ask and only brings me to the hospital. All night he stays with me and even most of the next day when they say they have to keep me and observe. Warren sees into me so deeply, and he covers my open cuts with his own hands, but in the end he is still only a doctor for the body.

> **perturbations:** deviations in the motions of the planets from their true elliptical orbits, as a result of their gravitational attractions for each other

S O L A ' S   N I G H T M A R E had thrown me off balance, and it wasn't until late morning that I remembered today was laundry day. I gathered my dirty clothing into my canvas bag and pulled on my green backpack, which held a box of detergent. The laundry bag had a sturdy shoulder strap, but today I carried it in front of me, against my chest. Sola wouldn't feel like this, I told myself, embracing the uneven lumps of the bag. But what did I know about how she would feel? I sent the thought of her away, buried it in the bottom of the bag.

The Laundromat was six blocks away, four to the south and two to the west; there was one traffic light and one four-lane road to cross, and I had to pass a place called Burger Depot that never had more than one customer inside at a time. The signs on its windows were all hand-written, promoting things like extra creamy milkshakes and homemade French fries. Inside, above the counter, I had seen a huge sign listing at least two dozen varieties of burgers, each with a name of a movie star or a city. I had never eaten there, but once I went inside thinking I might buy a milkshake; a man with a black baseball cap was sitting at the counter and with both hands was feeding himself an enormous ham-burger. The feeling of grease and smoke in the air combined with the smells of ketchup and what must have been recently fried bacon kept me from ordering a shake or anything else. Stick with Frank's, I told myself. Stick with the kosher deli.

But this time my route was blocked by signs for MEN WORKING; there was a hole in the street and a sidewalk gaped open, huge pieces torn up. I had to go around, go across to the other sidewalk, no other choice. The picture in my head tilted, cracked apart. I thought I might even get lost; this was not the way I knew in my sleep, with my eyes closed.

My bag felt heavier, I couldn't watch my feet to make sure they went straight. The noise didn't help, a drill at the side of my skull, the earth vi-brating up through my bones. I thought the man at the wheel of the ma-chine must have been crazy, even with the canary-yellow ear protectors and heavy boots. Could a body be expected to take that kind of pound-ing? Even the street looked distressed, stones broken against their will. Someone was working inside the hole of the street, his hard hat at the level of a parked car's tires. It confused me, a face down so low, his legs invisible underground. Like burying someone standing up. Like people in the camp who died standing up at roll call, like people in cattle cars who died standing up because there was no room to fall down.

A garage door opened by an unseen hand, the car approaching. The driver had pushed a button, activated the gears inside her house. I waited for her silver Buick to steer into its shadowy berth, a ship into calmer water. She nodded to me, a thank-you for letting her pass, and I waited for the engine to turn off before I continued walking. Red park-ing lights clicking to blank, the muffled mutter of a car radio. Behind me, the garage door hummed into action again, closing her Buick inside. We all could be safe from each other, doors could close without hands, like eyelids.

> **cycle:** a series of events that is regularly repeated, e.g., a single orbit, rotation, vibration, oscillation, or wave; a cycle is a complete single set of changes, starting from one point and returning to the same point in the same way

THE LAUNDROMAT was very quiet at this time of day, which was how I timed my trip. There were dozens of machines to choose from, with their round mouths open in anticipation of my sheets and underwear and T-shirts. A change machine filled my hand with quarters and I sorted my clothes into one load of color and one of whites.

There were two sets of four-unit orange molded-plastic seats along the window side of the Laundromat; since the seats were bolted together, when I sat down on one they all rocked in unison. I liked the soothing hum of machinery in motion and the smell of soap in the air, I liked that everyone there had a purpose: folding or sorting or waiting for the final spin cycle to stop. A pile of free newspapers provided me with reading material. Usually I studied the latest copy of the *Flea Market*, reviewing every ad while I waited.

But this time, I kept thinking about Sola, about the way her weeping had pulled me downstairs in the dark. My skin prickled at the thought of lying so close to her.

I needed to do something with my hands, so I stood at the long table down the center of the room for sorting and folding. I spread out my seven dark blue T-shirts, one gray cotton sweater (a gift from Paula), seven pairs of navy socks, seven pairs of blue jeans, 30 × 36.

I liked that people here seemed to pay little attention to one another; they calmly pushed their baskets on wheels and watched their wet clothes slap against the portholes of the machines. There was a dispenser for laundry soap, one for hot chocolate, and another for cold drinks. A pay phone by the front door rang three times, but nobody picked it up. There was a faint layer of gray lint on all of the surfaces, and between the machines years of buildup had been trapped. The periodic rush of traffic out on the street was punctuated by jangling coins and the occasional metallic spank of a button or zipper against the tumblers. Soak, rinse, spin. Everything had its own cycle.

"Somebody been lookin' fo' you," a voice says from outside my apartment door. I am finally finished with my cleaning and am stopping here to look at the mail and check the windows. When I open the door, I see that the voice belongs to one of my neighbors, a small Asian woman whose back curves like a hill behind her shoulders.

"Excuse me?" I say, opening the door wider to invite her inside.

"Somebody come lookin' aroun' fo' you," she repeats, and shakes her head at my invitation. We do not know each other's names. She lifts her hand in the air as high as she can reach. "Dis big, maybe bigga," she says, waving upward. "A man wid sunglasses."

"I am living somewhere else for a while," I explain, even though she is not asking any questions.

"He was heah thwee, fo' time last week," she says, turning away and heading for the stairs. "Nobody talk to him, but I see out my window."

"Thank you," I say to her curved back as she begins to climb the concrete steps. I want to ask her name, but it is too late.

"Neva min'," she says, waving her hand again. She is already up on the second floor, and I hear her voice echo in the stairwell. "No warry," she says.

At first, I do not worry, like she says not to. I think it has to be Warren coming to see what is happening to me. We are not seeing each other for almost a year, ever since I tell him I need to try to have a life on my own, without his help anymore. He says he understands, and I am grateful even more than before for his knowing when it is the right time to leave me alone.

"Don't go too far away," he says. "Okay?"

"Okay," I tell him.

I do not give him the address of the apartment I find for myself, because I want to make a space between us, at least for a while. Now, after what my neighbor says, I think he somehow finds me anyway. But the more I think about how this could happen, the more it seems to make no sense. My phone number is not listed and he does not know any of the people I work for. And so I start to think about who else it might be that is looking for me at my apartment.

I am legal: Warren has a lawyer who arranges for me to have political asylum. A month of interviews and many pages of documents prove I am in danger of being killed if I return to my country, so the American government agrees I have to be protected. The lawyer tells me that after one year I get a green card, and I can even apply for citizenship if I want, after living in the United States for another five years.

He winks at Warren and says, "Everything would be that much easier if you got married right away," and laughs like he is making a big joke.

We do not laugh. Warren says many times he is in love with me. He is a good man, a wonderful person, and he deserves for someone to love him completely, but it is not me.

"Forgive me," I say to him the night I get my legal papers. We are drinking champagne to celebrate my asylum, and I am trying to be happy. The bubbles catch in my throat.

"For what?" he asks me.

I want to say, "Forgive me for letting you save my life," but instead I say, "For not marrying you."

We are sitting on a couch near a vase full of different kinds of flowers. I concentrate on smelling them, to see if I can tell one from another. He places one hand on my cheek, so gently, and looks at me for a long time, like he wants to stop the time and keep everything frozen. "I'm not sorry I love you," he says.

I close my eyes because I cannot look at him. Tears begin to spill out of me. I am crying onto his hands, and that is all I can give.

W H E N I folded my laundry, I watched my hands and thought about Sola again. The clothes were still warm from the dryer and I had to peel them apart because of the static electricity; they crackled and floated like seagulls. She was not supposed to be caught like this in my head. I smoothed the corners of my T-shirts and rolled them into cotton logs, paired the socks into dark balls, stacked everything in my bag like I was a packer of groceries.

I thought about my father's suits, how they made no sense in my life. I kept my jeans in rotation, date of purchase inscribed with indelible ink on the inside of the left front pocket. One pair for each day of the week, and khakis to wear to the Laundromat. Every year on my birthday, I bought a new pair, and the oldest pair was retired, delivered to the Salvation Army. For the first three months, the newest pair got washed with all the others before ever being worn, to break down its edges, make it approachable.

I liked wearing the newest pair of jeans on Monday, stiffest at the start of the week, retreating into softer paler indigo as the weekend approached. Like dye fading out of the days, my limbs loosest on Sunday. Like aging toward gray hair in the whitening patches of denim on my knees and backside. I would fade like that too, lose my color and my sturdiness in time. It was okay with me.

I washed my hair every morning in the shower, shaved with a handheld razor. I flossed my teeth twice a day, kept my nails short and clean. When I needed parts for the televisions, I used mail order and UPS. I kept things alive by taking good care of them. I wanted to die with my original teeth, that didn't seem unreasonable.

Behind me, someone banged a machine to shake loose a stubborn packet of detergent; I heard coins in his pocket as he bent down to collect his prize. Everything felt lighter now: my own detergent nestled into the pack on my back, my embraceable bag of clean laundry. I headed for the corner of the street, where the light had just turned to green, and I walked all six blocks without waiting for anything.

As I drive back to Paula's apartment, I try to think about who is at my apartment in sunglasses if it is not Warren. Maybe he knows someone who is an expert in finding lost people, and does not trust that I can tell him in the end where I am and what is happening to me.

But what if it is not him or anyone who knows him? When they do all the interviews for my asylum papers, they ask me so many times if anyone from my village is still alive besides me. I have to say over and over that I am the only one, that every person is murdered but me, that I have to listen to all of them being killed by the soldiers. The murderers keep screaming that my village is protecting the rebels, that we are helping them fight against the government.

"I am the only one," I tell them. "The one who has to listen to the killing. So I can tell it to you."

They want to know if I am ever in contact with the rebels. As if maybe I am telling this story to help them, even now! It is so crazy I almost start laughing.

"I am not political," I explain. "I only hear rumors about groups of men and women who live in mountain caves and fight against the soldiers. They do not come near my village, at least I never know about it, we are all too frightened to get involved." And still the end is the same: everyone dead.

"Did anyone know you survived?" they ask me.

"No one," I say. "I am all alone."

But now that question begins to echo in my head. I do not feel so certain. I am staying in the forest for maybe a day or two after the killing. I am in shock, they tell me, the ones who take care of me in the hospital.

"But who were the ones who found you in the forest, who brought you to the hospital?"

I cannot remember. I tell them I think they are farmers, people who live outside of the village. "How many?" they ask me.

"I am in shock," I say, repeating what they tell me in the hospital, trying to make them understand. "I do not know them. I do not know who I am even."

Now I begin to doubt everything. The nuns and hospital nurses and even Warren never tell me who brings me there, they never care to know. I am almost dead myself, they tell me, covered with dirt and leaves and my eyes like a wild animal.

"We thought you were a madwoman at first," Warren says. "Someone crazy from living in the forest by herself."

Who is looking for me? Who knows where I live?

Madame le Fleur always said "Don't look back." She said it every time I left her house, threatening me with those words. For a long time I used to think she meant for me not to turn around to look at her as I was leaving, but eventually I learned it was much more than that. She wanted me to keep my gaze on the future and not to be afraid of having left my family behind, leaving Julian especially. "You can't hold his hand," she would say, and it was true, he wouldn't let me touch him. But also I had to live my own life, save the only life I could save.

I think when I sang as a child I was practicing leaving, practicing my flight into my own life. It took so much separateness to be able to sing. In that basement I imagined I was on a stage in a field of light and I didn't care if people were watching me or if there was no one. Just the image of a dark cave and one circle of light for me to stand in, my voice rising and filling the air.

I thought I had to forget about all of them so I could sing.

BACK IN my apartment, putting away my laundry, I kept picturing Sola's hands on the mango, the juice making her skin glow. For the first time in years, I felt a lurching deep in my groin. I stood with my hands full of clean clothes, willing myself to think about information, to focus on the tasks I needed to perform before the day slipped away from me.

The heat under my skin slowly faded when I realized with relief that it was time to collect the mail by the front door. For Paula: three promotions for credit cards, along with *Opera News* and *Time* and a bank statement. Among my own pile, I found a letter from Paula addressed to Sola

Luz Ordonio, in care of me. She had written my name in solid black letters, extra large, to get my attention. There was no postcard for me that
day, but I remembered what she'd written the last time about needing to
ask Sola to stay longer in the apartment. For a wild moment I thought
about hiding the letter, not showing it to Sola. If she never read it, she
would leave at the end of the month. I would cure myself of this terrible
desire and return to my ordered world.

I held the letter in my hand, studying the stamp. There was a por-
trait of flowers, blurry shapes of yellow and red and purple, and some
kind of ancient-looking church in the distance. Except for my name, the
rest of the address was full of Paula's flourishes and stretched-out loops.
Sola Luz Ordonio. In care of Julian Perel. I returned to my living room
and sat down to think things over. My wall flickered back to life, and a
room full of people began to laugh.

"I'm not that kind of person," a woman was explaining to the audience. She looked like an enormous bag of flour, packed too tightly into a
blue and white dress, a white bow at her throat. There were eleven of
her on my wall, and in each one she waved a hand to tell the people to
stop and listen.

"It's not like I'm a paranoid," she said. "I'm not like that."

The camera turned to the host for her reaction. "Oh, but I think you
are," she said. There was a joyous burst of applause and laughter. The
host held her microphone even closer to her mouth, and whispered into
it. "I really think you are," she said.

A series of commercials paraded by, multiplied eleven times. A
woman with a hairstyle from my childhood was tormented by two
ghostly versions of herself, until she was finally saved by a box of diet
capsules. An avuncular voice spoke lovingly and confessionally about a
recipe for baked beans: "Our secret is in the brown sugar." A zoo of
dancing blue geese and red teddy bears was held hostage by a seemingly
innocent roll of paper towels. In a vast expanse of turquoise water, a daz-
zling white cruise ship floated serenely. The message WHAT ARE YOU
WAITING FOR? sailed across eleven screens, hovering even after the ship
had vanished.

The letter in my lap weighed nothing; inside was probably some filmy airmail paper, the kind that you could see through if you held it up to the light. Why did she write open postcards to me and a sealed letter to Sola? Was there something she didn't want me to see?

The situation was ambiguous. Wasn't the letter addressed to me too, as the caretaker? Wasn't it my responsibility to read the contents and then pass them along to Sola? I studied the stamp again, in search of clues. Three flowers and a church. Splatters of red, yellow, and purple. The canceled stamp said Budapest, although some of the letters were smudged. I tried to imagine Paula mailing it, maybe handing it to some concierge who spoke no English, smiling the way she did so easily. "A float down the Danube," that was what she wrote to me before. And now she was in Hungary, singing. In the land of my father's secrets.

I was auditioning in my sleep, Isaac reprimanding me over and over about the smallness of my voice, the way it would never be able to reach the back rows of the concert hall, his baton raised as if to strike me. I could not hear the music from the orchestra, kept missing my cues, my first note arriving too late. The faces of the judges frowning in disappointment, my heart falling to the stage floor and shattering at my feet.

It was because of Isaac that I went to look for a place in Europe, as if my own country was declared off-limits, he had sealed all the entrances behind my back. He had come from there but wouldn't go back, choosing the refuge of America for the rest of his life. I needed to see if there was more room for me in the smaller halls, if my voice could fill a different space farther from my home. Between the agent and Madame, I chose my targets, made plans to reach into distant landscapes. When anyone said *"in bocca al lupo,"* I thought of my wolf-mother Madame, and the way she would have carried me in her mouth if I'd been her infant, the way she shaped my mouth with her fingers when I was learning how to open the sound, training my spine to straightness. I was looking

for a place where my voice could live and grow, like the plants inside Julian's head. To make music out of nothing, out of air.

semipermeable membrane: a membrane allowing the
passage of some substances and not of others

M Y P H O N E rang three times before I decided to pick it up. After
the second ring, I started to imagine Paula in a terrible accident on the
other side of the globe, someone calling to give me the news of her death.
My knees began to shake, and the need to know overcame me.

The voice belonged to Sola. "Julian? Is that you?"

"Of course." My heartbeat stayed fast, a drumbeat.

"Oh, good," she sighed into the phone. "I need to ask you to do
something."

I heard traffic in the background, maybe a truck turning a corner. I
took deep breaths. "Where are you?"

"A gas station. But listen, I need you to look out the front window
and see if there is a car on the street."

I waited, listening to the faint echo of another conversation trapped in
the phone line with ours. "There are always cars on the street," I said.

"But a car parked in front. With someone inside."

Her voice sounded strange, too tight in her throat.

"Julian?"

"Yes."

"Are you looking?"

"Is someone waiting here for you, is that it?"

"Please look," she said. "Please."

"I'll be right back," I said, putting down the phone. I went to stand at
the window for a few seconds, long enough to see that the only cars
were moving past the building, no one parking at all. The playground
had three children and two mothers, two strollers, no cars.

"Nothing," I said.

"You are sure?"

"No one."

"Okay. Thank you," she sighed again.

"Are you all right?"

"Yes. I think so. I can call you later."

She hung up without saying good-bye, and I held the phone for another few seconds, listening to the dead connection.

After I call Julian, I call Warren to see if he knows what is happening, but all I hear is his machine. "I'll be out of town the rest of the week, but leave a message and I'll get back to you as soon as I can. If this is an emergency, please try my pager at 415 861 2328." I do not say anything. I am not an emergency. His gentle voice calms me for a moment, until I remember it is just a ghost, and he is far away.

I remember how Warren makes me drink warm milk at night when I cannot sleep; he says it is what his mother always does for him as a child, and he drinks it with me for company. My own mother rubs my feet with oil, smoothing and pressing my skin with her strong hands. The warmth spreads through my whole body and makes me so sleepy I do not dream of anything.

One of those nights when sleep is not coming to me, as we sit at the kitchen table and hold the warm cups of milk, Warren says, "I keep thinking about having children with you."

I do not tell him again about my daughter, about everything that happens to me. He knows as much as he needs to know. It is still impossible for me to imagine starting over, creating a child with anyone. Especially in this strange world where everything is so fast and loud and electric.

"These kitchen lights are too bright for me, in the middle of the night," I say. "Can we talk in the bedroom?"

Warren is wearing a pale green T-shirt that makes his eyes look like pools of water. "We don't have to decide anything now," he says. "I just want you to know I think about it, about our children. Teaching them Spanish. Taking them to see the ocean. Wanting them to look like you."

We go into the bedroom, get beneath the covers and hold hands. He lets me be in my silence. The bed is wide and white and full of pillows; over our heads there is a window to the sky. At night I can see stars, and in the morning sometimes there are birds passing very high up. I can tell what time it is by the color of the sky.

"We don't have to talk about it," he says, whispering. I think he is afraid of me telling him I do not want any more children, afraid of what he knows is already true. I keep waiting to see if my heart can change, if I can find an opening in myself for loving him, but the opening is hidden from me, like the entrance to a cave that is a secret.

Now, I sit in my car and keep looking in my mirror to see behind myself. It feels like someone is watching all the time, even though there is no one there. I call Warren again, to see if I can tell him something. "I am all right and you should not worry about me," I say. "I am going to call you again soon." The hairs on the back of my neck are standing up, listening.

> **virtual state:** (in classical physics) a force between bodies
> not in contact, e.g., electrostatic repulsion, is represented by
> a field

I STAYED for a while at the window, watching the street to see if anyone showed up to park and wait for Sola—and also to see Sola when she returned. Brian rode away on his bicycle and after a while, the children and their mothers left the playground. Behind me, my televisions were muttering about prize money and floor polish and the war on drugs. Words floated across the screen: THIS IS MY NEIGHBORHOOD. THIS IS MY FAMILY. I heard a siren, a piano, and a brief burst of laughter; below my window, a taxi slowed to a stop. The driver consulted a piece of paper, looked at my building, smacked his head with one hand, looked up at my building one more time, and then pulled away.

Paula's letter was tucked under the cushion of my chair, still unopened. I was deciding to keep it hidden, and let Sola leave without reading it. Why did Paula need her to stay? I could take care of myself, I could keep an eye on Paula's place too, there was no reason for so much caretaking. Water plants? I could do that. I was already in charge of the mail, and what was so difficult about lunch? I could make more trips to the deli, even build the sandwiches myself. Thinking about it made it all seem possible, even though the more I tried to picture myself completely self-reliant and truly alone, the more the details eluded me.

The problem was that I had begun to taste new things; the gazpacho and its mosaic of flavors, the mango's juice and texture, even the tart surprise of lemons in water. My tongue and skin and all of these messages were waking up too much. The unreceived letter was a door I could close on everything.

> **causality :** the relating of causes to the effects that they produce; many contemporary physicists believe that no coherent causal description can be given of events that occur on the subatomic scale

Dear Sola:

I'm hoping that everything has worked out well so far and that you're enjoying the apartment. I have another favor to ask—that is, an extension of the favor you're already doing for me. Could you possibly stay another two weeks? I have a brilliant opportunity I can't bear to pass up, and it means staying away longer.

If you aren't able to do it, I'll understand, but I'm hopeful you won't mind staying. I just don't want Julian to have to be alone there.

You'll find Herman Roth's phone number in my address book by the bed; just let him know whether or not you can stay, and he'll get in touch with me. Thanks in advance for helping me out so much—and I'm instructing Herman to send you another check for the additional time.

A hundred thanks, Paula

I R E A D Paula's letter, folded it back up and put it away again. There was nothing surprising or secretive, nothing to make my decision any clearer. Herman Roth was the problem: he'd be waiting for the call from Sola, and wanting to tell Paula what was happening, because Paula was worrying. *I just don't want Julian to have to be alone there.*

Forget the wolf, I had said to her, the way she wanted me to. I knew how to be alone, that was the one thing I knew how to do. Didn't she understand?

I want to go home and take a shower, but I do not know what place is home for me. Paula's apartment is where I have some of my things, and the rest are at my own apartment. I keep hearing my neighbor's voice saying "Somebody lookin' fo' you," and I think about where I can hide, up in the park maybe, among the trees and deep into the dark, all I need is water and I can stay there for days, until they stop looking and it is safe again. Without really thinking, I start driving into the hills too fast, toward the forest, barely stopping at the signs, feeling my wild heart in my chest.

When I get to the edge of the woods, I park the car in a cloud of dust and look for anything in the trunk that can help me: a blanket, a water bottle, a warm sweater. My arms gather things while my mind is already flying into the trees. That way, I think, as far as I can go. When I hear noises behind me, I turn without breathing to see a group of children, maybe twenty, all wearing hats and bright colors and carrying little packs on their backs. They are going for a hike.

For a few seconds, maybe longer, I watch the children laughing and drinking water from a low fountain and tying their shoelaces. When the teacher tells them to line up in twos and hold hands with their buddies, I think that is what brings me back. I am here, in a town with no soldiers, no one is trying to kill me, there are no guns pointing at my head, no one screaming or bleeding or being cut open. Here in these woods people walk with their dogs and have picnics and pick berries; no one comes here to hide from murderers. I start breathing again. My arms are full of things; I put them back into the trunk and feel my heart become more quiet. Slowly, I climb into my car and drive back down the hill to the place where Julian lives, the place with the golden tree.

AFTER SOLA parked the car in front of the house, I saw her look up at my window as she locked the door; her smile made me flinch and step back, like I'd been caught at something. I turned up the televisions and changed all the channels, looking for something dimly lit and harmless. The noise was almost enough to make me feel quiet inside, but then Sola knocked at my door and made my heart leap.

"It is me," she said, shouting.

I turned the sound down again and went to the door.

"Okay," I said. My hand was on the knob but I hesitated, staying inside.

"I just want to say I am sorry for calling before," she said from the other side of the door. "I do not want to bother you now too. Just to say I am sorry."

"Okay," I said again. I heard her footsteps on the stairs, and my hand turned the knob.

"Are you all right?" I heard myself ask. The door was open enough for my head and shoulders to lean through, toward the stairs.

Sola turned around from halfway down the steps and gave me half a smile. "I am all right."

"What are you doing now?" I asked, leaning farther through the doorway.

"Now?" she shrugged her shoulders. "I am taking a shower. My skin smells like too many chemicals from work. Then I am eating a little something."

"Oh."

"What are you doing now?"

Waiting for you, I didn't say. "Just thinking," I said.

"Okay," she said.

"Were you scared about something before?" I asked her. The door was wide open now.

She looked away and shook her head. Her dark T-shirt was covered with splashes of white, like snow or stars. Bleach, I realized, had stolen the color. "It is nothing. I am just nervous a little bit."

"Who was it?" I asked, although I wasn't sure I wanted to know.

"I do not know," she said, and then went down the rest of the stairs. I saw the top of her head vanish. "Maybe later," she added from Paula's door. I couldn't see her there, I could just hear her voice.

SIX

ONE OF the televisions stopped working. In the morning when I turned them on, the third one from the right, bottom row, stayed stubbornly black, no picture and no sound. I adjusted knobs and reached for a signal, but the screen stayed dark and silent. It was like a missing tooth in a face, a mask with someone's eyeless socket peeking through.

I made my precise cup of green tea and timed my egg, sat in the kitchen with my back to the screens. Ten televisions muttered softly about morning traffic and breakfast cereal, and audiences laughed at the wake-up jokes. I didn't want to fix it, I decided, at least not right away. My alphabet needed attention, any letter would do.

I turned the sound all the way off, considered pulling the broken set out of the lineup, but it was too much trouble. At lunchtime, I heated up my soup and turned only once to see if it was still a dead eye, imagining for a moment that I saw Sola's face floating there, a ghostly smile appearing as she looked at me. And the blackness of her hair all around.

I heard the wheelchair ramp as it rocked beneath the weight of my neighbors, Elaine's footsteps and the clicking spokes of the chair. Often they sounded like they were laughing, but today all I heard was the sound of motion. The van door sliding open, the mechanical whir of his lift raising him inside. Then the slide and click, the engine sparking into life, the diminishing hum of their departure. Brian had already gone off to his library, and I was alone in the building, feeling our bones settle into each other.

The talk shows mimed happiness. I sat in my leather chair and wrote a letter to Paula in my head.

I surprised myself by having no interest in fixing the broken television. Its dark face reflected the room; from certain angles I could even see my own face, a blurry pale oval, moving from place to place. The light from the window made a rectangle of glare, like the gleam of light in a dark eye.

> **transition temperature:** the temperature at which one
> form of a polymorphous substance changes into another;
> the temperature at which both forms can coexist

Always the day before an audition, I spoke in a whisper if I spoke at all, resting my voice completely. The cords were so vulnerable, my scarf and Madame le Fleur such flimsy and invisible comforts. But somewhere in the midst of this journey, I had begun to be afraid of my own sound, as if I were listening for a mistake, an excuse to condemn myself to permanent silence. I began to feel afraid of my throat's narrow passage, as if my vocal cords had grown thick in the night and there was almost no room for the breath to pass through. One morning I woke with my hands around my neck.

What if I could not sing anymore, what if the judges could tell I was pretending to feel the pain of Elektra when in truth I was only making the sounds, wearing the mask of pain?

In the shower I try to wash every inch of skin, like I am trying to get the smells of someone else off my body. I scrub hard with a cloth and with a round sponge from the ocean that Paula has in her shower. I think it is funny that people want me to use chemicals to make their houses clean, and that the chemicals make me feel unclean, like I am dipping myself in invisible dye. I think of my grandmother weaving her baskets; she uses dyes to soak her reeds for weaving, bright pools of red and purple and yellow that she makes from vegetables and flowers. Her hands always have the stains of the rainbow.

I knock on the ceiling and after a silence Julian knocks back, then we meet on the stairs.

"Are you really all right?" he asks me. I tell him I am, because I am telling myself it is true. But I need some company, I am afraid to be alone. I ask him to come downstairs to visit.

When I say I am going back to my apartment soon, he does not say anything, just sits on Paula's couch with a pillow in his lap. "I am missing this place," I say, and then, because I am afraid of making him sad or uncomfortable, because I do not want him to leave me by myself, I go into the bright kitchen to put water on the stove. "I am making tea, okay?"

"Okay," he says from the living room, and then says something else while I am filling up the pot with water.

"I do not hear you," I say, going back toward the couch. "What are you saying?"

He will not look at me, but only stares at a spot on the far wall. I stay leaning on a chair, and make sure not to get too close to where he is sitting. "Never mind," he says.

"All right."

He seems satisfied then, and looks in my direction a little. "Do you want to tell me what was wrong today?" he asks.

I do not say anything at first. I do not know how much to tell. He waits for me to speak, and I wait for him too. The room fills with the hissing sound of the water cooking on the stove.

"I think it is just in my imagination," I say, wanting to believe it. "Or some ghost from my other life. It is difficult." I stop, listening to the water turn into steam. As soon as the kettle starts to whistle, Julian looks like he wants to jump up, but I am closer to the kitchen. When I come back with our tea, I see him holding his elbows like he is testing the hardness of his bones.

He takes a very deep breath. "When you're a witness, and you tell other people, you make them witnesses too."

Standing with the teacups in both hands, I feel my knees go loose for a moment. "Is that bad?" I whisper.

Julian shakes his head. "No," he says. "It's good."

> **light, velocity of:** the mean value is 186,281 miles per
> second; according to the special theory of relativity, the ve-
> locity of light is absolute and represents a limiting velocity
> in that the velocity of no body can exceed it; in the mass-
> energy equation, which follows from the special theory of
> relativity, the velocity of light appears as the "connecting
> link" between mass and energy

THE CONSTANT of c was the one solid truth I could count on, steady and perfect, beyond doubt. The note of middle C or high C, was that Paula's constant, the one truth she trusted? What if I lost my constant, unraveling every equation I'd ever learned? What would be left?

I wondered if Sola had a constant of her own, something she used to hold her core self in place. That buried language? Could it be steady if it was something abandoned, words that could no longer be spoken aloud? Or was it the blood in her that wouldn't let her die, even when she tried to release it? Maybe it was the story itself, whatever she had seen or heard that made her wish for her own death—and yet the thing that re-lentlessly demanded her fierce hold on life.

Was my father's unspoken past his constant, his secret center?

Julian and I drink our tea and sit quietly for a while, with our private thoughts. I remember again that interview, the one where they want me to prove I am the only witness; I picture the room with its blank walls and false mirrors, the way the three men in their ties and jackets take notes on yellow pads and never exactly look into my eyes. They do not want to believe me, I can tell by the hardness of their mouths and how they lean back in their chairs sometimes, like they are not really listening to me but instead thinking about what time it is and when they can have another cigarette. Warren has to wait for me outside, so I am alone with them in the too-bright room. Someone else is watching from behind the mirror, Warren tells me afterwards because he sees someone go into that room, but I already know when I am sitting there, I feel the presence of someone else watching.

Like now.

"Was it the doctor, do you think?" Julian asks me. I am surprised he thinks of it, because it is my first idea too.

"No," I say. "He is not the one. And not immigration either, because I have all my papers."

"Maybe it's nothing," Julian says. "Just a salesman or someone like that." He raises his eyebrows and shrugs.

I notice that my panic from before is beginning to drift farther away, and that makes me think I need to laugh more, to forget about the man in the sunglasses who is hiding his eyes.

"Tomorrow, I do not have any houses to clean," I say, and take a deep breath just to soak it in. "Maybe we can go out for a walk. Some place high up with a big view."

"A walk?" Julian says. "Together?" He looks like he is trying to remember something important.

"If you want to," I say.

He looks past me, out the window toward the golden leaves of the tree. "Not too far up," he says.

"Just to see the sea," I say. "Can you do that?"

"I think so," he says, and stands up to leave, even before the tea is ready. I cannot tell if he is still afraid of me or not. "Tomorrow we'll walk high enough to see the sea."

double decomposition: a chemical reaction between two compounds in which each of the original compounds is decomposed and two new compounds are formed

Dear Jules:

Did Mom ever teach you to count down into sleep? I think she said it was like walking down a long flight of stairs, using the numbers to help me descend toward my dreams. Then Madame le Fleur told me to picture a chromatic scale, notes on a staff stepping down through the lines and spaces. I've relied on that method for so long now, the dark disks floating in the space behind my eyelids, notes for my dreamlife. You wouldn't believe it, but I'm still so afraid of the dark, after all this time; I go to sleep with my hands clenched and my feet twisted together for comfort. I don't know what I'm so scared of, really. But I wrap my throat in soft cotton, I start at high C and hope my way downstairs into someplace safe for the night.

Love, P.

IN THE morning, I lay very still to remember my dream; if I moved, even turned over on my side, it would vanish. There was a long hallway, a series of eleven locked doors with light leaking in thin strips along the floor, and behind each door a different sound: an old man counting backwards very slowly; Paula singing "Happy Birthday"; a game show host introducing a surprise guest; my own voice saying "It's going to rain today." I walked down the hallway toward an open door in the distance, but as I walked, the door remained far off, moving away as I approached it. Behind me, I could hear footsteps but I didn't dare turn around to see who it was.

When I saw Sola at my door later that morning, I suddenly remembered another dream I'd had, a dream in slow motion with a background language I didn't know. The voice was full of clicks and rolling vowels and a melody that seemed familiar and strange at the same time. I thought this was another one of my imagined versions of Paula's journey, but I could see only one image from that dream: Sola. One hand covering her mouth, and the other hand beckoning toward me.

When Sola came upstairs at ten-thirty to see if I was ready to go, I noticed her studying the side of my face.

"What?" I said. She was wearing jeans and a sweatshirt the color of a peach.

"You are in my dream from last night," Sola said, touching the doorknob like a good luck charm.

"You took the words out of my mouth," I said.

"Took your words?"

"It means we were saying the same thing," I said. "You were in my dream too."

Sola came into my apartment and sat on the arm of the couch. "We are walking together on a long path in a forest," she said. "There is someone behind us, following, but we cannot see who it is. I do not know if you can see me or not, but I can see you. There are not any colors, everything is gray except for some green light in the branches."

"We dreamed almost the same dream," I said. "Even though that's impossible."

"Is it?" she said.

I didn't know. My heart was pounding, threatening to break out of its cage. Sola sat on the arm of the couch, waiting.

"My other dream is from home," she said. "My lost language."

"Really?" I said.

"Yes," she said, and for a moment she went so far away from the room I thought she had vanished. I didn't tell her I'd dreamed something like that one too.

"Are you ready?" she asked, coming back, brightening.

I checked all my pockets: keys, handkerchief, some money. "Do I need my backpack?"

"I have one," she said. "With a water bottle. Walking makes me want to drink water."

"Okay," I said. I checked my pockets again, to be sure. "It's not going to rain, is it?"

"No rain," she said. "Just light."

> **dynamics:** the mathematical and physical study of the behavior of bodies under the action of forces that produce changes of motion in them

WHEN PAULA took me on a birthday ride down to the dog park at the edge of the bay, I felt my heart thrashing against the bars of my chest. I wanted to grab the door frame on the way out of our building, brace my feet against the edges of the floor, the corners of my life.

When Sola pulled me out of my apartment I felt at first the same rising panic, the certainty I'd run out of air like a diver down too deep or maybe the opposite, getting the bends from rising too fast toward the surface. I didn't trust the stairs or the sidewalks, and when she opened her car door it was like being offered a visit to the inside of someone else's dream. I watched myself climb in, one leg followed by the rest of my body, the seat belt a kind of life jacket to strap around my chest.

"Are you all right?" she asked me, and I nodded as if it might be true enough by pretending. The car seat was warm from the sun. I had my hands on my knees and I could feel the bones cupped there. The windshield had three small cracks running at disparate angles and there was a small round hole that looked like it had been made by a bullet. Sola got into her seat and closed the door, buckled her belt and started the engine. I stared straight ahead, waiting for the road beneath us to begin to move.

It is a test for both of us, I think, to see if I can walk in the woods without my memories, and for Julian, to go so far from the place where he feels safe. In my car, he sits all the way next to the door, and he keeps checking his seat belt, making it tighter until I think he is hurting himself.

"Are you all right?" I keep asking him, and he nods, looking straight ahead through the windshield like he has to see what is coming. I remember before Warren is teaching me to drive, I sit like that too, thinking it is my job to make sure we do not drive off the road or hit something. Other cars always get too close, or stop too fast in front of us, and Warren puts his arm in front of me to keep me from flying into the window.

"Sorry," he says, even though it is not his mistake, and then says something about how many terrible drivers there are. When he teaches me, he always tells me to assume that everyone else is crazy and does not know what they are doing. "Be defensive, in other words," he says, laughing. "They'll never stop surprising you with stupid moves, so you have to be prepared."

When we start driving up the long hill of Marin Avenue, Julian looks at me from the side. "Where are we going?"

"All the way up," I say. "The park is at the top. And there is a trail we can walk on that looks out to the ocean."

"I've never been up here," he says quietly, and without taking his eyes away from the road. "It feels like we're going to fall."

The car pushes so hard at the hill, groaning like an animal. "I know," I say. "But we are not falling."

At the top of the hill, the road curves and makes the tires sing. There are bicyclists riding next to us on the road, and every color of green as far as I can see. We pass signs for STEAM TRAINS and BOTANICAL GARDENS, places I do not know anything about except their names. After I park under a tree, I get out of the car and walk over to the other side, where Julian is unfolding himself.

"Do you want a drink of water before we start?" I ask. He has to take his hands out of his pockets to hold the bottle, and when he swallows, the bump of his throat moves up and down like a small animal. He takes off his sunglasses, rubbing them with the bottom edge of his shirt. I see a little bit of his skin when he does that.

"It makes me want to touch everything," I say. I mean the grass, the branches of the trees, the sky. I swing the pack onto my back and we begin to walk to the place looking out to the sea.

I W A T C H E D the path stretch away from us, turning into stripes of light and shadow and light. There were side paths that curved mysteriously into dead ends, tricky rises that were never the top. We didn't talk at all. I watched my feet and Sola's feet, matching the size of our steps, and a soft film of dust began to paint our shoes the color of the earth. I thought about the uniform surface of sidewalks and the tile floor of Frank's Deli. There were no lines here to pay attention to, no blocks to count.

At the very peak of the climb, a scarred wooden picnic table stood in a circle of stones, and Sola sat down on the top of it, her feet on the bench. I sat that way too, and the astonishing world spread out all around us: water stretching to the horizon, green and golden hills squatting in the sun, the city in the hazy distance, the two bridges connecting everything.

The blue was so blue it seemed invented. I kept taking off my sunglasses and squinting to make sure the colors were real. All the live things were in motion, responding to the bursts of wind; even Sola's hair shimmered like the leaves, sliding back and forth against her brown shoulders. She lifted up the mass of black with one hand, and then twisted it into a knot that nested at the back of her dark head.

I heard but couldn't see an airplane overhead; two turkey vultures drew lazy circles in the sky. The breaths I took were deeper and deeper, filling my lungs with eucalyptus and pine. I kept imagining Paula's amazement if she could have seen me up so high, surrounded by so much open space. I was amazed too, struck dumb at the way everything felt perfectly connected, even me, like I belonged here. And I thought, *There are people who live like this every day, who know how to see and feel these colors every time they open their eyes.*

Sola climbed onto the table and stood, doing a slow turn in the wind. I wished I could take hold of her, at least touch her hand, but all I managed was to stand next to her and turn the way she was turning.

"It is like this is the whole world, right here," she said.

I closed my eyes and opened them, just to be surprised all over again. "I'm standing on a table in the middle of the world," I said, and we both laughed into the wild blue.

On the way down, small rocks skidded and rolled away from us. Sola said, "This is the part where you have to trust yourself. Being afraid can make you fall."

Leaning into the hill, our shadows bumped elbows; our edges blurred. The country between us kept getting smaller.

SEVEN

In Budapest, I kept thinking all the men of a certain age looked in some vague way like my father, even though hardly anyone had his red hair or his blue eyes. I felt as though someone were going to call my name and reach out to hug me, or dance with me, or throw something at me. Once or twice, I imagined someone dropping a net around me or shooting me in the back of the head. I wondered if this was anything like what Julian felt every time he stepped out the door.

It was Herman Roth who said I had to come, I had to seize every chance.

"This is it, baby," he said over the phone long-distance. "You might as well take every shot."

"I'm getting a little tired," I said to him, from yet another hotel room in yet another city. I always bought fresh flowers to keep in the room, but by the time I left, they were losing petals, fading, falling over.

"Well, don't let me push you too hard," he said, and I could just picture him tapping his big fingers against a desk, like he could take me or leave me. "If you want to turn around now, it's up to you."

"No," I said. "I'm not turning around." His tone was calculated, I knew that, but it still produced the right effect in me. It reminded me of Isaac, of the way he said I was nothing without him, the way he tried to hold me back.

"I'm still going strong," I said to Herman Roth.

"That's what I thought," he said.

After a rehearsal in one of the high rooms of the Music Academy, I walked into the neighborhood near the old synagogue. In the windows of upper-story apartments, I kept seeing elderly people looking down toward the street, wearing expressions of regret or exhaustion or dull amazement. A kind of permanent shock, as if they would never be able to tell you what day or even what year it was if you asked them. I kept my scarf tightly wrapped around my neck, trying to read the signs on faces.

My audition was scheduled for a concert hall in the castle. Jan, a young Hungarian musician, offered to take me on a city tour the day I was resting my voice. He was in his early twenties, wearing imported Levi's and a leather jacket; he must have cut himself shaving that morning, because a small scab was trapped on his jawbone. He had thick eyebrows and a nervous habit of pulling on one ear.

At my request, he took me to the opera house, to see where I wouldn't yet be singing. They were doing *Carmen* that evening. Inside, it was all gilded and ornate and vast, full of places for my voice to get lost in. We stood in the wings, looking out toward the tiered seats; I saw countless red velvet boxes rising toward the gold chandeliers, griffons and gargoyles adorning the balconies.

"Please, do you like to sing something just now?" Jan asked, and gestured for me to go out on stage, facing the imaginary audience. From where I stood, the balcony set up for that night's opera looked dangerously rusted and fragile, like it would never hold anyone's weight.

"Oh, no," I whispered, shaking my head.

"Please," Jan said again, smiling, holding out his hand.

"No," I said again, watching his smile disappear. He thought I was being rude. "Today I'm trying not even to speak," I explained.

"Of course," Jan said, his blush pouring down his throat and beneath his shirt collar. "I'm sorry," he said, pulling first on one ear and then the other.

"Say something in Hungarian," I whispered, feeling a need to be nice again. Maybe this was why I wasn't famous: no courage to be mean.

Jan looked at me, smiled, and released a stream of sound that was at one moment completely foreign and strangely familiar. "What did you say?" I asked him.

"I said, 'Maybe one day I will be hearing your beautiful voice.'" He blushed again and bowed a little. My first Hungarian audience.

I begin preparing myself for going back to my apartment. I order a new lock for my door, and I leave two messages for Max Stein, the lawyer who helps get me my papers.

"You're perfectly legal, Ms. Ordonio," he tells me when he finally calls back. "No one is interested in having you deported or changing your status in any way."

I let out the breath I am holding inside and say, "Okay." I can hear him shuffling papers, maybe looking at the files with my name. I remember the polished wooden furniture of his office, and him sitting behind a wide desk with his neat beard and curly hair. His nose is bent a little to one side, like it is broken from something hitting him.

"Are you worried for any particular reason?" he asks. "Has anyone been harassing you?"

"Harassing? I do not think so. No, not harassing." I am in Paula's apartment, safe. But I am holding the phone very close to my lips, whispering. "I think maybe someone is following me."

"You're being followed?"

Do I sound crazy? I cannot tell anymore. "I think so. I am not sure. But yes. I think so." Outside, there are no parked cars.

"Who do you think would be following you?" Max Stein sounds curious, not worried. Do people tell him things like this every day?

"I do not know who," I say, not sure I can say the words out loud. *Maybe someone is trying to kill me.*

"I seem to recall that no one knew you were a witness, am I right?" Stein says, sorting papers again. I hear another phone ringing somewhere in his office. "You hid and were discovered by the Red Cross, then taken to the hospital, wasn't that it?"

"Not the Red Cross. Nobody knows who they are. I do not remember that part. Who finds me, I mean. I do not know who it is."

"You were in shock."

"Yes." Shock, shocking, shocked. Electric shock. Treatment for shock. *Suffering from severe shock,* it says on my chart.

"But surely, Ms. Ordonio, no one knew that you ended up here in America. Did they?"

"Outside of the nuns from the hospital? No. Nobody else." Warren tells them I cannot be left behind and I am going home with him.

"Was there anyone in the hospital who might have been, say, suspicious? An informer for the government or something like that?"

"How can I know?" I want to shout at him. *You see? I am almost dead there.* "I am not political, I keep telling them. Do you remember?"

"Yes, I remember what you said. But here is how I look at it. You were a witness to the murder of your people by order of your own government. That, by definition, makes you political. Do you see?"

I do not see, I do not want to see. But I have to say it anyway. "Yes, Mr. Stein. I see."

I DIDN'T know where Paula was exactly. Herman Roth knew, I was certain of that, but I didn't want to call him, I didn't want to give him the chance to ask me about the letter for Sola, or about anything else. I met him once, in front of the building, and he made me nervous, with his too-loud voice and his constantly moving eyebrows; I felt him sizing things up, including me. I guessed that he thought I was crazy. He spoke to me as if he wasn't sure I understood English and only communicated with mathematical symbols. Why Paula liked him I couldn't understand, except she must have believed he was a good manager, knew how to do his job and take care of her. Somebody had to do it.

Dear Julian:

I'm staying in Pest, singing in Buda, crossing the Danube to get from one to the other. Today, wandering around the back streets of some old neighborhood where Daddy might have grown up, I actually bent down to touch the cobblestones. They were all rounded and smooth and looking like they were the same ones he would have walked on as a child. I felt so close to him and so far away. I think my wings are getting tired. . . .

Love, P.

P A U L A   W I T H tired wings was a difficult image for me to hold on to. She always soared so effortlessly, and went so far without stopping. Buda and Pest: I couldn't imagine them either. My father never spoke about his childhood, as if it had been drowned behind his back, swallowed by a liquid darkness.

That one time I heard him speaking Hungarian to the woman with the matching tattoo, it was like watching my father become another person, a stranger. His mouth moved in a way I had never seen, the words in his throat rose and fell, a gargling sound. Paula could sing in four languages, but none of them sounded like his Hungarian. When I looked it up in the encyclopedia, I found out it wasn't related to any other language; the Hungarian tongue lived in a world of its own. English was all I knew, except for the language of science, which wasn't really a language at all.

I knew one word for *star* and one word for *heart* and one word for *laughing*, even though I knew there were hundreds, maybe thousands of ways to speak about these things. The televisions spoke to me best with silence. And Sola's wordless voice sobbing in the middle of the night would stay with me for the rest of my life.

total internal reflection: when light passes from one medium to another that is optically less dense, e.g., from glass to air, the ray is bent away from the normal. If the incident ray meets the surface at such an angle that the refracted ray must be bent away at an angle of more than 90 degrees, the light cannot emerge at all, and is totally internally reflected

O N   T H E last Wednesday before Sola's departure, I began to practice my independence. First, I ripped a hole in my schedule by going to the market on a day that was not designated for shopping. I needed supplies; I was going to make the sandwich myself today. In the middle of the night I had decided to make lunch for Sola too, and crept downstairs in the darkness to leave a note under her door saying "Lunch will be brought to YOU today." Now, leaving for the store, I felt the stirrings of panic. What made me think of changing my own rules? I told myself to back off while there was still time. Tiptoeing, bending like a spy, I checked to see if the edge of the note was still visible beneath Paula's closed apartment door. There was no piece of white, only a blank, shining floor.

In the store, I felt disoriented. This was not my day for being here under these fluorescent lights, among this determined throng of shoppers. My usual memorized list was no good either: I couldn't follow my practiced route through the aisles. My hands were shaking, my feet wanted to point their way out the door and onto the street toward home.

I thought people were staring at me because I was standing still for too long in this place of movement and action. A young man in a green apron was spraying vegetables with a hose, the mist making transparent rainbows. I gripped the handles of my plastic basket, headed for produce, and concentrated.

One perfectly yielding avocado. One tomato. Bringing the rounded shape to my nose I tried to find its earthy smell, but there was too much wax in the way. I weighed the tomato, predicting its price, trying to see if I could make my totals come to perfectly even numbers. In dairy I located a brick of dill Havarti cheese; and in baked goods, I reached for a fresh loaf of dark rye, aromatic even through its plastic bag. Finally, I agonized over a quart of lemonade, reading the ingredients and wondering if Sola's taste buds would find it too sweet. What was white grape juice and what was it doing in lemonade?

By the time I checked out it was nearly ten o'clock. The register receipt had the zeroes I'd arranged, and my backpack was laden with ingredients. I walked home with my burden, making plans.

Sola's car was still out front and the blinds were closed; I waited in the hallway, listening for sounds of her before going upstairs. The water was running. Relieved, practically buoyant, I climbed the steps so fast I got winded. There was plenty of time before one o'clock, but I needed to get everything just right.

The televisions were off, but I longed for sound, sensing that my panic was about to return. I put on a tape, a recording in my sister's familiar voice. Mozart arias from *Così fan Tutte* and *Don Giovanni*. The notes entered the room as tenderly as rain.

Calmer now, able again to focus, I unloaded my backpack, covering the entire counter with food. I devised a system for assembling the sandwiches: the bread lined up and waiting, the tomato and avocado sliced into crescents, the cheese in precise rectangles.

Dipping my knife into the jar like a brush in a pot of paint, I spread mustard to the very edges of the bread. The ochre stain was flecked with seeds and textured like a waiting canvas.

Slowly, carefully, I arranged the tiles of my mosaic: yellow and red and green. The design was a relief map of squared-off islands and oceans and continents. When I cut the sandwiches into triangles, the layers were geological deposits on the side of a mountain, history laid down in relentless stripes.

Allegro, Andante, Adagio.

I sleep very badly and dream of screaming—or trying to scream and making no sounds. I wake up with my mouth open, and for a few moments I cannot remember where I am. My sheets are twisted into knots around my legs and the pillow is on the floor. Slowly, faces come into my head: Warren, Mrs. Barrett-Jones, Paula, Julian. I have to fit them into my life, one by one, until I am back in the present. Only one of them speaks to me. Julian is saying "When you tell other people, you make them witnesses too." I try to think of how to say *witness* in my old language, and it takes me several moments to remember. An image of my grandmother comes at the same time: she is weaving a basket, the reeds dancing in her hands, the basket cradled between her knees as she squats on a flat rock beside the river.

"Who is following me?" I ask her, but she does not look up from her work. I sit in Paula's bed and hug my knees, wishing more than anything that I could learn how to weave a basket with my hands.

My heart starts beating like a trapped animal when I see the note on the floor inside the front door of Paula's apartment. I think it is a message from the man in sunglasses: he is here, and before he kills me he is going to tell me why he wants to kill me. I run to look out the front window for his car, but only see my own banged-up Ford. I crouch down on the carpet, thinking there is no place to hide. After three deep breaths, I pick up the note, and when I see what it says I start laughing. "Lunch will be brought to YOU today," I say out loud, so relieved I sit down on the couch and throw the note in the air. "Lunch."

Just in that moment, the phone rings and makes me jump. My heartbeat is still not all the way slowed down. Paula wants me to answer the phone whenever I am in the apartment, even though she has a machine, so I put my hand on my heart to make it quiet and I answer.

A man's voice I do not know says, "Is this Sola Ordonio?"

I want to throw down the phone right away, and I turn again to look out the window for the car with the murderer inside. No one is there.

"Who is this?" I whisper.

"Ms. Ordonio? Are you there?" I do not say anything else, just wait for him to tell me. "It's Herman Roth, Ms. Perel's manager."

For the second time, I sit down on the couch laughing, thinking I am finally going crazy after all this time. "Herman what?" I say. "Perel's what?"

"Roth," he says. "Manager. I'm the one making her famous. Well, no, she's making herself famous. I'm just the man behind the curtain." He laughs, even when I do not. "You are Ms. Ordonio, right?"

"Right." He says my name like it does not quite fit in his mouth. Oardonnyo.

"I'm calling because Paula told me I'd be hearing from you about staying on at her place, and I hadn't heard yet. I wanted to make sure everything's okay, I don't want her to have to worry about the apartment while she's under so much pressure. This isn't really my job, you understand, but she asked me as a favor to check on things. Because of her brother and so on."

He talks so fast I cannot keep up with all he says, so I go back to the beginning. "Staying on?"

"I believe she wrote a letter. You didn't get one?"

"No, no letter."

"Well. She's extended her trip and wants you to stay in the apartment another two weeks. You were supposed to call and let me know if you can do it."

"I am sorry, this is the first thing I am hearing about it." My head is still thick with thoughts about being chased and followed. Staying is something new. "I am planning to leave in a few more days," I say. "Go back to my apartment."

"I know. But that's why I'm calling. Can you stay?" He is waiting for me to answer, but I have to slow down, try to think in a straight line. "Two more weeks?" I say.

"Right."

"I think I can stay," I say, carefully. "But you know I have to check on some things first." There is Julian and there is my apartment and there is still someone looking for me. I do not know what is safe. "Can I call you later?"

I hear him take a breath and blow it into the phone. "Sure, later's okay. As long as it's today. I'm faxing her this evening, so it would be good to have the word by then. And she told me to give you another check too, if that makes a difference."

Herman Roth gives me the number to call him later, and I write it down on the back of Julian's note, which I pick up one more time from the floor. *Lunch. Two more weeks.*

The mail that Julian collects every day for Paula is piling up in a big round box on the floor by the front door. Even though at first it feels like I am doing something wrong, I spend a few minutes looking through all of it, in case there is something for me. I remember how for the first few months I am living with Warren, I always look in his mail for a letter with my name on it, thinking that one day someone is writing to tell me to come home, it is all a mistake, a dream, everyone is alive, and everyone is missing me. I watch for stamps from other countries, and handwriting in the script of my mother. But after a while, I have to stop expecting anything. No one is left from that place who knows me, who knows my name. And here, in this great pile of papers, everything says Paula Perel, or Ms. Perel, or Mademoiselle Perel. No one knows my name.

YEARS AGO in a backstage dressing room, I was watching Paula brush out her hair when a woman came in with her blond little girl, a child maybe five or six. The mother explained that her daughter was autistic, and I could see how the girl stood so stiffly, as though her body didn't really belong to her. There was a blankness in her face, a flat, sky-blue gaze.

Her mother said, "She always relaxes completely when I turn on the stereo, especially when I play opera. When I brought her here today I thought maybe you wouldn't mind singing just a few notes for her right now, so that she can be this close to you? I want her to see where the singing comes from."

And of course Paula let the child do it; she sang a few lines from the program she'd just finished. And what was amazing was that the child went straight to Paula and placed her small fingers on my sister's lips, very gently, but quite seriously too. And the girl's mouth opened just a little, not to make a sound but as if she wanted to feel the shape of the air on her lips too, the feeling of the music coming out.

Once when Paula was practicing in her apartment I saw a man on the sidewalk stop in midstride as he heard her voice, a look on his face like he couldn't quite believe what he was hearing. I watched out my window and saw him lift his hand to his chest, a gesture that made my own hand float up too in a sympathetic echo.

She was holding notes at the top of an arpeggio, a sound as pure as a blade of light. He stood there like his knees were broken, like his hips had locked forever into place. I saw his eyes close, I thought he might lie down on the cement and die there. *Her voice could kill with beauty*, I thought, *lift you right out of your skin.*

> **zodiacal light:** a faint luminous patch seen in the sky, on
> the western horizon after sunset or on the eastern horizon
> before sunrise, believed to be due to the scattering of sun-
> light by meteoric matter revolving around the sun

I clean Paula's kitchen sink and bring myself back to peace again, the smooth places on the counters make me feel I am wiping away my dreams, my tears in sleep. Inside myself I go clear and empty, no voices or fear, just the sound of water rinsing everything.

Julian tells me about his bottles of vinegar and lemon and no chemicals, nothing to burn your skin and make your breathing choke up. "It's called Green," he says.

I think of my grandmother and my mother, the things they know about the earth, the flowers, the herbs, the body of women, the cycles, the emergence of a child. I have not learned enough from them. The voice of my grandmother in my dreams cannot teach me how to live in this world of glass and steel and poison. I have to learn this world for myself.

AT EXACTLY one o'clock I stood at the door of Paula's apartment with a sandwich plate in each hand, silverware rolled inside napkins that were stuffed into my back pockets, and the glasses of lemonade still upstairs on my kitchen counter. I had no free hand to knock on the door, but Sola opened it anyway to let me in.

"Just on time," she said.

"I'll be right back," I said, setting down the plates on the coffee table and bolting upstairs for the lemonade. The glasses were filled to the very brim, so I had to take the steps more carefully coming back down. "I guess I need a tray," I said.

Sola closed the door behind me, and we stood looking down at the sandwiches on the table. "They look like a design of something," Sola said. "I am so hungry but I almost do not want to eat them. You know?"

"Oh, it's just food," I said, feeling my face go red.

"But you are making it especially for me," she said. "Which makes it almost like art."

We sat opposite each other—me in the chair and Sola on the couch—and ate. After her first bite, she said, "Wonderful," and then we didn't talk. From time to time I watched her mouth while she chewed and her throat when she swallowed. When we were both finished, she put her empty glass in the middle of her plate, and said, "I have a phone call from Herman Roth."

Right away, I knew that she knew, but I pretended. "What did he want?"

She was leaning forward, with her elbows on her knees, her face supported by her hands. "Your sister wants me to stay here another two weeks."

"Oh." I counted the crumbs on my plate.

"I am thinking about it," she said. "I have some mixed-up feelings."

"Mixed-up?" Twenty-seven crumbs and one tomato seed.

"I think it is good for her, but I am not so sure it is good for me."

"Why?" Sola's plate had a streak of mustard on one edge.

"Maybe I am already staying here too long. Maybe I am not living my own life."

I looked at her bare brown feet against Paula's green carpet, thought of the roots of trees.

"You know, I am just visiting here. My own place is over there." She gestured vaguely with one hand. "On the other side."

"Other side of what?"

"You know. The other side of everything." She sat up straight, used her hands to draw pictures in the air. "Where things are not so nice and quiet. Where children play with guns they find in the garbage, and shoot each other by mistake. Or not by mistake. Where women sell their bodies to pay for a place to live with their babies. Where—"

"Wait," I said, leaning forward, trying to stop her hands with my voice. "What makes that other side your place?"

"I do not know." She sighed and began folding her napkin into smaller and smaller triangles.

"Do you want to stay?" I asked.

She tilted her head to one side. "Maybe you do not want me to," she said.

Go. Stay. Go. "It's just two weeks," I said quietly.

"Your sister worries about you," Sola said.

"I know. But she doesn't realize . . ." I couldn't finish my sentence. *Doesn't realize how much safer I am by myself? Doesn't realize that with Sola here I'm forgetting how to be alone?*

Sola dropped the folded napkin into her glass, where it slowly unfolded against the melting ice. "I could say yes to Herman Roth and then leave anyway. Make Paula feel better and let you stay by yourself." She shook her head, touched her throat with one hand. "But I do not want to lie."

"No," I said.

"No to which thing?"

"No to lying," I said. "I'm sorry. I knew about Paula wanting you to stay. I got the letter and hid it from you."

She nodded her head, turned the empty glass around on the table so we could watch the napkin as it absorbed the icy water. I stood up to take the dishes to the kitchen, needing to do something that would make a small but distracting noise. "It is all right," Sola said, and looked up at me. "You have mixed-up feelings too."

I stacked the plates and grabbed the glasses between my fingertips, walking away from her. "Yes," I said. "Very mixed-up." That didn't begin to describe it: the electric ache in the center of my body whenever I thought about Sola, the way I dreamed her dreams, the way I wanted to touch her. If I didn't send her away, I would be turned inside out.

I sit there watching Julian struggle with his monsters. My own fears are about the outside, the ones coming after me, and his are about the inside and underneath, the sufferings people spend all their lives hiding from others, or maybe hiding from themselves. He is doing a good job so far, keeping everyone at a distance and locking himself up in his apartment, not even his sister is really allowed inside, where he lives. It makes sense to hide Paula's letter, to make me go away. But the problem is, I want to stay. I need to stay. I think maybe he needs me to stay too.

> **velocity, relative:** the velocity of one body relative to another is the rate at which the first body is changing its position with respect to the second

"IT'S YOUR decision," I said to Sola. She was watching me too closely, I could feel it on my skin.

"In a way."

I began to wish I were back in my apartment, washing the dishes. Making sure I had sealed all the edges of the plastic containers in my refrigerator. But when I looked at Sola, I remembered that phone call, when she wanted me to check in front of the building for a car. "Are you afraid to go back?"

"Yes," she said, lifting her shoulders in a helpless gesture. "But I can manage," she added.

I nodded.

"And you can manage too," she said. Her voice was a smooth round stone. I didn't say anything. She pulled her bare feet onto the chair and folded them neatly beneath her. Sitting that way, she seemed so self-contained, compacted into a knot.

I heard a faucet dripping in Paula's kitchen. Outside the window, I could see the fog was just beginning to dissipate; patches of blue sky floated among the gray and white veils. The room was getting brighter.

"I'd like to see your place some time," I mumbled, because just then I had been trying to imagine where she lived, what the "other side" looked like.

Sola's mouth opened in surprise. "You want to see my apartment? Really?"

"It's probably not convenient," I said, backing off. "I was just curious. Never mind."

Sola shook her head, smiling. "No, I think it can be nice for you to come." She reached behind herself and began braiding her hair; her fingers worked blindly, expertly. "I am just embarrassed," she said. "No one ever visits me there."

"No one?" We both must have been thinking then about whoever it was that was looking for her. But neither of us said anything about him.

"You want to stay here, don't you," I said, thinking, *It's just two more weeks.*

Sola held on to the end of her braid with one hand, like it was a rope. "Yes," she said.

I already know that I have to stop myself from touching him, because he is so frightened. But using my hands is like language for me, or better; words are so small, so far from what I want them to mean. I can never say exactly what I am feeling, not even in my old language, and especially not in this newer one. There are too many places only skin can reach, only the feeling of fingertips and the endings of nerves. Electricity is the closest idea, or vibrations, or maybe chemistry. There is so much I never study because my schooling is so broken into pieces and in so many different places. Many times Warren tells me I have a quick mind, that I can learn anything I want, but the question is, what to learn? I think about that student Brian and his fascination with weather, then Julian with all of his science books; Paula is training and learning about music for many years, and of course Warren studies so long to become a doctor.

It is so different where I come from, people do not select a subject to become an expert, but we do what our hands and our lives require. It does not seem as if there are choices about it. My grandmother makes baskets because she needs them for her use every day, and so do other people in our village. There are weavers who make fabric for clothing and men who carve tools for farming; someone always has a special gift for animals and someone like my mother knows how to help women give birth. Everyone fits together, all the parts helping each other, all of us turning like a smooth wheel.

Am I remembering it too perfectly, making it seem like I come from a garden of paradise? It is hard to know anymore. The past is becoming more and more like a story I am reading or even making up myself. How does anyone know if they remember the truth?

The truth in present tense is that the world I come from is gone, burned into ashes. I want to show my apartment to Julian, partly to see it through someone else's eyes, to see what it can tell about my life. To remind myself again and again that this is where I live. Now.

I kept feeling drawn back into the Jewish quarter, haunted by images I'd somehow never considered before. Here I was, my feet on stones my father might have stepped on, and the great synagogue rose in front of me like some oversized stage set, Moorish towers and mosaic stonework. Inside, I was stunned by the ornateness, almost as grand and gilded and tiered as the opera house, just a few blocks away. I gazed at the thousands of empty seats, wondering when they would be filled again.

Outside, alone in the shady courtyard, I found my answer. A garden of gravestones: small moss-covered slabs tilting toward one another, most only as high as my knees. I thought they looked like children huddled together to stay warm, touching shoulders for comfort. The air felt cool; I tightened my scarf around my throat as I bent down to read the inscriptions. On each one I noticed the same date repeated over and over: 1944. Then without warning I saw my family's name Perel engraved on two stones leaning side by side. When my fingertips touched the damp cold of those letters, the shock went through me so hard I heard a moan rise from my throat, and I thought I might fall down.

There were records, it turned out. History climbing toward me like a rope, braided with details that took the breath right out of my chest. My father's father was a cantor. There was a sister too, who would have been my aunt, a violin player. A girl with one hand curved around a delicate skeleton of wood, the other holding a bow like it was made of glass. My grandfather singing in praise of the god he died believing in, chanting all the way into heaven. A red-haired girl dying like the broken string of her instrument, snapping forever with one terrible note.

I sat at a wide oak table with the papers spread out before me, names written incongruously in that beautiful script of a murdered world. "Jacob David Perel, age 51, deported to Auschwitz. Sarah Rebecca Perel, age 14, deported to Auschwitz." My grandmother had been spared the deportations and the gas chambers, dying earlier from tuberculosis. What I was reading on those pages meant my father went to Auschwitz at the age of seventeen, orphaned on arrival.

It was after my mother's death that my father stopped going to synagogue. It must have been the final insult, the last shred of faith torn away. God was dead or at least turned away, he told us, there was no point in trying to reach him. "You might as well pray to a stone or pray to the dead. Don't you see? If they couldn't save themselves, what can they do for any of us?"

He ripped his clothing in the tradition of mourning, he grew a beard for several months. But there was to be no more praying, no more voices raised in the name of God.

Walking in the Jewish quarter, I tried to picture my father as a child, imagined him walking with his family to the synagogue where his own father's voice would rise toward the vaulted ceiling, imagined his mother and sister veiled behind the opaque curtains of the women's section. I wondered if the violin-playing child asked why she couldn't play her instrument on the Sabbath when father played the instrument of his voice? I wondered what they told her when she tried to pack her precious violin into the one suitcase she was instructed to bring along on the morning of the deportation, if they had enough foreboding to let her choose whatever she liked, if they knew it didn't matter what their suitcases held because no one ever returned to unpack them again.

It seemed that every opera I knew was too small to contain this story, not just the tragedy of a single family or even a community but an entire world erased, millions of voices silenced. I had sung of betrayals, abandonment, even murder, but nothing compared to this. My aunt's violin and my grandfather's voice had been stolen from the world; I could not begin to understand why. I felt my throat closing in shame, that I had made beautiful music in the face of this nightmare. The losses filled me up, choked me. And I feared I could never sing another note.

SOLA CALLED Herman Roth while I was still with her in Paula's apartment.

"I can stay for two more weeks," she told him. Even from across the room, I could hear his booming voice respond to the good news. Sola smiled.

I was drying our dishes from lunch, getting things ready to go back upstairs. Sola was listening to something else on the phone.

"Oh," she said. "That is very generous."

She listened again, looking at me sideways. "He is fine," she said, so I knew he had asked her about me. For Paula. "Yes," she said. "Please tell Paula everything in the apartment is perfectly all right and Julian is doing well too."

I turned to leave, feeling the odd shiver of being talked about in the third person when I was still in the room.

"He is right here," I heard Sola say.

I turned quickly to shake my head but it was too late.

"Do you want to talk?" she said, both to Herman on the phone and to me in the room.

I shook my head, but she was already holding out the phone for me to take it. Reluctantly, I set down the plates and glasses, feeling doomed. Herman Roth's voice in my ear.

"Julian!" he said loudly. "How the hell are you?"

"Fine," I said, holding the phone away an inch or so to soften the sound.

"Good to hear your voice," he said. "Your sister's trip is going great. She's gonna be a star, right? And I'm glad to know everything's all right over there at home. Paula was asking about you."

"I'm just fine," I said.

"She'll be glad to hear it! Anything else you want me to tell her for you? I'll be faxing as soon as I hang up the phone."

A hundred images flickered before me, none in words. I saw myself taking a walk with Sola into the high green hills, making sandwiches, lying curled against Sola's back in the middle of the dark night. Paula didn't know about any of it. "Tell her hello," I said. Mouth of the wolf.

After talking with Herman Roth I have to go clean a client's house. Before Julian leaves with his plates and glasses, he tells me he is glad I am staying longer, he says he does not want me to be afraid.

"It is nothing," I tell him, realizing when I say the words that this is the sound I keep repeating in my head over and over: It is nothing nothing nothing. Like a prayer.

"I wish I could help," he says, one foot already on the stairs to go up.

It is nothing, nothing, nothing, says the voice of my grandmother. "Thank you for the lunch," I say to Julian's feet as they climb away from me.

The four hours of cleaning go by quickly, like a blank page

in a book; my hands do what they are supposed to do, and when
Mrs. Olivier asks me if I happen to need an answering machine
because she is giving one away, I have to pull hard at my mind
to bring it back from the surfaces of counters and sinks and
bathtubs and floors, back to the place where people talk to one
another.

"Answering machine?" I ask.

She is pointing to a shoe box that is sitting on the kitchen table.
"There's nothing wrong with it," she says, lifting the lid to show me
the machine inside, its black cord wrapped neatly around its shiny
middle. She has three gold rings on one hand, each with a different
color of stone; her peach-painted nails tap on the black plastic lid of
the machine. "My husband wanted a new one, a digital one or
something, and so this one is apparently obsolete as far as Daniel's
concerned. I was going to drop it at the Salvation Army, but since
you're here, maybe you need one?"

"I do not think so," I say. "But it is nice of you to ask."

She smiles at me like I am a small child. "Well, you might need
one more than you think. I know I've wanted to leave you a message
on occasion, and I've been surprised you didn't have a machine.
Don't you find them useful? I can't imagine being without one
anymore."

I think of Warren's message, how comforting it is just to hear his
voice. But who needs to call me when I am not at home? Clients
who really want to talk to me can just keep trying.

"I do not know," I say, and then I think of the man in the
sunglasses. If he knows where I live, maybe he knows my phone
number, and I want to hear his voice, see if it has an accent, some
note that can help me know who he is. I feel suddenly like a spy with
a way to get information.

"It's up to you, Sola," Mrs. Olivier is saying, replacing the lid on
the shoe box.

"Maybe I will just try it out," I say. "If I do not like it, I can always
give it away myself. Right?"

"Good for you," she says, tapping her perfect fingernails on the box and sliding it toward me. "I bet you'll find you can't do without it after one week."

S O M E T I M E S I wondered why I didn't have a more deliberate system for generating definitions for my dictionary, but it seemed necessary to allow them to rise up, allow one set of meanings to lead to another in a cascade of random surprise. The only question was how to determine when the work was complete—when had I covered enough territory? Surely there would always be something else to add to the *E* chapter, or the *T* chapter, or the *M*. Legitimately, the dictionary could be revised indefinitely, at least through my lifetime, since discoveries were being made every day, every hour. Somewhere in the world a new understanding of a particle was being scribbled into a notebook, an atom was being smashed into yet unnamed pieces, a star was dying or being born. And those were only the observed events, the things visible to human or telescopic or microscopic eyes. In other dimensions, universes unfolded themselves, evolved, transformed. At times my dictionary seemed to me like a child's game, chalk drawings on a sidewalk between rainstorms.

All I could do was attempt to keep just ahead of the rate of change, admit the impossibility of being truly current. By the time the dictionary was printed and bound, some number of terms would be obsolete, science moving faster than the printing press, mind over matter, again.

affinity: (in chemistry) chemical attraction; the force binding
    atoms together

It is the anniversary of my baby girl's death, seven years ago. I clean the house of a man with four cats, letting them rub against me one after another as I move from room to room. There is a piano in the living room whose keys make a soft cry when I dust them. Paula has a piano in her apartment, but the cover is closed and the keys stay hidden inside like a woman ashamed to show her teeth when she smiles. I wash the man's kitchen floor and dust the shelves of books about art and antiques, I make the stovetop gleam like it is new from the factory.

I keep myself in motion all day, focusing on my hands and their tasks, stopping just once to stroke one of the cats who wraps its body around my ankles and will not give up its search for my attention. Instantly in that touch I feel my heart go soft, I feel the bones of her body under her loose fur, and I think of Camucha, the weight of her when she is still so new from inside me it seems we still share the same blood, the same breath. I hold her all day, wrapped against my body while I help my mother with the house or the cooking, pounding the flour for tamales, washing the steps outside the front door, going to the market for some tomatoes and chilies. Camucha curls against me like we are the same being, like our skin is the same skin. I stroke the cat and crouch in a stranger's kitchen, counting seven years in my heartbeats. Seven long strokes along her small silky back.

I pull myself back to my feet and rinse my hands in the sink, amazed to have the same hands now as I do in that time seven years before, when I hold my child at my breast, when she drinks from the liquid of my body.

> **alternating current:** a flow of electricity that, after reaching a maximum in one direction, decreases, finally reversing and reaching a maximum in the opposite direction, the cycle being repeated continuously

I F I could have gone backwards, reversing everything about my life, would I start over? Erase it all? And if not all, what would I keep? The nights of lying with my head on my father's barrel chest, listening to his heartbeat until I was asleep? And then, barely conscious, being carried in his arms back to my own bed? Wouldn't I keep that? What if, when Paula was born, I had remained silent? Or what if Paula had been born first, and I was the one who began singing before I had words? Would my voice be the one pouring into the ears of Budapest right now?

Once, in secret, I wrote with blue ink the date of my birth on the inside of my forearm. When I scrubbed at it with soap and water, fading it more and more until it vanished, I imagined what it would be like to make the pain and the sorrow disappear like that too. When my father's language remained submerged in silence, was he erasing his past? Trying to stop the current? Instead, the flow continued, electric and relentless, in me.

There was a survivor visiting our house who had had her tattoo removed, burned away. But I still saw a scar, a mark to show that something had been there, some echo still carved beneath her skin. What we hold on to, we can't choose. Reversing and reaching a maximum in the opposite direction. And the cycle repeating continuously, without our permission.

To record my message on the answering machine I have to practice many times. The directions say to tell my name and number so people know they are reaching the right phone, but I do not want to say my name. My voice does not sound like my own when I play it back, there is something rough and a little scratched in the edges of the words. Once, I try the message in Spanish, but I know it is confusing for my clients, all of them Americans who know only how to say *por favor* and *gracias*. Finally, I leave the machine with its glowing red light, and I leave the apartment, locking the new lock behind me. When I go to collect the small pile of mail from my box, I see my Asian neighbor in her robe and slippers at the bottom of the stairs, watching me.

"That man, he foun' you?" she asks.

"No," I say. "Not yet."

"You maybe wan' me to tell him someting I see him 'gain?" She tilts her head to one side, half smiling.

"Thank you," I say. "But I do not know who he is."

She turns sideways to look at me, and I see again how her back curves like a hill. "You in trouble witta gov'ment, someting like dat?"

I shake my head.

"Okay. None a' my business," she says, shaking her own head, turning to go back upstairs. "But you be cayful, anyways." She holds the hem of her robe with one hand and the railing of the stairs with her other hand, slowly pulling herself up the steps. I hear one sharp sigh when she gets to the top; it echoes down to where I am standing with my mail in my hands, the sound like a small wind caught in a cave, and then gone.

I found him in the Jewish museum beside the synagogue, in a series of rooms filled with the heartbreaking relics of the dead. I was searching for stories about the cantor from Debrecen, my grandfather, and when I mentioned his name, Joszef Huber looked at me like someone studying a map.

"Perel?" he asked, his brown eyes widening behind his thick glasses. "I knew one man named Jacob. Some relative of yours?"

When I said I was Jacob's daughter, Huber came out from behind a display case filled with folded prayer shawls. He wore a dark blue suit, shiny at the lapels, and when he introduced himself to me, his smile revealed several gold teeth.

"Your father must have married a pretty woman to make a beauty like you," he said. Then he reached out and pinched my cheek, something I hadn't felt since I was a child.

"You knew him?" I said.

He was leaning on a cane, but with his free hand he rubbed his heavy gray eyebrows, nodding vigorously. "In the camp," he said, his voice dropping down. "You know."

I shook my head, felt myself reddening with shame. There was so much I didn't know.

Huber gripped my arm with surprising force. "So Perel made it all the way to America. He did well there?"

"He did well," I said, my voice catching a little. "He had work he cared about, he made a family. I have an older brother, Julian. But both of my parents are dead now." It was still hard to say this out loud, even here, even in this museum full of ghosts.

Huber suddenly pulled me toward a small alcove, away from the flow of visitors passing through the museum entrance. There was a pair of wooden chairs leaning against a wall. "Sit down," he urged. "I need to rest my legs anyways."

He kept looking at me, as if trying to connect the pieces. "I see him in you," he said. "The redhead." The way he grimaced when he sat down on the chair made me want to help him somehow. But what did I have to offer? His fingers were twisted and swollen at the knuckles.

"Tell me something about him," I said. "Can you? From that time you knew each other?"

He sighed and shook his head; I saw the deep lines in his forehead. "You know enough, I bet."

"No, I don't. I really don't."

"The things I could say to you, it wouldn't be good for you to know," he said, rubbing his eyebrows again.

"I need to hear," I said. "Now that he's gone, I can't ask him anymore." The silver objects in the museum cases gleamed. I felt cold again, wishing my scarf were made of wool instead of silk.

Huber stared at my face for a long moment. "Your father was *Sonderkommando*, don't you know? Don't you know what it means?"

I shook my head.

He grabbed my arm for the second time. "I don't want to say it to you," he said. "This thing is gonna break you to know it." When he let go of me, I saw crimson fingerprints on my skin. So this is what they mean by a rose tattoo, I thought, and I watched it fade away.

"It's for a reason he didn't tell you," Huber said. He massaged his crooked fingers, grimacing. "The words don't work. It's like the sun. You can't look directly or it burns your eyes."

Almost involuntarily I closed my eyes for a moment, as if to protect them. "But the silence is worse," I said. "Can you understand? When the family keeps trying to imagine everything they don't know?" Of course I was thinking of Julian then.

He sighed, and I felt the throb of my heartbeat. Disembodied voices from the museum floated nearby; I heard the melody of Hungarian, so familiar and so strange. The language of my father's secrets. I reached out to touch one of Huber's hands. "Please," I said, almost whispering.

When he looked at me again, Huber's expression was full of pity. "*Sonderkommando* was the Special Group," he said. "The Special Detail."

I shook my head, not yet understanding.

"These were the people who worked in the ovens," he said, and took a deep breath. "They took the bodies from the gas chamber, stacked them up, made sure they burned the way the Nazis liked, efficient. With the right combination of fat and thin, so the fat would drip to collect for the soap."

I seemed to lose my hearing for a moment when he said the word *soap*, as if on the way toward passing out. I dropped my head toward my knees, muttering something like *Oh, my God*, over and over, not even sure what language I was speaking.

"I said I didn't want to say it to you, remember? 'Cause it would break you." Huber touched my shoulder, gently this time.

I sat with my head almost between my knees, feeling like I wanted to fold myself in half, like I wanted to curl into a ball and never stand up again. Finally I found a word, one he had just used, one that suddenly seemed more monstrous than the word *oven*, or the word *soap*.

"Special," I said. I still couldn't lift up my head to look at him, but I heard him sigh again, I heard his chair creak. The cane with its rubber tip pounded once on the floor.

"Ach," he said. "They used words like that to kill the spirit even worse than the body. It was like the selections, where no such thing as a good choice could come to you, except that for a while it seemed like being selected to live was better. But it wasn't really better, you know? Your father—" he stopped himself this time. "I won't say any more. I said too much already."

"No, don't stop," I said, looking into his watery eyes. "You have to tell me the rest, now I've started to know. Finish what you were saying. Please."

The chair creaked again as he leaned close to me. "Listen," he said, his voice almost in my ear. "There are things we can never understand about that place, about what people did there. To stay alive, it wasn't even a choice sometimes. People didn't ask to die or to live either. The *Sonderkommando*, they only knew that it could be them in that pile of corpses, and almost every single one of them was ending up there anyway. The Germans made sure of it. And even if you were strong enough in your body to keep working, when your soul was dead you couldn't keep doing it anymore."

I dropped my head again, feeling my neck couldn't bear the weight of it. "What about you?" I asked, even though I wondered if it was fair, if I had a right.

His voice changed pitch again, into a lower whisper. "My job was only a little bit different, I was with the people just before the gas, when they were going in. And every once in a while, when I thought I could take the chance to speak to one of them, a woman with a baby in her arms, or a young boy ..." His voice trailed off, then returned when he cleared his throat. "I told them where to stand, where it would go quickly for them. That was the only mercy I could give."

monotropic: existing in only one stable physical form, any other form obtainable being unstable under all conditions

Eduardo's death is the first one. He leaves us when I am still pregnant with Camucha, promising to return before the baby is born. But the image still sealed on my eyes is his back, walking away, and dust flying up around his feet. He does not turn around to wave at me, and I stand with one hand on my belly, comforting the unborn child, comforting myself for the feeling of dread I have. One month later Eduardo is crushed to death in a mining accident, and his broken body is returned to me in a wooden box. My mother wants me to open the coffin, to see that inside is only his empty shell.

"Looking at his death will help you believe the spirit is still alive somewhere else," she tells me. But I cannot bear to do it. In my mind I hold on to the picture of Eduardo from before, from when we are lying in our bed together, and I try to erase everything else, even the picture of his back as he is walking away from me. His death is the first one, and I think, when I give birth two months after his death, at the start of the rainy season, that his loss is replaced by her.

The second death is the death of my baby girl, one night in her sleep, the night of her first birthday. For no reason and without a single sound of leaving the world. When we bury her, the women of my village say we are "planting an angel in the ground." I cry for two months without stopping, I think I will never be able to stop. And then for one full year I do not laugh or even smile, not because that is the tradition but because I cannot find anything in me that remembers happiness. When my village is murdered, it is the first time I say a blessing for the death of my daughter, because she is spared the killing blades. But with the other deaths, everything begins to melt together, two streams forming a river, and I feel as though the water is pulling me under, there is too much sorrow to hold up against. So I let myself be swallowed up. The river washes over me and over me.

For a while I am thankful that Camucha does not reach the age of asking where her father is. My brothers play with her so much, she probably thinks she has three fathers, and sometimes it is a knife in my heart to see how she laughs when they lift her up. But now they are together, Camucha and Eduardo, meeting in a place where I cannot see them.

The day before I leave my village forever, I go with Warren to the graves of my baby girl and my husband to say good-bye. They are buried side by side.

Warren drives me in his jeep to the burial place, but I go by myself to the graves. It is very early morning, when the sun hides behind the hills, and it is so cold I have to wrap myself in one of the hospital blankets, with some of it over my head like a shawl. This makes me feel protected, because no one can see my face—that is, no one except the dead, who can see everything. I am shivering even beneath the blanket, but when I stand at the side of the graves, something strange happens, and I feel an intense heat spreading over me. It is not like the heat of the day, under the sun, but more a warming from inside. I feel I am glowing like a pile of embers.

"I am not forgetting you," I whisper, the same thing I say later that same day at the terrible place where my mother and my brothers are buried on the western edge of the village, together with all the other victims of the massacre. There is no marker for the dead, only a mound of earth covering them all. I say the names of my family out loud to myself, one by one, trying not to choke on the sound of my voice in this silence.

By then the sun is higher in the sky and blazing down on me, but I do not feel it; instead of the wool blanket around my head, I have a white scarf covering me like a shroud, reflecting the sun back on itself, not soaking it in. Afterwards, Warren says I look like I am floating, not touching the earth.

But my feeling is not about floating. There is an ache in me so strong it fills the emptiness. I wish that day I could simply collapse into the dirt and never rise up again.

How can I be the only one left?

In the hospital I am asking myself this question so many times it is the first thing I think in the morning and the last thought in my head at night. But when I lift my eyes, there is Warren, standing beside his jeep and waiting for me, to take me away and keep saving my life over and over. I say good-bye to everyone, and then I walk away forever from that place of death.

Falling asleep that night, or trying to, I couldn't stop thinking about it, the word *Sonderkommando* in my head like some horrible drumbeat. It was such a dark sound, not like Special Detail. I had translated the German word for myself, I knew German well. But there were always those surprising combinations, words invented by splicing others together, creative license in a way, I admired it sometimes. But this wasn't creative, it was sinister, atrocious, and I kept thinking of how my father must have suffered to hear me sing in German that time at Madame's house.

Then I thought of him being a vegetarian, and when I realized what it meant, I gasped out loud in the dark of my hotel room. It was the one thing he couldn't ever allow to touch his lips: flesh. Burned.

How could I sing after that, standing so close to these dead relatives? And now this: my father's hands lifting the corpses into the ovens, the tattoo on his own arm to remind him he was next, any moment, there was no one else to save but himself. A phrase came into my head that night: The life you save may be your own. But I couldn't remember where it came from. I thought of television, and then I thought of Julian, his mesmerized look, and then I wondered what was behind it all, his disappearances, his vanishing act. To escape this? I wondered, for the first time. The knowledge of this? If he already knew, I couldn't guess how, since I couldn't imagine my father ever speaking about it. To anyone, not even my mother. How could it be said out loud?

Not simply "I knew what it was like, in hell, I lived there." Maybe he did tell her that much, once, or maybe he chose to let her use her imagination. Maybe she never asked, maybe she trusted his silence to be what he needed, and if he'd needed or wanted to say more, it was up to him. I thought of her advice columns, the clippings I read in the year after her death, a collection my father had saved in a big white envelope. She encouraged her readers to talk things over with their loved ones, to make sure they were as open and forthcoming as possible. But once she wrote, "First do no harm," like we were all doctors for one another. Maybe she couldn't convince him, even in that indirect way, to share what couldn't be shared. Wasn't it enough that he had to live with the memory of what he'd seen, what he'd touched? It was seed for a lifetime of nightmares, I thought, and maybe even now, in the ground, he could not find rest.

i wept then, and wept and wept, keening into my starchy hotel pillowcase, making sounds I couldn't hold inside, even when I felt the pain in my vocal cords, even when some part of me wanted to stop, to protect my voice. I heard Madame in my head, her warnings at me never to cry, never to scream out. But this time I had no will against the sound, it came out of me like rain.

EIGHT

SOMETHING ABOUT Frank's Deli seemed different that Thursday, as if some lightbulb had burned out, making everything slightly dimmer than usual. When I gave Frank my order, he wrote it down on his pad like I was some stranger calling on the phone instead of the person who came in for the same thing every week. The color in his face wasn't quite right either. Some shadow of gray had collected there.

"You all right?" I asked. He looked at me for a moment as if trying to figure out a puzzle. "It's Julian Perel. Large soup and half a broiled chicken, remember?"

"Oh, yeah, Mr. Perel," he said. "Sure, sure." He tucked the pad back into the pocket of his apron, replaced the pencil behind his ear. I saw him wince as he poured soup into a container and began to wrap my chicken in aluminum foil.

"Are you feeling okay?" I asked him.

He answered without looking at me. "Oh, sure. You get older, things go wrong from time to time. The usual stuff."

The deli was surprisingly quiet; only a dark-haired woman with a little boy beside her stood at the far end of the display case, deciding what to order.

"Sweetheart, you do like the potato kugel," the woman said to the little boy. "Don't you remember?"

"It's none of my business," I mumbled in Frank's direction.

"Nice of you to ask anyways," he said, sliding the wrapped chicken into a foil-lined paper bag. "But no one really wants to hear about an old man's arthritis or bad knees." He handed me my food and grinned a little. "It's what comes with old age. The body breaks down, bit by bit." He managed a quick wink. "Enjoy while you can," he said.

Before I had even turned away, the woman—who was standing too close to me—began to tell Frank what she wanted, the little boy now wrapping his small arms around her leg. I paid the cashier with exact change and left the deli, its tinny bell ringing behind me as the door closed. Out on the sidewalk, I stood for a moment watching a young man at the flower stall arranging a bouquet of roses the color of piano keys. The bag with the food was warm in my hands.

My father slowed down in stages the year before he died: only taking his neighborhood walk once a week, and later only once a month, the mile taking him longer and longer to cover. He began pausing more and more often to catch his breath on the hill, mopping his forehead with a handkerchief. The spring he died was supposed to be his last year of teaching; he had planned to retire after thirty-five years and spend his time reading.

"Maybe I'll take up gardening, who knows?" he said. But I understood when he died that without teaching to wake up for in the morning, he might have been in danger of staying in bed all day, the newspaper studied column by column, every word read twice. The summer of his retirement would have been the first time he didn't have to stay in the present, or focus on the future and his incoming students. The past would have threatened to sneak up from behind.

So many evenings after dinner he sat in his chair reading the afternoon paper, muttering "It's crazy out there," over one article or another. I usually sat across the room on the couch, reviewing my homework.

"People are animals. Beasts," my father said, more than once. Then he would shake his head, frowning at the evidence on the page, confirmation of everything he already knew about the world.

I picture myself doing this: lifting the heavy wooden lid of the coffin, gazing at the face of Eduardo, even picturing a spot of dried blood at the corner of his mouth. But I truly do not know if this is a memory or if I am dreaming it, because I also remember telling my mother "I cannot" when she urges me to look at him inside his box of death.

Is Eduardo here? Alive? Trying to find me?

The idea is too impossible, it means not only that Eduardo is not dead in the accident, but that someone else's body is in his grave, that he is managing to find me all the way in California, that now he is a man wearing sunglasses and searching for me at my apartment. It cannot be true, and yet I cannot stop it from being in my head, making me crazy and sleepless and terrified.

Eduardo not dead.

It is like unraveling the knot at the beginning, because his death is the very first one, followed by Camucha and then everyone else. If he is not dead, it takes away the foundation for all the rest of the deaths. Except that all the rest of them, I still see and hear.

M Y   N O T E S for the dictionary were arranged in the piles of the alphabet, twenty-six stacks in four rows (six in three and eight in one). Around the room I had a circular arrangement of other scientific dictionaries, sources for physics, chemistry, biology, astronomy, and so on. In my chair on wheels I rolled across the bare wooden floor from one book to another as I gathered my information, made my notes. The laptop rolled with me, and I played on its silent piano keys.

Ten entries began with her name: solar cell, solar constant, solar day, solar energy, solar flares, solar parallax, solar prominence, solar system, solar wind, solar year. I made a twenty-seventh pile, to make her name its own category.

> **solar wind:** streams of electrically charged particles (protons and electrons) emitted by the Sun, predominantly during solar flares and sunspot activity; some of these particles become trapped in the Earth's magnetic field (see MAGNETISM,

TERRESTRIAL), forming the outer Van Allen radiation belt, but some penetrate to the upper atmosphere, where they congregate in narrow zones in the region of the Earth's magnetic poles, producing auroral displays (see AURORA BOREALIS)

In the shocking light of morning, I pulled paper from the desk in my hotel room, thinking I had to write something to Julian, write down what I had heard from Huber at the museum—as if otherwise it would vanish like some kind of dream. But I could barely hold the pen steady, and besides, what could I write? It was like Huber said, the words didn't work.

Dearest Julian:
   I'm getting more and more afraid. Of everything. Of Budapest, and these terrible dark secrets being pulled out of the stones. I have so much to tell you Jules, and you won't even get this letter until after I'm already home.
                              Your loving and confused
                              sister, P.

I climbed back into bed and pulled the covers over my head. I couldn't stop thinking about my father, about his hands that had held me and had held the bodies of so many dead. I heard Hungarian voices in the hallway outside my door; I heard a distant radio playing a waltz. And for the first time in my life, the music hurt. All I wanted was silence.

The day I finally meet the man in the sunglasses, I am driving with the radio on very loud; it seems a good way to keep myself from thinking about all of my fears. The windows are open, and when I pull up in front of Julian's building, there is no time to protect myself. He just comes out of nowhere and before I can shout or roll up the window, he removes his glasses and shows me his face. I know him right away, even though his face is so much thinner and older, and even though something about his eyes does not match the face I know from my other life.

"Diego," I say, the name leaping from my mouth in the same second he says my name.

"It's really you," he says next, surprising me even more by speaking in English.

I climb out of the car and stand facing him, my keys cutting into my hands because I am holding them so tightly. The ground seems unsteady. I feel I need to lean against the side of the car. "What are you doing here?" I ask him, and then he reaches out a hand to touch me on the shoulder, like he needs to make sure I am real.

"I can't believe I finally found you," he says, his hand still on my shoulder.

I look down at the sunglasses he is holding in his other hand, and then back into his face, searching for an explanation. "I do not understand," I say. "I cannot even remember . . ."

Diego smiles with half his mouth, his teeth revealing gaps and a small glint of gold. "It was a party for Eduardo," he says quietly. "You remember?" I nod, not able to speak.

Diego continues. "You know I spoke to him about you the day he died, he was telling me about the last time he saw you, about when he would be going home. . . ." His voice goes down and down to nothing, into silence, and his face turns dark. "I saw his body when they brought it up from the mine. . . ."

I touch myself on the heart, knowing that my dream about Eduardo being still alive is never something I can believe, even for a moment. Diego stops speaking. He is not here to tell me about Eduardo, there is something he wants from me, I can see it in his tired eyes.

"What are you looking for?" I ask him. "Why are you following me?"

Diego sighs. "I'm sorry," he says. "I didn't mean to make you frightened. But I have to talk with you, about many things." He pushes one hand through his dark hair. "I saw you one day, by mistake. You were putting some groceries in your car outside the store, just like anybody, and I could not believe my own eyes. When I decided it was really you, I followed you to your apartment. After all the time of searching for you, I truly couldn't believe it. And also I couldn't talk with you, it was too much shock at first. I just kept going back to your building, waiting for courage. Because seeing someone from my old village, my old life, I felt I was going crazy. I thought everyone was dead and so you were a ghost. . . ."

His voice stops again, like a stone in a well with no echo. I feel the heat of the car through my back. "Maybe we should go inside," I say. "Let us talk inside." I start to walk toward the front door, but Diego does not follow me.

"This isn't where you live," he says. "Why go in here?" He sounds suspicious, almost angry.

"I am taking care of this place for a while," I explain, waiting for him to believe me. "That is why you are not finding me at my apartment."

"You knew I was there?"

"My neighbor tells me someone is looking for me. A man in sunglasses, she says. I could never guess it is you."

Diego smiles his half-smile again and puts his glasses back on, becoming someone I do not know. "It is me," he says, removing them again. "Your husband's old friend."

I try to say something, but no sound comes out. I feel a pain in my heart for Eduardo and his friend, born in the same month, I remember now. They are together from the time they are babies. Other things come rushing back to me. Diego leaving the village first, to find work in the mines, then returning with his stories of money, filling Eduardo with ideas about getting rich. "It's hard work, brother," he tells my husband, "but they pay you enough to make up for the sore muscles. Trust me. Come."

Eduardo promises to be back for the baby, in time to see the baby's birth. I try to believe him, but something in me knows it is not right. Diego's stories are too shiny, too full of easy hope. I wait and wait, until the box comes to me with Eduardo's body inside.

"Today I knew I would find you," Diego says, finally walking with me to the door. "I woke up and there was a bird singing outside my window. I couldn't see it but I could hear it. I knew if I waited for you at the apartment you would come. Then when you didn't go inside, I just had to follow you wherever you went, all day if I had to, until you stopped." He touches me again on the shoulder while I place the key in the lock. "I must talk to you. It's the only thing I can think about since I saw you with the groceries one week ago."

Inside, in the entryway, Julian leaves for me a stack of Paula's new mail; it sits by the door to her apartment like an offering, like a note saying to me he is there. I pick it up and tell Diego to come inside and sit down.

"Do you want something?" I ask him, not sure what I have in the refrigerator except water and grape juice, maybe some cheese, some vegetables for a salad. "Are you hungry or thirsty?"

"Do you have coffee? I need something strong."

I notice that beneath his eyes are dark smudges like someone has bruised his face. He sits down in the chair with a sound of pure falling, everything landing in one exhausted piece. He is so much older now. It makes me wonder what Eduardo's face could be like if we are standing face-to-face. If we are alive together.

"I can make coffee," I say, going into the kitchen. I hear a sigh from Diego and a creaking sound from the chair; from the doorway I can see his head turning to look at everything in Paula's living room, the curtains and paintings and collections of glass.

"Who is she?" he asks.

"A friend. She is away." For some reason I do not yet feel like telling him too much. Not the details. I want him to talk first, tell me what he is doing in America, how he is living. It is strange that we are speaking in English, but I have my reasons and maybe he has his too. It is better this way, I think, more true to the strangers we are now. The village is so far away.

While the water boils and the coffee drips slowly into the cups, we do not say anything. I notice Diego's head drop slowly to one side and then onto his chest. He is asleep so quickly, like he has no choice about it. I do not know what to do, so I stand in the kitchen, waiting. Upstairs I can hear the televisions, and I think maybe Julian sees us come into the building together. I feel like I have a secret.

"Wake up, Diego," I whisper, leaning toward him but not getting too close. "Diego."

His eyes come open fast and wide, and I can tell from his expression that he is forgetting where he is, what he is doing here with me. "It is Sola," I say. "Remember?"

"Sola. I know." He rubs his face, runs his fingers along his jaw. "I'm sorry. I'm just so tired."

"Do you still want the coffee? Do you want to come back another time?"

"No, no. I want to drink the coffee, and I must stay here now. Do you see? Do you have to go anyplace? Or can I stay? Can we talk?" He speaks rapidly, his tongue tripping over the sharp edges of English like he is afraid I am running away unless he holds on to me with his words.

"We can drink the coffee," I say. "And talk."

I ACTUALLY had my window open by the time the man approached Sola's car, although I had no plans for what I would do. When he took off his sunglasses and Sola faced him without being afraid, I decided that she didn't need my help. Then I laughed at myself for thinking I could be heroic. Would I shout from the window for him to leave her alone? Threaten to call the police? He could have her down on the ground before I finished my sentence, and from the upstairs and the inside I was powerless.

I watched them speak briefly and then walk through the door together, and I had to believe that the man was someone she knew, someone she trusted enough to bring into Paula's apartment. I strained to listen for their voices from downstairs, but they were so quiet. And then I told myself to stop. I was paying too much attention to Sola's life, wanting to know too much.

I closed the window and went back to my chair, turning the sounds of the televisions up high enough that I didn't have to think about her, or the man in sunglasses, or anything.

When I sit on the couch across from Diego with our cups of coffee, I feel like I have to be dreaming. The room is filled with beautiful things; behind Diego's head I can see a vivid watercolor painting of tulips and under our feet is a soft carpet in a hundred shades of green. And none of it belongs to either one of us. I can tell by the way Diego sits so stiffly, without leaning against the pillows, that he must be feeling as lost here as I still am.

"It was the nun at the hospital who told me about you," Diego says. Sister Isabella, the one whose hands I remember, who holds my fingers very gently in the bowl of warm water and scrubs at the dirt under my nails.

"I went back there, looking for something. Trying to find ghosts." He stares at me. "And she told me about you, about you being here in California. I got so excited I grabbed her hand by mistake. I had to apologize for offending her, but she was so kind, she didn't mind, she gave me her forgiveness. She shook her head when she said your name, and then she crossed herself out of pity. When I told her I knew you she looked at me with pity too."

"I remember her," I say. "I remember asking her to cut off my hair, but she will not do it. She says only the nuns are allowed to deny themselves that way."

Diego brings the coffee to his lips and takes a long swallow. It is too hot for me to drink, but he seems not to notice it burning his throat. "I'm sorry I made you afraid," he says.

"I think someone is still trying to kill me," I say quietly, stunned by my own words. We look into each other's eyes for a moment.

"Yes," he says, as if what I say is the most natural thing, and then turns his head to see the room we are in. There is no curiosity in his eyes, just a blank staring.

"I have to know," he begins, then stops and takes a deep breath, wide enough to spread his ribs. "I have to know what happened to my family," he says, and that makes me take a deep breath too. "You must know something that you can tell me. About how they died, about who did it to them. If I don't hear the story I'll keep going crazy from imagining it all my life."

I close my eyes and hold the cup of coffee close to my face so I can smell it. Somehow this makes me feel better, like it is a real moment and not a nightmare. I can breathe that dark and bitter liquid.

"It is true I know the story," I say. "I am still carrying it around with me, all of it."

I think the lines of Diego's face become deeper right then, like some invisible hand is pressing down on him. He puts his cup on the table and leans toward me, reaching out a hand like he wants to touch me. But his hand stops in the air.

"I know it's a terrible thing to ask," he says. "It's not fair for me to ask you. But when I saw you alive, I felt you were the only chance, my only way to get some pieces of that story." He takes another deep breath, releases it like a moan. "When I returned to the village after being away for so long, working in those mines, I could not believe what I found. Instead of the simple life of my childhood, there was nothing, not even a chicken or a goat to show that anything had ever lived in that place. I saw squares of black ground where buildings used to be, and everything turned into ashes. The few houses still standing were so empty I thought I was a ghost too. I kept touching walls, trees, my own arms and legs to see if my fingers would just pass through."

I nod.

"Then I went to that place, that one awful grave, and I understood where everyone was, the entire village buried together like that. I think I lost my breath and fell down, but I don't remember falling. I woke up later with my head in the dust, my hands full of dust. It was dark, and I was alone."

When he stops talking, the room becomes very silent, until I hear again the voices of Julian's televisions over our heads, like a distant crowd of people murmuring to each other.

"How are you getting here, to California?" I ask Diego, and for the first time he leans all the way back against the pillows.

"My pockets were full of money," he says, and smiles a sad half-smile. "I was finally coming home with my fortune, but there was no one to share with, no one to admire me. What good was it? I almost envied Eduardo, for dying before all of this, for not having to stand like I did at the graves of all his family." Diego coughs, like he is choking on his own story.

"I am ashamed of what I did next," he says, not meeting my eyes. "But I was alone in the world, out of my head. I went to the nearest city, and for several days, maybe even weeks, I stayed drunk enough to forget even my own name. One morning I woke up in bed with someone I had never seen before, and on the radio was someone talking about California. 'I'm going,' I said to her, this strange woman who looked like no one to me. 'I'm going to California.' "

Diego holds up his hands for me to look, and I see how bent and broken-looking his fingers are, how much like an old man's hands they are. "It was what I had left when the money was gone," he says, dropping his hands back into his lap. "My old tools. I found work in the fields along with all the other people searching in the dirt for their dreams."

"Even now?" I ask.

"No," he says, and I can see his missing teeth when he smiles wide. "I work in a store now, selling all the fruits I used to pick. It's better for an old man like me."

Again I think of Eduardo and what he could be looking like. He has such beautiful hands: long, slender fingers and perfectly round nails, little half-moons on each one. He dreams of being a musician someday, playing his own compositions on the guitar. And then I think of us picking fruit under the hot sun.

"That's my story," Diego says, and rubs at a stain on his pants. "It's not as hard to tell as yours, I know. But I'm asking you."

We both hold such envy for the dead, and yet it is not our time to be among them. I touch the insides of my wrists and feel the thin roughness of my scars. *The voice of my blood.* "I can try," I say.

S O L A   W A S downstairs with the man in sunglasses, and I couldn't get the questions out of my head. *Who? What? Why?* They were the shimmering chorus behind every image on every screen. Before she had been afraid, and now she was downstairs with him. *Who? What? Why?* The truth was, I knew almost nothing about her life, about the people she loved or feared or hated.

I began pacing around my apartment, feeling caged inside my own mental boxes and wanting out for the first time I could remember. I read the fortunes on my refrigerator, one after another as if they held the answers I needed. But what came to me was the longing for Paula's voice in my ears, a steady flare of sound pouring from the one throat I ever allowed myself to love. Even when she was gone I still had her recordings to hold on to, music that made me feel as close to peace as I believed I could get. So I filled my apartment with Paula, into every spiderweb. *Sing to me like ice.*

When the music starts, Diego sits up straight on the couch, alert like an animal to a sound of danger. It is very loud, louder than I ever hear from Julian's apartment.

"What's going on?" Diego asks.

"It is from upstairs," I say. "The brother of the woman who lives here."

"He must be waking up the dead." Diego almost laughs.

"That is her voice," I explain. "The sister. She is a singer."

Diego and I both sit listening for a few more moments, but the sound is too much even for us downstairs. Something has to be wrong. "I need to check on him," I say. "To see if he is all right."

I have to bang on the door with a fist to make more noise than the music, and after a moment Julian comes to open it. His face looks full of fear.

"Are you all right?" I say, and in the same moment he asks me the same question.

"Wait," he says. "Let me turn it down."

I do not follow him into the apartment, but stay in the hallway at the open door. The music drops to a softer level, although Paula's voice is still there in the distance, pure and sweet. The words are in a language I do not know.

"I'm sorry," Julian says when he comes back to the doorway. "I didn't mean to disturb anyone. But are you really all right?"

"Yes," I say.

He looks at me, not into my eyes but off to the side a little. "And the man? He was the one following you?"

"He is all right," I say. "It is someone I know from a long time ago."

"Not the doctor," Julian says.

"No, not the doctor," I say. Julian seems to be waiting for more, so I tell him it is someone from my village. "His name is Diego. He is a good friend of my husband."

Julian's eyes open wide when I say the word *husband*, but at first he does not say anything. I notice his hands dig down and make fists in his pockets like he is holding on to some small stones.

"I didn't know you had a husband," he says very quietly.

I nod. There is so much he does not know. In the background, Paula's voice rises up to a beautifully high note and stays there for what seems like an impossibly long time. Julian's eyes close until the note disappears.

"My husband is dead for many years," I tell him. I am puzzled to realize that I am not certain anymore how long ago it is since his death. But the memory is in my bones, not my head. "A mining accident," I say.

"I'm very sorry," Julian says. He pulls a hand out of his pocket to push it through his hair; some strands fall across his forehead like streaks of dark paint.

"I should go back down," I say. "Diego is waiting for me."

Julian nods, sweeps the streaks back away from his face. There are lines on his forehead I do not remember seeing before. I do not know how old he is.

"You can come with me," I say, surprising myself as much as him. But when I say it out loud it is true: I want him to listen. "I am telling Diego the story about our village, about how I am a witness there." Julian's eyebrows lean toward each other as I say that word, *witness,* and Paula's voice begins again. I imagine I can see his brain working inside his skull.

"Come," I say.

> **earthshine:** a faint illumination of the dark side of the Moon during a crescent phase, due to sunlight reflected from the Earth's surface

AT THE bottom of the stairs I had to prepare myself for several moments to be able to sit in Paula's apartment with Diego there. It was as if someone had rearranged the furniture or painted the walls: everything felt mixed-up and turned over. I tried to make room for him in my mind, create space for an object that didn't belong but had to be there. Diego was the one asking for the story, Sola told me, and maybe without him I would never hear it.

He was on the couch; I sat in one of the chairs facing the door and Sola sat in the other one. Watching the door made me feel as though I could leave at any time, just get up and walk out, as long as no one tried to stop me. Diego's face was sun-darkened and deeply lined; he had hair as black as Sola's and a mustache that disguised most of his mouth. I didn't get a good look at his eyes, didn't want to be caught studying him.

When Sola introduced us, we nodded at each other. She told him she wanted me there to listen, and asked if it was all right with him.

"*¿Por qué quieres eso?*" Diego asked her.

Sola looked over at me, as if to acknowledge I had heard the question too. "He understands," Sola said to Diego, referring to the Spanish and maybe more. "And he is a friend. I want for him to hear."

Diego shrugged, pulled with misshapen fingers at the edges of his mustache. I wasn't looking straight at him but I could sense his eyes on me, examining me. Paula's living room felt small and my skin felt too tight for my body. The door looked very close; I calculated how many steps it would take to get me out and to the staircase. Six, six and a half.

"I've been waiting a long time for this story," Diego said, and he sighed.

"I know," Sola said.

"It's up to you how to tell it," Diego said. *"Como tú quieres."*

Sola folded her legs up beneath her on the chair and smoothed the fabric of her skirt across her lap. I saw past her to a framed photograph on the mantel of the fireplace: our family one of the last times we were all together, on my father's birthday. We were still celebrating on the wrong day, his backwards birthday. Even after my mother died, we kept doing it, either because it was too hard to break the habit or because we wanted to believe in the lie. Maybe there were other lies we never knew about, would never know. In the photo both my mother and my sister were holding on to my father's arms, all three of them wearing similar smiles. I was standing off to the side, half-turned away from the photographer, my mother's best friend Betty. *"Say champagne,"* Betty had said.

The room was so quiet I could hear my pulse throbbing in my head.

Sola said very softly, "I do not know if I can do it. Say everything out loud."

I watched the door again, thinking I wasn't supposed to be here. I pictured the insides of Sola's wrists, the mango juice staining her skin yellow orange. I remembered my father's silences, louder than words.

Six and a half steps.

"Este dolor," Diego said, *"necesita una voz. Su voz."*

This sorrow needs your voice.

Sola looked at him. Diego lifted his hands to his heart. *"El silencio magulla el corazón,"* he said.

The verb was a new one for me. I turned to ask Sola what it meant, and saw tears on her cheeks, shining rivers of salt. "Bruises," she whispered, without my asking. "Silence bruises the heart."

If that was true I thought my father's heart must have been completely black and blue from a lifetime of wordless grief banging around in his chest. At once I pictured myself moving so quickly I'd be through the door before anyone knew what had happened. But nobody stirred. Sola's rivers poured down without making a sound. Far away, across oceans and continents, Paula was singing in a hall filled with light.

At first I could see how Sola didn't want to tell Diego her story. I imagined bands tight around her heart, a conviction she had to keep the story inside in order to save him from its truth. I knew it so well, that fierce refusal. Like some permanently wrapped gift, but a gift the receiver wanted to exchange, the truth instead of silence. My father had given us the same gift, and inside the silence the knives were sharp anyway, that was the part he couldn't or wouldn't understand. I was cut open by that silence, and I knew Diego needed Sola's words the way I needed them too. We were all black holes, dense with the nightmares we invent when the stories are kept hidden from us.

Paula had filled the silence with her own voice, and I had filled it with the voices of science and the electronic air, and what we really needed was the voice of our father telling us his story, giving us at least that much of himself, the life he'd nearly lost. But he couldn't speak, the horror was bigger than anything he could name with words, and we were left to find out for ourselves what had been burned into his skin forever.

When Diego speaks of bruises, I think I see a shudder run through Julian's body, something like a current of electricity. Maybe Diego is only trying to describe his own suffering, but I know he is right about all of us. I think of the night my sadness is pouring out of me after breaking the dam, how Julian lies next to me while I fall asleep. How many years is it since I am crying like that? And still tears never feel like enough: they rinse something away, but only the surface, not whatever is underneath.

Now Diego and Julian both sit with their hands open in their laps, like they are waiting to receive something. From me. I imagine I feel a soft caress on my cheek, the touch of my grandmother, her tender weaving fingers. Outside the window of Paula's apartment I see the tree that Julian is helping to grow, full now with green leaves. I take a deep breath.

First I tell about the morning of that day, how beautiful the colors of the sky are, how I work with my mother to pound the tortillas. Describing it to them I can almost feel the sweet coolness of the adobe house and the steady rhythm of my hands and my mother's as we work together. Diego is not looking at me; I think he is probably imagining his own mother and sisters doing the same thing in the house next door to mine.

When the sun is lifting high enough to cast smaller and smaller shadows around the houses and the trees, most people are inside, finishing the work of the morning and preparing the midday meal. I have a headache, something I am suffering from ever since the year before when my baby girl dies. I go down to the river to see if the fresh water might soothe my face, remembering the way I go there to hide the stains on my blouse when my breast milk keeps coming in the first weeks after Camucha is gone.

That is when I hear the army trucks skidding in the dirt and then the sound of heavy boots, sharp voices of soldiers ordering people to come out of their houses. I am behind some thick bushes that grow along the edge of the river and cannot see what is happening, but I hear a few children crying and that makes the soldiers shout even louder to be quick and gather in the plaza. There is something about the sharpness of their voices that makes me wait where I am for a little while, not moving. I hear someone shout for all the men to line up separately, and then that same voice begins yelling about the guerrillas in the mountains, about how he knows we are giving them food, about how our husbands and sons are joining to fight along with them. Then I hear a woman's voice—this is the voice I recognize as Diego's mother—trying to explain that her son is working in the mines, that she does not have any sons fighting in the mountains. They are innocent people, she says, just living from day to day. Diego's eyes begin to fill with tears. I do not want to tell him the rest, but I have to: that she is in the middle of another sentence when I hear a bullet fired and then her voice is silent. More people begin to wail, and the soldiers keep shouting that everyone is going to die unless we tell them where the guerrillas are hiding and how we are helping them.

I feel a powerful longing to go into the plaza with the rest of them, that whatever happens I do not want to be alone with the river, but as soon as I hear the shooting and the screaming I know that I cannot move from where I am, I will not be able to make my legs hold me up. The horrible popping sounds of the guns seem to last for hours, mixed up with screams and crying. Some of the younger girls are taken away to the chapel at the edge of the plaza, and the screams coming from there are horrible. Diego's sisters I am sure are in that place too, violated again and again before being finally murdered.

It is the longest day of my life, the sun does not seem to move at all but stays blazing up in the sky like the eye of a demon, burning and burning.

I tell about the branches of the bushes against my arms and legs, the river moving next to me like it always does, like it is an ordinary day. I keep thinking the waters are turning red, filling up with the blood of the dead, but they stay clear like some strange and impossible dream. I crouch very low in the dirt, holding myself into a shape like a rock, wishing I am not a woman, not even human. For the first time I think I know what it feels like to want to kill someone, because I want to kill all of those soldiers with my eyes wide open, I want to point those weapons at their own hearts.

All day long the guns make their killing sounds. My family, my friends, all the people of my village cry and pray and choke into the thick silence of death. At one point I hear the voice of my own mother, I know her cry better than my own. After that, I push my fist into my mouth to keep myself from screaming.

Afterwards, after everyone is dead, the soldiers stay in the village destroying things, stealing what they want from the store and from people's houses, eating and drinking into the night. They sound like a pack of wild animals. Someone shouts about an order for *"operativo de tierra arrasada."* It is the first time I hear that phrase. That is when they begin to burn the houses of the village, and I am terrified that the fire is coming down to the bushes where I am hiding. Every so often I hear someone crying out from a hiding place or from the doorway of a house because the fire is burning them alive. Sometimes there is gunfire after that and other times the voice just keeps going until the fire consumes it.

A few times I hear footsteps come very close to where I am hiding, and my heart is beating so loudly I think they must hear it. I know that if I make any movement at all, a soldier can find me and kill me. I stay in the bushes long after the stars come into the sky, until finally I hear them leaving, and the engine noise of the last truck echoes in the distance. The air is filled with the terrible smell of burned flesh, I have to hold my shirt over my mouth to keep from gagging.

And there are no more sounds after that. Even my own throat cannot make any sounds.

NINE

AFTER SOLA stopped talking, the three of us sat in silence for several minutes. Diego had his eyes closed and his hands balled into fists; there might have been tears at the corners of his eyes, but I wasn't sure. I didn't dare look at Sola but kept my head low, only glancing under my brows to see if Diego was going to be all right. I had the impression he might explode.

I remembered Sola in my apartment saying that the heavens wanted to break into rain, and we had disagreed about whether the rain was the laughter of the angels or their tears. It didn't make sense to me that angels laughed. *Risa.* Laughter. *Sonrisa.* Smile. *Lágrima.* Tear.

Diego cleared his throat before he spoke, brought his fists to his chin and then slowly opened them. I imagined the blood flowing with relief toward his fingertips. He was not going to explode.

"I kept trying to picture it in my head," he said, looking at Sola. "But I didn't know who died first. It's better that my mother did not live to hear the screams of my sisters being . . ." He choked on the word *raped*. I saw his fingers squeeze back down into fists. "If I were back there now I would join the guerrillas in the mountains. I would beg to kill for them." His voice was low and dark. "If they wouldn't give me a gun I would gladly murder with my hands, I would like to break the necks of those soldiers like they were sticks in the field. . . ."

"Diego," Sola said quietly, forcing him to take a breath. They looked at each other. I thought about leaving right then, running from the heaviness in the room. But I didn't move.

Sola took a deep breath of her own and said, "We cannot bring them back. What can we do but let it rest?"

Diego squinted his eyes at her as if he couldn't believe what he was hearing, and his voice began to rise. "Is that what you did? Make it *rest*?"

I saw her touch the insides of her wrists, where the scars were. "I am still trying," she said. I realized that my teeth were pressed against each other so hard my jaw ached. Sola continued. "I do not pretend it is all right. I do not try to forget. But for some reason I am still alive. Here in this world." She got up from her chair and slowly approached the couch, touched Diego on the shoulder and sat beside him, close enough that their legs were touching. She kept one hand on his shoulder as he bowed his head toward his knees, folding onto his own lap like a piece of melting plastic.

"You cannot help it that you are alive," she said, and her hand stroked his rounded back. She whispered something I couldn't hear, and then I saw his shoulders begin to shake until his whole upper body was heaving, and a muffled moan rose into the air. As Diego's cries grew louder, I got up from my chair. Quietly, quietly, I took those steps to the door, which opened and released me.

As I touch Diego's back, I think again about Eduardo, about his leaving me while I am pregnant with Camucha. That picture I am holding for so long of his back as he walks away seems to be the one I can hold forever, not the way he lifts me up and carries me to our own bedroom for the first time, not his face underneath me while we make love. Diego does not resemble Eduardo, but somehow my hand on his shoulder feels familiar, maybe because I am touching someone from my home for the first time in years, maybe because of the closeness of his blood to my blood. I remember playing with his sisters when we are small, and our mothers are going together to the market, sometimes trading stories and laughter in the evenings after the last meal of the day.

The strangeness of his finding me is striking me harder now. After losing so many of the people we love, we are in this room together in a city neither one of us belongs to. It does not make sense to me, really, that I am in the same body, the same person from then until now: here on Paula's couch, while the best friend of my dead husband cries beneath my hands.

When I see Julian get up from the chair I do not even think to try to stop his leaving, I am not sure anymore that it is right to invite him to listen. What does anyone do with another person's story? I am speaking in his language, but there are so many ways the words cannot say what is true. Still, the past keeps forcing us to listen.

I S T O O D in my apartment with my back to the closed door, letting my eyes find comfort in the wall of stacked televisions. Their blank screens reminded me that I could turn myself off too, stop all of the flashing color and vibrating noise inside my head.

It was their story, I kept telling myself, hers and Diego's, not anything for me to hold. What did I know about villages where the women made meals out of corn flour, or where there were guerrillas in the mountains? The details were like something I might see on the news, or a National Geographic special, a world that couldn't have a message for me. But when I thought of soldiers, massacres, burning . . . I had to put my hands over my ears, I had to change the channels fast.

In a near panic, I went for an aimless walk in my neighborhood, the first time in my memory that I walked without a destination in mind, without a task to orient my route. The sycamores lining my street looked so solid, so permanent, their invisible sap rising against gravity, their feet planted in the cement sidewalks. I stepped on cracks, heard the sharp collapse of dead leaves beneath my shoes, felt the brief rustle of wind thrown against me by passing cars. The sky was a flat blue, palest at the horizon. Joggers and walkers repeated themselves on a track by the school, moving like wind-up toys with different sets of batteries. One man ran on the grassy field at the inside of the track, his arms pumping wildly and his head thrown back in a weird look of ecstasy and pain; he wore only a pair of shorts and his chest gleamed with sweat. I could not begin to imagine what pulled or pushed him with such velocity, what made him long for that kind of speed. I thought of Brian and his bicycle, his beaver head bent with purpose over the handlebars. People used their bodies in ways that astonished me, ways I didn't even move in my dreams.

I continued walking past a tennis court, a café, a bakery, a fish market. There were people everywhere, talking politely to each other, scolding their children for running toward the street, tying their dogs' leashes to a bicycle rack, loading groceries into an open trunk. I kept thinking that this was the world my own stories would be about, if I had any to tell. Maybe I was a character in someone else's stories. Maybe Frank told people about the man who always ordered the same meal on the same days of the week, regular as the delivery of mail. Maybe at the Chinese restaurant, they counted on my arrival like I counted on them to include my fortune cookie and my chopsticks with my food. Maybe we all shared electrons the way molecules did, participating invisibly in each other's chemistry experiments even as we moved through our separate and untouched universes.

Once Paula told me she never really knew what her voice sounded like when she sang. She said Madame le Fleur explained that we can never hear ourselves the way others hear us, through air waves reaching the eardrums. I remember Paula touching her face with her fingertips, feeling for the map of her skull. "We hear ourselves through our bones," she said.

I read an article about singing, written by a doctor of the larynx. In it there was a formula for pitch of the voice, which I memorized.

$N = 1/2\pi \ \sqrt{E/M}$. N is the frequency. E is the elasticity coefficient or tension. M is the vibrating mass.

Madame le Fleur told me the voice starts in the mind, not in the body. "The throat does not exist," Madame said. "The vowel drops from above. The words drop from above onto the lips." Placing her palms under my chin, she would cry "Sustain! Sustain!" Now I was learning that the voice could be stopped in the mind; my fears could close my throat like a fist.

I tried to recall every one of Madame's lessons, repeated her cries of "Sustain! Sustain!" like a chant in my hotel room. I turned away from the mirror, pictured myself standing next to Madame's piano, half gazing out her living room window onto the street. When breath filled me I was buoyant, exhilarated, on fire. I felt a vibrating column of air that shook me internally. Isaac used to say I was making love with the air, turning the wind into music.

But here I was in Hungary, unraveled. The secret mechanisms that powered my voice had been disconnected. Terror was riding my bones and I couldn't make it stop.

> **demagnetization:** the process of depriving a body of its
> magnetic properties. The *demagnetization energy* is the en-
> ergy that would be released when a body is completely
> demagnetized

THE MAIL cascaded through the slot in the front door; it was wait-ing when I returned from my walk. Inside Paula's apartment, it was so quiet. I wondered if Sola and Diego were asleep, or sitting silently inside the echoes of Sola's story. Maybe they were gone.

There was a letter to me from Paula, the envelope so thin and weightless it seemed empty. One filmy page and her familiar looping script, but somehow pushed at an angle across the paper, as if wind-blown.

Dearest Jules:

I must tell someone and you're the only one who can keep this secret. Truly if I don't say it or write it down I'll go out of my mind. But I have begun to feel such stage fright it's impossible for me to function. Before my turn to sing, I spend terrible minutes—sometimes hours!—in the bathroom, sweating and shaking and even vomiting once or twice. It's like I've been possessed by some sort of monster, a beast inside that shakes my faith so completely I become convinced that when I open my mouth, either a horrible croaking roar will come out, or maybe even silence. I've decided to cancel the rest of the trip, it's really only two auditions but I can't bear even the thought of going through the panic and drama anymore. I don't know what else to do except come home.

There's so much more to tell, Jules, but I have to wait until I see you, until we are in the same room.

Love to you—P.

I TRIED to imagine Paula shaking with fear, but the image refused to come. My sister had never been afraid of anything, as far as I knew. I remembered her backstage at a recital in the symphony hall. We were in her dressing room almost two hours before the performance, and Paula was in a red silk bathrobe, seated in front of an enormous mirror rimmed with glowing lightbulbs.

She was rubbing some kind of lotion onto her face and throat, gathering a pool of creamy liquid onto her palms and seeming to be entering a kind of trance. I stood somewhere behind her, watching her in the mirror, the red robe catching the light and throwing it back. She had no makeup on yet, but she let me stay while she put it on: blackening her eyelashes, rubbing something like clay into the fold of her eyelids, powdering her forehead and nose, streaking rose-colored shadows onto her cheekbones. Her hair was pulled back from her face and gathered into an elaborate knot behind her head; a trio of clustered diamonds nestled in the center of each earlobe, as if holding messages there, notes to be whispered as she sang.

"You can sit down if you want to," Paula said over her shoulder, gesturing toward a plush blue chair with a white scarf draped across its back. "And could you hand me that towel? I need to keep my throat warm." She took the soft cloth from my hands and wrapped it twice, loosely, around her neck, tucking the ends into her robe and sighing. "Much better," she said. She poured from a gleaming black thermos on the table in front of her into a mug the size of a cereal bowl. "Hot water with lemon," she said. "Want some?" I shook my head into the mirror, and she nodded at my reflection.

A notebook-sized speaker in one high corner of the room began to report that the orchestra was gathering; we could hear chairs and music stands scraping against the wooden floor. Low voices murmured to one another as the musicians unzipped and unsnapped their cases, pulled instruments free of their wrappings. I heard strings plucked and played, notes tested in the air, a blooming cacophony. Paula outlined her lips with a red pencil before filling them in with lipstick the color of that silk robe. I kept my hands in my pockets.

Later, I took the seat she reserved for me behind the orchestra. I wanted a high view of the musicians and to imagine as I watched the conductor that I was taking instructions from him like the rest. This meant Paula's back was to me, of course, but I preferred not seeing her face; it was more amazing to study the back of her neck, the way her head tilted gracefully to one side, the way her arms rose and fell like wings curving around air.

I liked the way the musicians all in black seemed to disappear behind their instruments; the chestnut glow of the cellos was so much more vivid than the people playing them, as if to emphasize that it was their shapely and hollow bodies that were primarily responsible for the sound. And weren't they? The conductor silently told everyone what to do, how to breathe, where to slow down, but even he held a baton in his hand.

Paula was the only one whose instrument lived inside her body. The only one whose music spilled out of her simply because she opened her mouth.

temporary magnetism: induced magnetism; magnetism
that a body, e.g., soft iron, possesses only by virtue of being
in a magnetic field and that largely disappears on removing
the body from the field

"You have to be careful," Madame said. "There are so many ene-
mies of your instrument. Dampness, wind, dust. Never leave the
house with wet hair, never sleep near an open window. Never
shout or scream, never sing a note without warming up first, never
sing full voice in a rehearsal, especially on the day before a performance. Never reveal how much you want something, never let
them see your fear."

And now I knew about fear.

Did I have to endure some period of waiting? It seemed impossible that my voice could be dead forever, but I knew it happened
to people, that kind of loss. I tried to imagine dormancy, a time
for my voice to be asleep, underground. I remembered the way
Madame wouldn't allow me to sing for anyone but her during the
first three years of my training; she was my only audience, not
even my family was permitted to listen. Now, I couldn't even
imagine singing for her.

I dreamed about Isaac, about packing and unpacking luggage,
getting onto trains and buses and airplanes. Anxiety, a panic about
what to bring, what to leave behind. Tickets got misplaced, sched-
ules were wrong, I was so late that I nearly missed the departure.
Isaac was seated next to me, staying in the hotel room adjoining
mine, I couldn't see him, I just knew he was there, like electricity
in my skin.

I called Herman Roth from the airport in Budapest, and told
him I was coming home; the auditions had already been canceled
and my bags were safely on their way to the belly of the plane.

"What do you mean canceled?" he asked me.

"The last two," I said. "I'm exhausted."

He gave an exasperated sigh into the phone. "You canceled them yourself? Without even checking with me?"

"I had to," I said, starting to feel defensive. I told myself he was my manager, not my owner. I had every right.

"I've got a reputation too, you know," he said, edgily. "If you're gonna do stuff like that, you need to talk it over with me. I've got a perspective on your career maybe you can't see so clearly." Then he mumbled something under his breath.

"What was that?" I asked.

"Nothing. Do what you gotta do."

He didn't sound like he meant it, but I didn't care. "Everything went great," I lied, wanting to change the subject.

"Yeah, sure," his voice rumbled in my ear. "Why walk away now?"

"I'm not walking away. It's just been a long trip, longer than I'd planned for, remember? And I pushed it too far."

"Canceling always bothers me," he said, his voice dropping low again.

"I told them it was doctor's orders, my throat was inflamed." That part wasn't really a lie. The fear filled my throat like a virus. "They seemed to understand."

"Singers get away with murder sometimes," Herman said.

I touched the scarf around my neck and checked the departure time on the board to make sure I still had time to go through customs. "I've got to go now," I said. "I'll talk with you when I get home."

"One more thing," Herman said as I was about to hang up. "Isaac's been asking me about when you'll be back. Do you want me to tell him you're on your way or what?"

"Just call Julian and tell him I'll be home tomorrow night," I said. I wasn't ready for Isaac in the flesh, not for a while. On the plane, I was blessed with a row of empty seats. I wrapped myself in a blanket and slept.

I N   O N E of the boxes of my father's belongings that the housekeeper sent to me after he died, I found a set of three reel-to-reel tapes held together with a disintegrating rubber band. When I started to pry it loose, the rubber crumbled into pieces, a few stray fragments stubbornly adhering to the plastic edges of the reels. The tapes were labeled in my father's precise block letters: dates of the recordings, a simple title for each one. THE PERIODIC TABLE. MOLECULES AND ATOMS. BASIC LAB PROCEDURES.

He had never been my teacher, but I used to see him through the small window of his classroom door when I was walking to my own chemistry class in the next room. My teacher, Mr. Kohn, knew I was the son of a fellow teacher, but he never spoke about it with me, which I appreciated. In the beginning of the year, he offered me a single raised eyebrow each time I made perfect scores on tests. After several weeks, he allowed me to work independently in the back of the room, quietly performing my own experiments and recording their results in a blue spiral notebook that Mr. Kohn read and responded to with small red plus signs as an indication of his approval.

Now, with these tapes in my hands, it was easy to picture my father standing behind a small wooden lectern, resettling his glasses onto the bridge of his nose, his red hair glowing under the fluorescent lights of his classroom. October 1, 8, 15. The introduction to the noble gases, the inert gases, the explanation of positrons and electrons, the logic of combining and separating chemical universes, how to stay in control of a Bunsen burner, how to measure with precision.

I heard his voice without playing a single tape: the gravelly pitch as it rose and fell, the rhythmic clearing of his throat at the start of a new topic, the small pauses so that the students could finish copying a particularly complex drawing from the blackboard. I could imagine the precise lines he made with his cylinder of chalk; no squawking from his board, no tentative whisper, just the steady tapping code of blocked-out words and mathematical symbols, the purposeful pointing of arrows.

Why there were only three of these tapes, I couldn't figure out, until I found a copy of a letter to the school in which my father explained that

he had to have surgery for the removal of a gallstone. He had there-
fore prepared a series of lectures for his substitute teacher to use in his
chemistry classes, so as to relieve his replacement of the burdens of
preparation.

According to the dates, I was eight years old at the time. I suddenly
remembered the snaky-looking red scar on my father's belly, the one he
used to point to and say "This was where I was cut by a sword." I remembered how Paula would giggle and embellish the story, saying "He
was a giant, wasn't he. With enormous yellow teeth and a way of smiling that made all the plants wilt when they smelled his breath. Right?"

"Food always got caught in his beard," my father said, playing along.
"And flies were always following him around. I was lucky he didn't get
any closer to me than the tip of his sword."

I had been scheduled to sing Elektra's first monologue from the
Strauss opera, where Elektra remembers her father's murder and
imagines revenge in chilling detail. I sat before my hotel room mirror, thinking of all the times I'd watched my mouth and throat and
eyes to practice hiding all visible traces of the strain, evidence
of what the sound cost me. But even as I stared calmly at my own
mask in the mirror, I felt a lurching in my belly, as if someone had
reached inside and grabbed hold of me. I took a sip of warm water
and watched my throat as I swallowed. I thought at first it wasn't
stage fright in the usual sense, not the kind of fear that singers talk
about where they are terrified they will open their mouths and
nothing will come out. It was more the kind of fear that I wouldn't
recognize my own voice, that some demon was inside me and singing through me, and I was no longer in control.

Breathe, breathe, breathe, I whispered to myself. But something
was rising inside me, some kind of darkness I didn't recognize. I
kept trying to picture myself at the edge of the stage, preparing
for my entrance. Could I will myself out through the dim backstage light, touch the heavy velvet curtain to my heart for luck the

way I always did? And when it was time, and I had to sing that line *"Agamemnon, wo bist Du?"* could I find that elemental sound?

> **image, real:** (in physics) an image formed by a mirror or lens at a point through which the rays of light entering the observer's eye actually pass; such an image can be obtained on a screen

> **image, virtual:** (in physics) an image seen at a point from which the rays of light appear to come to the observer but do not actually do so, e.g., the image seen in a plane mirror or through a diverging lens; such an image cannot be obtained on a screen placed at its apparent position, since the rays of light do not pass through that point

THERE WAS a woman my father knew after the war. She had lost her entire family, including her two children, her husband, and both her parents. Years later, after she remarried and had a little girl, she began to suffer from severe depressions, black moods that would force her into bed for weeks at a time. One day the husband came home from work and found the two of them, the wife and the little girl, dead in the kitchen, the house filled with gas from the gaping mouth of the oven. Before she killed them both, she had shaved off all of her hair. "She was still in the camp, you see?" my father said when he told me this story. "She never really left. She was all the time waiting for her turn."

On the plane, I dreamed of a very old man with arthritic hands fumbling through piles of brittle papers, as if he is searching for something hidden. I have given him a note with my father's name and date of birth—the true one, not the backwards one—and I am waiting for him to look up at me and signal that he knows where to look. But he holds the note and studies it for several silent moments, his lips moving very slightly as he pronounces the name. He looks at my face, and his eyebrows lift along with the corners

of his mouth. I smile back, hopefully, and watch him as he rises
and turns his back, reaching painfully toward a shelf against the
wall behind his desk that bends under the weight of too many
thick volumes. There is a date stamped in gold on the leather
binding, 1920–1933, and I can see when he opens it that it must
be the register of births, each entry written in a fading inky script.
He begins to turn the pages, but he's looking in the wrong year,
and I think it's perhaps impolite to tell him, so I wait. His misshapen finger slides across the page, and he says something, not
my father's name but another Perel. There was another child, a little girl, he says, born three years after my father, and his finger taps
on the lines. He says he remembers her, a beautiful child that everyone in town knew because she had very red hair and very blue eyes.
The old man looks at me. She used to play a very small violin, he
says, one made for her, and she made the music of an angel.

> **zones of audibility:** an intense sound, e.g., due to an ex-
> plosion, can usually be heard or detected at all points in
> a large area around the source of the sound, and also in dis-
> tant zones of audibility separated from that area by regions
> in which the sound cannot be detected. Sound waves
> can reach these zones by reflection down from the upper
> atmosphere

I WORKED on the dictionary less and less because I knew it was
nearly complete. If I waited long enough there would always be new
terms to add, an infinite alphabet of discoveries widening every day into
a slightly new version of the physical world. I remembered when I believed myself a part of that discovering edge, when all I could imagine
caring about was the reach toward some unique angle on the universe,
discerning a relationship between stars that hadn't been comprehensible
until now.

I wasn't worrying about money so much as time, how to turn my attention fully to something new when I'd learned so well how to work

with this alphabet, these scribblings and abbreviations, these pages to fill. My dissertation felt like an ancient relic, a trunk in someone else's attic with no decipherable meaning anymore. If I talked with my advisor she'd urge me to return to it, or even to start over, apply for grant money.

It was, as always, a question of desire. What did I want or care about or need to know? What questions would be potent and irresistible enough to wake me from a dream and pull me to my desk in the middle of the night? All I could think about was Sola's black hair, the absence of Paula's voice, the last pages of the last letter of the dictionary. My fortunes promised me good news, a surprising discovery, a true friend.

I turned off the televisions. I sat in the room with their blank faces, their silenced voices. I waited for instructions from my heart.

Julian is back in his apartment, I hear the doors open and close, then his footsteps over my head. Diego is asleep on the couch in Paula's living room, as if the weight of everything I am telling him is pushing him down under water. I hope he is not dreaming.

The phone rings but I do not want to answer it, I think it is all right this time to let Paula's machine pick up. I feel the need to be silent for a little while longer, to let the sound of my story soak back into myself. I do not turn on any lights as the sun goes down and it gets dark in the apartment, I just want to let the day turn over into night while I sit there, watching Diego sleep, and listening to Julian's chair roll across the floor.

Diego moans a little in his sleep and turns over, pulling one of the cushions over his head as he turns. I wonder if I should wake him up, but I know I cannot stop him from dreaming when he goes to his home and for every night after this one. My own nightmares are still coming to me, not all the time but often enough, and if not for the visits of my grandmother sometimes I do not know if I can stand it.

I remember Julian saying I can make other people witnesses by telling them, but I still am not sure I am doing the right thing. What I do not yet know are the stories that Julian carries around under his skin and in his bones, but I know there is something, I can see it every time I look at his face.

W H E N I got back from my walk I wondered if Diego had left or not; there was no light leaking from under Paula's apartment door, but that didn't mean anything. I went upstairs with the mail, rereading Paula's letter as I climbed the steps, feeling a strange combination of relief and fear about her saying she was coming home. It was as if years had passed since she left, and I felt a mixture of excitement and dread about what it would be like to see her again.

Then my mind fixed itself on the idea that Sola would be leaving, going back to her apartment somewhere on the "other side," as she said, and the thing that I thought I'd wanted, to be returned to my previous life before I knew her, was going to happen after all. Paula would be below me, singing, and I would be sitting like a stone in front of my televisions, lost to the world I was just starting to discover. I went to my desk, and placed my hand on the pile of dictionary entries that began with Sola's name.

The blank faces of the televisions told me nothing. I had to go downstairs to tell Sola that Paula was coming home and everything was about to change. My phone rang, making me jump. I thought maybe it was Sola calling, although I didn't think she'd be calling from downstairs, or maybe it was Paula from some faraway place. Something wrong somewhere. I rolled my chair to the phone.

"Herman Roth here. Hope I didn't interrupt anything important?"

I thought about telling him he had the wrong number. "No," I said.

"Good, good. I just got off the phone with your sister, she wanted me to give you a call. You know she's coming back?"

It bothered me that he got to speak to her and I didn't. But I told him yes, I knew.

"Right. Well. She's already in the air, I think, then she's got a layover in New York and lands in San Francisco around nine tomorrow night. That sound good?"

"Fine," I said, getting ready to hang up. But Herman wasn't going anywhere yet.

"She sounded a bit down, you know? Low energy at least."

"I know," I said. What did Herman Roth know about Paula's energy? He didn't have to call me to talk about energy. I wondered how Paula could stand to talk to him about anything, but maybe all that boisterousness in his voice was what made him a good manager. I wished I could turn down his volume.

"That woman staying in the apartment, what's her name, something like ordinary, even though it's not ordinary, get what I'm saying? Anyway, you've got to let her know Paula's coming back so she can clear out of the place, right?"

"Sola Ordonio," I said, liking the way the vowels rolled.

"Right, right," Herman said. "I tried calling but she doesn't pick up. So you've got to tell her. Okay? Can I count on you?"

"I'll tell her," I said. "Good-bye, Herman."

When I hear Diego say my name, I realize I must be nearly asleep myself. I reach over to turn on the lamp and see Diego flinch from the sudden light.

"Sorry."

He rubs his face with one hand, massaging the skin around his temples. "Never mind," he says.

I want to touch him again, partly to make sure he is real, and partly to see if we can bring each other back to the present.

"Are you all right?"

Diego opens his mouth and then closes it again, shaking his head at what he cannot say. I wait. "Nothing is all right," he says finally.

I nod.

"Did you tell me all of it?" he asks, his hands opening in the air toward me. "I keep thinking there must be more that you can't even say out loud."

I nod again. "It is always that way," I say. "You can never say everything in words." I think about how I am screaming into the earth, about the impossibility of speaking about that to anyone. "But about that day, all I can give you is what I am giving you."

We both sigh, and then halfway smile at each other. Diego begins to massage his hands, rubbing and pressing on the knuckles and in the soft places at the base of his thumbs. It reminds me of my mother kneading dough. He says, "I could tell you some things about Eduardo and the mines, maybe that would be like giving you a story in exchange for the other one?"

I understand why he wants to talk about my dead husband, but I shake my head. "Not now," I say.

Diego stands up, brushing imaginary dust from his pants, suddenly seeming quite nervous. I stand up too, and we take a step toward each other. "Are we saying good-bye now?" I ask him. "Already?"

He reaches for one of my hands and clasps it between his own, then brings it to his lips for a very brief moment. "I don't know how to say thank you," he says. "I asked for something I needed even though I knew it would be very hard for you."

My hand tingles a little where he is kissing it. I am struck again by how old he looks now, and I wonder if he sees the same in me. I think that loss always shows in the eyes, the way Julian's eyes do, when he almost lets me see them. "It helps me to know that you know," I say to Diego. "For such a long time, I am the only one."

He looks at me, and I think to myself that it is still true, I am still the only one. Telling the story doesn't give it away, just gives it a sound. But perhaps the spirits of his mother and his sisters are a little quieter now because he does not have to keep imagining the story of their deaths.

O N   T V, I had seen what they do with wild horses to gentle them: they herd the animal into a holding box that's quickly filled to the top with grain so that he's completely embraced by this soft but unyielding mass. His body can't move. Because he's desperate to find a way out, he sticks his head through the opening in the gate, and that's where he can be whispered to. Someone stands there, at his head, and his body is safe and still, he's trapped but not in pain, and the whispering is what slowly calms him. So after an hour or two he's become gentle.

It's like the hugging machine made by that autistic woman. She figured out the only way she can stand to be hugged, and it's exactly how she needs it: a contraption perfectly designed for the pressure and intensity her body wants, without the problem of including another person at all. She hugs herself with machine arms.

I thought of myself walking to the Laundromat with my bag of dirty laundry, testing what it would feel like to embrace a person wanting to be held. It seemed impossible to imagine a body, with arms reaching around me too, holding me back.

More airplane dreams, fueled by the droning engines. I was warming up my voice, but there were all sorts of hands on my throat: Isaac's, Madame le Fleur's, my mother's, Julian's. The hands of a red-haired, blue-eyed girl that had to be my dead aunt, the one I never knew and whose music was murdered before I was born. Her hands were on her own throat, and she was staring at me. In the background was an orchestra, Isaac was conducting, and they were playing the overture to that Strauss opera, then the measures just before my entrance to call out to Agamemnon. A bird flew out of my dead aunt's mouth and landed on my shoulder, whispered something in my ear and flew off again. When I woke up all I could think about was trying to remember what the bird said to me, but I couldn't hear it anymore. It was gone.

Awake, I tried to remember the time before my voice, before that was the center of my life, but I couldn't find a memory that made any sense, there was no *me* before my voice, no other point of reference. To have sound coming out of me, to feel notes vibrate through my body, to open my mouth and release that sound, those notes. If anyone ever showed me how to begin it was the canaries, those tragic and brilliant yellow birds, their feathers so bright against the white bars of the cage, their small chests fluffing and filling with air, that delirious burst of music. I must have watched them from my high chair, must have seen how they used their bodies as instruments. And when my mouth was open, waiting for the spoonfuls of mashed bananas or peas, I breathed into my unfeathered chest and tried to imitate those canaries, tried to send my voice as high and exuberant as they aimed, past the cage and out of the room, out into the wild blue of the sky they could only see through a glass window on the other side of their barred world.

> **eutectic point:** two or more substances capable of forming
> solid solutions with each other have the property of lower-
> ing each other's freezing point; the minimum freezing point
> attainable, corresponding to the eutectic mixture, is termed
> the *eutectic point*

Julian comes downstairs just a few minutes after Diego's car pulls away. I am staring out the window in the direction of the yellow tree, although it is not yellow anymore but green and I am not really seeing it anyway. The street is dark and quiet. Julian knocks twice, and I sit for another moment before getting up to let him in.

He says, "Herman Roth called," while still in the doorway, and I almost cannot see his face in the dim light from the hall. "He says Paula is on her way back. She'll be here by tomorrow night."

"Is everything all right?"

Julian shrugs and slides his hands into his pockets. "I think so," he says. "I think she's just tired."

I cannot really imagine it, every day performing for strangers in different cities, always moving to a new room in a new hotel. She must know how to take care of herself, but still. "I can leave in the morning," I say. "And of course I can clean before I go . . ." I take a step backwards into the room. "Do you want to come in? For a little while?"

Julian stays in the doorway, rocking from foot to foot like he is trying to find his balance. He shakes his head. "It will be strange now to have her back," he says.

"Yes," I say, thinking of how dark my apartment is after this one, and feeling suddenly that I do not want to live there anymore. "I think I am moving somewhere else," I say, not quite meaning to say it out loud. "To a place with more light." I wave my hand in the air of Paula's living room, see again how the simple world of colors lifts my heart.

Julian frowns. "You're leaving town?"

"Just my apartment," I say. "To live in another part, maybe closer to this side. Maybe near a park or something green. A place with lots of windows."

"Where's your friend Diego?" he asks, looking past me into the living room.

"Gone," I say. "It is a hard day for him."

Julian nods, keeping his eyes on the room behind my back. "Hard for you too, I'd think," he says.

"It is like you say," I tell him. "Making other people witnesses too."

He pulls his hands from his pockets and rests them on the frame of the door above his head, almost as though he wants to hang from a tree branch. We both say nothing for a little while, and I feel all of the heavy invisible pieces of our silence. Then he turns to walk upstairs, ducking so the top of his head will not hit the lamp hanging by the front door.

"I'll miss you." He says it so quietly I almost do not hear him at all.

TEN

At dawn, before I was fully awake, I heard the sound of tree cutters at work up the street; they were trimming sycamore limbs that had grown too close to the phone wires. Branches were lifted free and fell in slow motion away from their source, a metallic arm reached high into the density of green, and a man with a hard hat wielded the blade as it sang and moaned. I felt it cutting into my bones if I allowed myself to listen carefully, and decided that even the TVs wouldn't be enough. Even full blast, their volume couldn't mask the sound of those blades.

I kept thinking I had to do something with my head and my feet, even traffic would be a relief. Even the sound of buses and the crying of brakes, horns, a siren. When the tree cutters stopped, gave way to silence, I thought of Sola weeping in the night, her sadness like a bridge between us.

On the anniversaries of the different deaths, I do certain things to mark the day. For my Camucha, I sing her a song, the one I use to make her fall asleep when she is still small enough to hold in one arm. She looks like Eduardo so much, her eyes very wide apart like his, and her fine hair almost coming to a point at the top of her forehead. He does not ever get to see her, so I sing to her about the father far away who loves her, and the rain in the mountains and the river always running down over the rocks to the sea. I sing to her in her grave and picture myself kissing her head, smelling the sweetness of her.

On the day for Eduardo, I light a candle and tell him I am not forgetting him, I tell him he is my only husband and father of my only child. I tell him I remember the way he puts his fingers into my hair like a comb, and I tell him I am sorry that his body is broken but happy to know his bones are resting in the earth.

For the rest of my family, for the village, I stay awake all night in silence, watching the darkness fill up with their faces, fill up with ghosts. I wait for each person to sit next to me in the dark, wait and listen for anyone to speak from the land of the dead. The universe of the dead. I stay very still, breathing softly, keeping myself awake until the sun comes back. I pretend I am on the front steps of the dead house, politely waiting for an invitation. Trying to kill myself is rude, I understand now, I have to wait for permission to enter to where they are. Somewhere in the rooms of the house, the dead are all together, laughing and playing games, telling each other stories about their lives on the earth. I cannot hear them but I know they are just on the other side of the door.

Maybe it is like the voices on Julian's televisions when he turns off the sound, they are still there inside the box but he cannot hear them, they are stopped by glass and distance and a wave too wide to catch with our simple half-closed ears.

I wanted to go home and sleep for days, weeks even, if I could keep the world out. I pictured my apartment with the curtains drawn, blackout style, the phone turned off, my eyes and ears shielded with masks and plugs. I thought maybe if I died into silence for a while, my voice might come back, I might be saved.

It occurred to me that I now felt envious of Julian, because he knew how to keep the world away, he knew his own flight distance. I'd been tamed, singing to other people for so long I forgot how to be alone, how to stop listening for applause. What did it mean to pay attention to silence? I didn't know. All I did was fill up with sound, my voice needing release, that was how I knew I was alive. My father in the audience, weeping, my mother giving him comfort. Julian all the way in the back, soaking my voice into his frozen skin. If I stopped singing I would disappear under the lake, a stone in the water, sinking.

It's not only that I was afraid to perform. I felt that I could not sing, would not, should not. That singing was an affront to the dead, the ultimate betrayal—not only to sing in German but to sing at all, to make music in the world as if beauty made sense, as if beauty belonged here. To us. No, I would fold my songs into silence, refuse to pretend I was filled with light. There was no room for my voice anymore, no place for that translucent sound. There could only be cold earth, empty graves, ashes, and darkness. No rightness or wrongness to any of it, simply the silence of the dead. Violins broken like bones.

BEFORE SHE started writing her advice column, my mother's religion was gardening and food; she worked with her hands in the earth and fed us from the ground. Tomatoes, squash, herbs, greens. She believed in the things that grow, filled us up with chlorophyll and sunlight. Swiss chard, garlic, sorrel soup. I saw her pause sometimes to admire a tomato before she picked it, she knelt sometimes near a bunch of sorrel and touched it with her fingertips like she might stroke the fur of an animal. "Food is alive," she told us. "We are part of the same cycle, the same taking in and growing in seasons, all of us back into the soil in the end so we can push through to the air one more time."

When I ate, I wanted to look at my food, keep my eyes open before I took a bite. When I watched my mother holding a tomato like it was a work of art, I wanted to see what she saw. There was a negative space that I kept my eyes on too, the shapes between things like the infinite distances inside our own bodies, particles moving at the speed of light.

sublimation: (in chemistry) the conversion of a solid directly
into vapor, and subsequent condensation, without melting

I WAS not in the building when Sola left, I didn't want to watch her
drive away. Instead, I held on to the image of her face, the profile of it,
her lips forming the story of the massacre to Diego, to me. We had made
ourselves witnesses, Diego and I, we had listened. It was a story so much
like the ones I'd heard from survivors of the camps, but it was unlike
them too, because it belonged to Sola. I thought about how my father's
story was the only one I could never know, and how it was the only
story I truly carried inside my body, the one I had lived so close to, and
so far away from. The distance between my skin and his skin, the distance between molecules. A universe apart, and unsplittable.

I walked away from my apartment so I wouldn't have to see Sola
walking away, and I didn't know how I could see her again. She told me
she wanted me to come to visit her, she asked me to go again with her for
a walk up into the hills. I didn't say yes because I didn't know if I could
do it, didn't know if I had already stretched my reach too far and had to
contract again, back inside the safe places of my life.

Paula was coming home, her voice returning to my ear. I still had my
dictionary, the piles of definitions covering my table. But somehow I was
learning how to feel, the very thing I'd been teaching myself against. I
hadn't fixed the broken television, didn't even know yet what had gone
wrong.

I cracked open my window, remembering the way Sola's black hair
caught light. I wanted to feel the touch of fresh air on my face.

I bring my bags to the car and check everything one more time. The
apartment is clean, full of light, the bed has fresh sheets and there are
no signs I am ever here. I have a bag of lemons for Julian, I am
writing a note for him, some words of leaving, some hope for our
friendship. I am already missing him, the heaviness of his heart, the
way I see him in his leather chair next to the wall of televisions, the

way he walks downstairs in the daze of heat. I bring the bag of lemons to his door, leave it where he can see it when the door opens. The box of mail for Paula is on the table, the paper with Diego's phone number is inside my wallet. I am going home to pack my bags again and find another place to live, a place with windows facing east and south. My skin is filled with the light of this place, the green of Paula's singing. I take with me the voice of my story, the look on Diego's face when I tell him about his mother and his sisters, the shape of his crooked hands. I take with me the blood inside my heart that still pushes me to be alive.

Diego meets me at the café wearing sunglasses and carrying a basket filled with fruit: ruby grapes and bananas and oranges small enough to fit in a child's hand. Mandarins, he calls them. He is smiling when he takes off the glasses, apologizing for being late.

"I have so many customers today," he says, half-proud and half-embarrassed. He places the basket on the table in front of me. "These are for you."

I bend my head and say thank you. The gift makes me feel that my own hands are empty; it is easier to give than to accept a gift, even from a friend. "Let me buy you a coffee," I say, rising when he sits. "With sugar and milk?"

"For me, black," he says. "I like it bitter and dark."

"Yes," I say. "Me too."

The café is full of people, a line curving past the pastries and sweets. A young woman in purple is talking on a phone she pulls from her backpack, a man in a gray suit is tapping messages on a computer. I see Diego through the window, looking out at the street, one hand rubbing the back of his neck. I wonder if he is thinking to himself like I am that this place is still like the moon, and he and I are the astronauts. How do we get back home? And then I think: it is not that we are so changed. It is that home is no longer there for us to return to it.

Over the coffee, we talk about ourselves as we are now, I tell him about my work, my apartment; he tells me about a woman he lives with who has a little boy named José.

"She wants to get married," he says. "I'm thinking maybe," and he shrugs to finish the thought. "José's father is in jail. Maria doesn't want anything to do with him. I say good for her. But for me, taking care of someone else's kid, it's not so easy."

The coffee tastes good, I feel it warming me inside. "You love her?" I ask.

Diego looks at me and then away, cars sliding past our table on the edge of the patio. We are no more strange than anyone else here, I remind myself. We are drinking coffee, speaking in English. It is just an ordinary dream.

"I love her," he says. "And I love the kid too. He's crazy about baseball, collects autographs. I take him to games sometimes, even when Maria doesn't come along. I feel . . ."

He stops, looks over my head at someone, shakes his head as if to clear it. "I feel lucky," he says. "That's all."

"Yes," I say. "That is all."

I HAD an idea about going to the deli on the wrong day, looking to buy a whole chicken. I thought I might see Frank's eyebrows shoot up into his forehead, but maybe he wouldn't ask. For once I wanted him to, wanted someone to know about my life.

When I got close to the deli, I saw a sign stretched like a banner across the door. It was handwritten, a letter to the customers explaining that Frank had suffered a fatal heart attack the day before. WE'RE COMPLETELY BEREFT, the sign said. WE CAN'T EVEN SAY WHEN THE DELI WILL BE OPEN AGAIN. PLEASE BEAR WITH US. THANKS FOR YOUR UNDERSTANDING.

Already some cards had been left leaning up against the door, and two other people came up to read the sign while I was standing there. Frank's extended family. I edged away, not quite taking in the news.

"What a shame," a woman's voice behind me said. "He was such a lovely man."

I saw Frank in his apron, the pencil tucked behind his ear, his winking eye. *What else can I get you today?* The world was moving so fast, changing without warning. I felt myself disappearing, unraveling inside my clothes, particles colliding and breaking apart.

In the week of shivah after my father's death, I tore my clothes, stopped shaving the stubble from my face, imagined myself going ashy-looking in the mirrors I kept covered with black cloth. We were old enough this time to be mourners. Paula kept candles burning, and three times a day we recited the Kaddish, murmuring side by side. I knew the Hebrew words by heart, having learned them in synagogue all those Saturdays, but Paula read them in transliterated English from the pages of our father's old prayer book.

The sky was clear blue or heavy with clouds, the trees held their leaves or dropped them. We were orphans now, held together by the invisible strands of DNA that we almost shared among the secrets of our cells.

Glorified and sanctified be thy name . . .

The rules said no music during the week of shivah, because music is for happiness, for distraction. Paula was supposed to close her throat, stop up the sound. I wondered if it was going to suffocate her, like keeping the towel over the birdcage even in the daylight. Wouldn't the birds realize that this night was lasting too long? Wouldn't they begin to sing against the dark?

The wind chanted at the windowpanes, my dreams filled with my father's looming figure, his hands too large for his body, his feet bare and blue from the cold. He had the look of someone who knew he was dying, but when he tried to speak to me, his mouth opened like a black hole and swallowed all the stars.

Now Paula was on her way home, I had to repeat it to myself as I walked away empty-handed from the deli. Sola was leaving and Paula was coming home, the world was shifting back into its original arrangement, planets back in their orbits. I wondered if someday I could make a chicken dinner for three, serve it to us as though we made a family around a table, dish up coleslaw onto three white plates, scoop potatoes like I'd been doing it all my life.

I wanted to hear Paula singing again in the morning, and I wanted to see Sola's hair down the back of her blue dress. I wanted to see if I could learn how to touch the skin of a person who called hummingbirds the birds who kiss flowers.

The sidewalk laid itself in front of me like a row of tiles on a game board, like a plan for going straight as far as I could. Brian wheeled past me on his bicycle, earlier than I'd ever seen him leave the building. Maybe there was a weather crisis, or he was close to finishing his thesis. I thought about my own thesis, and my advisor hoping I'd take time off but come back, the unfinished chapters sealed tightly in a cardboard box I never wanted to open again. I had my dictionary, and when that was done maybe I'd figure out how soon they would need a follow-up edition, or I'd start selling off televisions so I could begin to hunt for more broken bones to repair. I still wanted to put things together, find the blind road to being whole.

Could I take Sola to the observatory to look at the stars, point my gaze with hers into the black distance? She already knew about infinity, I could hear it in her story about the massacre, the impossibility of bringing together what had been torn apart, the uncrossable river between the past and the present. She already knew where I lived, but maybe I could show her something about space and time that only the stars knew how to explain, maybe I could show her a map of the sky. It was the only language I could speak in silence.

I believed Julian was the only person in the world who would understand this terror, even if I didn't say a word about it. He would read it in my face and recognize me, the sister who had forgotten how to be afraid and now remembered. The voice might come back if I stayed very quiet in my room, if I soothed my throat with nothing but hot water and lemon. My mother was long dead, Madame le Fleur was in a nursing home, my father was dead. And for the first time in my life I was losing my bearings. I needed to stare out the window at Julian's ginkgo tree, learn the pattern of its branches, its attachment to the ground. I wanted to be back on earth again, singing into the chamber of my own room.

On the plane, I slept and didn't talk to anyone, even kept my sunglasses on like I was an old-time movie star. Let them guess and whisper. I dreamed about flying underwater, moving faster than the fish, covering vast distances with ease. There were dark caves on both sides of me, I knew they weren't empty and when I reached a hand inside one I felt something soft brush against my fingers. I wasn't afraid, but I didn't go inside; I thought maybe if I waited at the mouth of the cave whatever was inside would come out to find me. But the water carried me away, I washed up on shore, and I found myself all dry, breathing air.

We were landing.

I W A S inside my apartment before deciding to buy something for Paula's return, turned around and walked all the way back to the flower stand near the deli. I wanted color for her homecoming. I had passed this place hundreds of times but never once approached closely enough to smell a single fragrance. Now I knew I wanted something red and yellow, a promise of light.

I remembered commercials on TV that talked about communicating with flowers, sending messages to people you loved. I told the woman I wanted to look around first. I watched her taking care of other customers, snipping and arranging, gathering bouquets into her arms. It all seemed possible, the blues and purples, even white and pink and orange. I thought maybe one of each flower, a bouquet of everything, almost too enormous for a single vase. Paula's apartment would look like a diva's dressing room after a performance, the praise of a hundred admirers.

The woman in the apron held her clippers in one hand like a question mark. "Ready yet?" she said.

"Okay," I said, and began to point. There were eighteen different flowers to collect; I selected a pair from each silver bucket.

"That it?" she asked, her armful hoisted on her hip like too many groceries.

"What do you think?" I asked her. This was a new language for me, to speak in color and smell. I didn't know what I was saying.

"I think it's terrific," she said, grinning. "Want me to arrange it for you?"

"Please," I said, and fumbled for my wallet. Suddenly I remembered I would be walking all the way home with these flowers, more vivid than a laundry bag clutched for safety in my arms. But it was too late to turn back now, the bouquet lay blooming on her cart. Welcome home.

When I passed into the airport through that floating tunnel, I wore my sunglasses and kept my head down, ignoring the limousine drivers who stood with cards bearing other people's names. On a better day I would have looked for my own name there, PEREL in block letters held between gloved hands, a name I suddenly thought of as belonging not only to me and to Julian but to my father and his father and all the ghosts I had so recently discovered. A name on too many gravestones. A cantor with a dead voice, a violin player with broken hands.

I found my luggage and a cab. I felt as though I'd been gone so long I didn't recognize the shape of the hills or the quality of the light. I thought to myself *crepi il lupo* (may the wolf die), wishing myself strength as if about to face an audience for my final aria. Except I hadn't sung a note since Budapest.

Looking in my purse for a handkerchief, I came across some Hungarian coins I'd set aside to give to Julian. That would be the easy part. What I didn't yet know was how I'd tell him these stories of the dead, and about what happened to our father. What if my telling sent him into a cave from which he'd never emerge? The list of losses had become so long for me so quickly, a list I hadn't allowed myself to keep track of before. It used to start with my mother and end with my father, but now it began so much earlier, stretching wide into the backstage of my life.

On the Berkeley side of the bridge, I took a deep breath and released it slowly, closing my eyes like a curtain. *Almost there,* I thought, my scarf around my throat as though I'd never taken it off. I pictured Julian waving good-bye from his window, hand pressed against the glass, I thought of Sola bringing his lunch and trying to decipher the strange language of his world. I wanted to tell him I was beginning to understand what it was like to be wrapped in fear, but I worried that maybe he still needed me to be the one sending my voice out into the world, maybe the weight of my silence would make his own impossible to bear. I didn't know how to come home.

I H A D my arms full of flowers, and somehow walked home without noticing the cracks in the sidewalk, without counting the trees or the blue cars. I was surprised by my front door appearing too soon, as if the building had been moved closer to the street. My key still fit into the lock, the handle still turned the way it was supposed to. I stood in the foyer for a moment, debating, then let myself into Paula's apartment, standing in her doorway for another minute to wonder about Sola.

Maybe she was doing the same thing just now in her own place, reminding herself that she lived there, noticing its familiar and unfamiliar arrangement of things. Paula's rooms looked calmly expectant, all of the surfaces bright with Sola's cleaning. I found a wide-mouthed crystal vase in one of the kitchen cabinets and filled it with water, unwrapping the bouquet and plunging it in. In my pocket was a small notecard where I'd written something for Paula, a formula for her voice and its perfect pitch. Then I went back upstairs to my leather chair, to wait for the sound of my sister.

I am on my way back to my apartment carrying almost exactly the same things I have in my hands when I leave: a suitcase and one green plant. Now I think its leaves are even brighter than before. Because of the light, and because I believe they can suffer from a lack of what they need to survive. They can feel peaceful too.

The thing I carry that is new is a basket of fruit from Diego, still full. I place the suitcase and the basket in the trunk and keep the plant on the seat next to me when I drive, back to the place I want to leave behind. And I think of the bushes that hide me from the soldiers, the ones that are surrounded by fire and yet do not burn. (The screaming I cannot remember. The idea of it, yes, but not the sound. It is a sound impossible to listen to, impossible to forget. But I cannot hear it at all.)

I want to live in a place where there is at least one beautiful tree to see from my window, or maybe a hillside covered with trees, or maybe the sound of water. Warren's house looks out across the bay, high like a lighthouse but far from the rocky edges of danger. I try to imagine myself there, waking up in bed with a man who loves me in my sleep, but I cannot feel my heart.

W H E N I closed the door of Paula's apartment after arranging the flowers in the vase, I climbed the stairs and saw a brown paper bag leaning against my door. Inside was a pile of lemons, maybe a dozen of them, yellow as canaries. When I pulled one out I saw it had words written on its skin, it said, YOU ARE. I pulled out a few more and saw each lemon had been inscribed with a word or two, all of them adding up to sentences, a letter in lemonskin. FOR NOW, one said. GOOD-BYE, said another, and I liked that the meanings were the same no matter which way I read them, a kind of forward and backward game like making up palindromes late at night when I couldn't sleep. COME SEE ME. Tattoos for happier days, an alphabet to remember her by. I THINK OF YOU, YOUR FRIEND and SOLA and DEAR JULIAN.

Inside my apartment I lined them all up on my worktable, this story of lemons, written for me. SOMETIME SOON, it said. WITH LOVE.

The first different thing was Julian coming downstairs to meet me at the front door when the cab driver was still pulling my luggage out of the trunk. I had my key in my hand when I saw his astonishing face appear in the open doorway. He was smiling.

"You're finally back," he said, keeping his hands in his pockets like always. No hugging.

"Hey there, sweet brother," I said, not sure whether to say anything about meeting downstairs like this, outside even. "I'm finally back." I took off my sunglasses and squinted up at him.

"It felt like a long one," he said.

"To me too."

My apartment door was open, he must have used his key. Another first, I thought. Julian followed me inside, and the driver came in behind us with my bags. I tipped him and thanked him, still watching Julian with private disbelief, waiting for him to start jumping out of his skin. But he stood in my living room like everything was okay. Then I saw the flowers in the kitchen, the brilliant profusion.

"For the prodigal diva," Julian said, dipping his head.

"From you?" I asked, trying not to sound as shocked as I was feeling. He nodded, not looking at me, as I went closer to admire the colors, the fragrances, all of it so vivid even in the dark kitchen. I didn't feel like turning on any bright lights, but I could tell that Sola had left the place shiny, not a fingerprint of her own. She'd given it back to me, the way she always gave me my own place exactly as it was supposed to be yet slightly changed, made more perfect. And now Julian. Something had happened to him while I was gone, but I had no idea what it could have been.

"The flowers are beautiful, Julian. Nicer than anything in all the dressing rooms between here and Budapest." I felt like crying, wished I could lean up against my brother's back and collapse.

"Are you okay, Paula?"

"Not really," I admitted, not knowing how much to say. "I got scared," I whispered.

Julian looked at me then, right into my eyes, though just for a moment. "Of what?" he said softly.

"It's gone," I said. "The voice. Everything." I leaned all my weight against the kitchen counter, dropping my jacket onto the floor in a heap, wanting to land there myself.

"It can't be," Julian said. "I don't believe it."

He picked up my jacket and went to hang it in the hall closet. I forced myself into the living room and landed on the couch like something dropped from a great height. "I made a mess. I lost my nerve. I canceled a performance and broke a promise. I found some ghosts and they got inside me." I closed my eyes and pushed myself down into the cushions of the couch. "I never want to get up," I said. "Is that okay?"

Julian stood near the edge of the couch, his hands back in his pockets. I opened my eyes and saw him looking at me with so much tenderness I thought I might break.

AT FIRST I thought Paula looked beautifully tired, smudged around her eyes when she took off her sunglasses, and smaller somehow than I remembered her to be. I felt a split second of wanting to touch her face, make sure she was real and not the sister in my dreams. But I stepped to the side of the door and let her inside, watched her accept what Sola had given back. The flowers made her happy, I felt good about that, but I began to see there was something else, something weighing her down. I'd never seen her with such a dim light, like she had begun to bend away from the sky.

When she mentioned the ghosts, I caught my breath as though I'd been shot. And it occurred to me that this was the first time Paula had ever felt the breath of the dead inside her, at least it was the first time either one of us had spoken out loud about it. I didn't know if I was allowed to ask, but I wanted to know.

"Who were the ghosts?"

She placed her hands on her face, gently covering her eyes. "Our family," she said. "Grandfather, aunt. I found out who they were, what happened to them."

I sat down in one of the living room chairs, the same place I'd been sitting when Sola told her story. Paula pulled her hands away and stared up at the ceiling as if it were a movie screen.

"In Budapest?" I asked.

She nodded, loosened the scarf around her throat. "Grandfather was a cantor, can you believe it? He sang, he chanted prayers for a living. And Daddy had a younger sister who played the violin." I listened, but at first it was just words, nothing real. I didn't see anything on the ceiling where Paula was watching her film scene by scene. The room was quiet for a little while.

"I never knew there was music back there," she said, "although I've wondered. But no one ever said, you know?"

I nodded, although she probably didn't notice. I felt so many things shifting inside me, sliding like pebbles on a hillside. I thought of my father saying he wouldn't let me have a bar mitzvah, wouldn't listen to anyone pray to an absent God. I thought of the look on his face when he heard Paula singing. "What else?" I asked.

"You can guess the rest," she said. "Can't you? Because all the stories ended the same way, pretty much." She made a gesture with her hand, floated it into the air. "Auschwitz," she said.

I knew, of course, although I didn't know. It was like everything in my father's head, passed into me in a molecular code that hadn't yet been translated. But my body knew the sequence, knew it all: loss, loss, loss.

"The only thing I found out about his mother, our grandmother, is that she died of tuberculosis," Paula went on. "And I really didn't mean to go on an expedition for any of it." She shrugged her shoulders, closed her eyes and opened them. "I just felt so strange there, so close to the past."

What did it mean, the past? What made it separate from the moment just behind me, the moment after that one and before the next one? I knew that people traveled to find their roots, as if there was a difference between life in one place and life in another. I knew Paula had been on another continent, beside another sea, and I knew that was where my father had been born, where his family had been killed. But none of it felt measurable to me, close or far. It felt as real as my heart pumping blood or my cells dying and rebuilding themselves, as meaningful and meaningless as time.

I looked over at the flowers, remembering color. "What about your voice?" I said.

She took a deep breath and let it out slowly. "I left it there," she said, nearly whispering. "Like maybe they killed me too."

I looked at the blue of my jeans and pictured the shape of my father's tattoo, the number I couldn't remember. I knew the periodic table but not a single fact of my father's scars. Suddenly my hands felt so cold I had to tuck them under my legs to make them warm again.

"What about now that you're home?" I asked. "Remember the time you flew too far north, into the cold and out of your habitat? Maybe that's what happened."

Paula smiled a little, touched the edges of her scarf with her fingertips. "Birds of a feather," she said. "Maybe I've got an indoor habitat like you after all, Jules."

Her eyes were closed again, and I thought maybe I should leave her alone to rest, maybe she was trying to talk herself into falling asleep. But I couldn't imagine Paula's voice abandoning her, or Paula abandoning her voice. It made no sense.

"How much did you cancel?"

"The last two auditions," she said. "I told them it was a virus, which was true in a way. Something invading my body, an intruder. I couldn't tell them, could I?"

I tried to hold on to what she'd said about our grandfather and aunt, about their music and their deaths. I thought about Sola's family murdered so close she could hear them crying for mercy, and I wondered if my father had been a witness to the killing of his father and sister. Maybe it didn't matter how much he saw, or maybe not seeing was worse, kept him caught like Diego in having to imagine it over and over for the rest of his life. I would never know.

"I'm so tired, Jules," Paula said softly. "And I feel all broken, like somebody took me apart."

I didn't know what to say to her. What she described was the way I had felt so much of my life that I couldn't understand it had a beginning, a first time. Paula always had wings and I watched her from the ground. It was so strange to hear about her not knowing anymore how to fly.

"I'll let you sleep for a while," I said, getting up to leave and feeling too large for her apartment, too close to the ceiling. "Is there anything you need right now?"

Her eyes were still closed in profile, her hands holding each other on her chest, rib cage rising and falling without any sound. She shook her head, the couch swallowing her up. "Maybe later, Jules," she whispered. "I think I need to sleep for a long time."

I returned to my apartment and the higher branches of the tree, closing the doors between Paula's apartment and the stairs, between the stairs and my rooms. There was a darkness inside her now, a history that had lived namelessly under my skin all these years.

ELEVEN

My apartment needs more windows, that is my first thought when I walk in the door with my suitcase and my plant and my basket of fruit. The curtains are closed and the rooms look so dark and small. Diego lives somewhere like this too, I am thinking, somewhere too close to other people whose names we do not know. When I picture his hands filling up baskets in a market, I imagine him telling people how to select a ripe mango. I wonder if he cuts it the way I do, making shapes of diamonds. This makes me think about Julian, about the day he sees the scars on my wrists and I tell him about slicing myself open. I do not know why I want to tell him so much, but somehow I find myself doing it. Then Diego in Paula's living room, needing to hear about how his mother and sisters are killed, and Julian sitting so quietly as he listens. Until I feel like my story is being drawn like a map inside Julian's heart.

T H E B R O K E N television still looked like a gap in a set of teeth, the face I vaguely remembered looking back at me from the mirror when I was a kid. I stared at the black screen and let the other colors blur at the edges of my vision, watched it as if a movie of my own life might begin to appear there.

I kept thinking about those ghosts finding Paula all the way in Budapest—but maybe it was more amazing that they had found their way to me in Berkeley, traveling across so many stretches of ocean and mountain and wilderness. My father carried them here, I suppose, carried them on his back like some beast of burden, weight so familiar he didn't remember how to stand up straight.

And then there was Sola with her own bundles of grief, living in the world as if the grief was part of everything too, no choosing to pick it up or put it down. What I saw in Diego's face, the torment of not knowing, I recognized too. But something happened when Sola told him about the massacre, something peeled him open and climbed inside, a liquid of truth that could make the other nightmares stop. Because now there was something with edges to hold on to, a story with a shape made by words: screams, gunshots, sky, river.

In my apartment I see the red light on my machine is blinking. On a streetlight the same message means stop, look both ways, go ahead with caution. This is what I do: put down the basket of fruit and the green fern, look around the rooms to be sure everything is all right. Empty, quiet, the same as if I am never away. I press the button to make the tape go backwards until it finds the place to begin. The voice belongs to Warren, I recognize the way he clears his throat before the words come out.

"Hi Sola, it's me. Strange to be leaving you a message on an answering machine, I didn't know you had one. Anyway . . . I've been away and now I'm back. . . . It's good to hear your voice, I'm glad everything's all right. . . . You know you can call whenever you want . . . I miss you."

He sounds like himself, and a little sad maybe, a little tired. I remember when he takes trips he comes back feeling excited, but then he sleeps a few days with so much deepness, like all that flying means his body needs to spend more time in stillness afterwards. After we fly together to this country, I remember doing the same thing, sleeping even in the daytime at first to give myself a chance to come all the way into this new world, my dreams helping me through the doorways of his strange house.

The machine stops at the end of Warren's voice and plays a low note, then it erases him like wind blowing away tracks in the sand. Julian is finding my lemons now, blue words on yellow skin. There are so many languages, and so few ways to say what I mean.

There is a high wind tonight, it pushes through the branches and leaves of the trees, and I am dreaming about Julian's golden tree, all the yellow leaves are coming down like rain and they have words written on them in blue ink, they are the words of my story that I am telling to Diego and to Julian, the story of the killing. And all the words are pouring down like falling water.

I dreamed my voice came back except it was a different voice; the sound had changed inside me somehow and I no longer recognized myself. For a while in the dream I was back again as a young girl with Madame, I was in her living room pushing at the piano the way she had me do to strengthen my abdominal muscles. So I was pushing against her piano, my hands on the shiny black wood, leaning into it with all my weight, and Madame was sitting on the bench next to me, tapping out a beat with her pencil on the closed lid of the keyboard.

A sheet of clarinet music was on the piano, it was the one I'd been having trouble learning, and Madame was frustrated with me, I thought any moment she would start hitting me with the pencil too. And then the scene changed and I was giving a note to my father and he was scowling and shaking his head, saying "No German music. No German music, no no no." And then he was on the couch with his head in his hands, he was weeping, and his hair was so red it looked like he was on fire, and then I heard Jules in my bedroom saying "It's eleven," and I woke up.

And I was still afraid to sing.

PAULA WAS still sleeping downstairs; she had asked me to try to get her up at eleven unless she came earlier than that to find me. I wasn't sure exactly how to wake her. At first I wanted just to knock on her apartment door, but when I didn't hear any answer, I used my key and went all the way inside. Her bedroom door was half-open, the curtains in the living room closed against the light.

"Paula?" I leaned toward the open door, toward the dark shape on her bed, and I had a flash of remembering Sola's hair spread like feathers across her pillow. "It's eleven."

"Already?"

When I stepped back into the hallway, I heard the covers being thrown around. "I think I slept fourteen hours. Is that possible?"

"You must have needed it," I said.

She had her feet on the floor now, I heard the closet door sliding open, banging against the wall. "I need tea," she said, coming toward me in her bathrobe. "I need it badly."

I followed her toward the kitchen, half-expecting to see Sola there, slicing lemons. But there was just the shiny empty room.

Paula put the water on to boil, stretched her arms and then sighed. "This is when I'd be testing my voice, that first morning sound to make sure it's there. And I'm afraid to try."

I looked at her hands, their smallness. "Mouth of the wolf," I said.

She looked at me as full of fear and sadness as I'd ever seen her, one hand at her throat like she might stroke the sound out of it. "I can't," she whispered.

I looked at her without flinching away. Her expression reminded me of that night she asked me what we could do about our father's nightmares. "That's not your line," I said, and gave her the cue again. "Mouth of the wolf."

She cracked a smile then, halfway at least. "Forget the wolf?" she asked. "Maybe tomorrow."

"What about seeing a doctor," Julian said when I went to visit him upstairs later that afternoon. I just couldn't stand to be alone in my apartment. He was sitting in his usual place, Daddy's old chair, but he had the televisions turned off, which was so strange I didn't know what to say about it.

"What kind of doctor?" I asked. I vaguely remembered the time Julian went to see a psychiatrist for a while. It had never seemed to have any visible effect on him.

"I don't know. Ear, nose, and throat?"

I sighed. "It's not there, I don't think. I mean, the problem isn't in my throat, like a nodule on my cords. It's me, it's the fear in me. I just don't know how to shake it." Standing near the doorway, I realized that something else was different, not just that the televisions were dark. One of the windows was open, allowing the sounds of the street to drift up.

Suddenly Julian stood up and gestured to me. "Sit here," he said, and went into the kitchen, fumbling inside his cabinets. "I'll get you a glass of something."

"Just water would be good," I said, and I took his place on the soft brown leather, sinking into its comfort. That's when I noticed them on his worktable, a row of lemons tattooed with blue ink. There was Sola's name on one; on another, a phone number was engraved, curving around its middle. One of the lemons said LOVE.

Julian came out of the kitchen holding my glass of water; he must have seen my open-mouthed wonder. "Sola left them for me the day you came home."

I took a long sip, and Julian placed one of the lemons in my empty hand. YOUR FRIEND, it said. A pair of bright green leaves was still attached to the stem, and I raised the fruit to my nose, inhaling its tangy aroma.

"They're Meyer lemons," he said. "Almost as sweet as oranges."

I went back to sit in Daddy's leather chair, cupping the lemon in one hand. I stroked its soft skin and thought of our canaries from all those years ago.

He smiled in the lopsided way he used to when he watched me in our basement while I practiced my scales. It occurred to me for the first time in my life that maybe if he was nearby nothing bad could happen to me. Maybe he could be my guardian angel.

And then he did the most astonishing thing. He sat down on the floor near my feet and leaned against the chair, close enough that his shoulder was touching one of my knees. I was so surprised by the contact I almost stopped breathing. Looking down, I saw his shoulder blades through his shirt, those bones that reminded me of wings. He held a lemon in his hand, the one that said SOLA.

Eleven blank TV faces reflected us sitting there, my brother and me. The scent of lemons filled the room.

"Every star eventually reaches a stage in its evolution where it collapses due to the gravitational attraction of its particles," Julian said, reciting from the dictionary in his head. "An event horizon forms around the star because no signal can get away from it to communicate any event to the outside world."

Then he twisted around to look up at me. "You're not that kind of star," he said, and he grinned as widely as I'd ever seen. "You're the other kind, that shines."

I T   W A S late evening, full dark. I'd gone down to knock on Paula's door, still worried about how I might help her. The only other time I'd come down like this, in the dark, was the night of Sola's weeping, the night I lay beside her on the bed.

Remembering it again, I thought it might not have happened, I might have dreamed it up, watched it on my broken TV screen. Every time I tried to picture that night, I saw myself from the outside, as if through the lens of a camera or someone else's gaze, myself watching myself.

Now my feet played the notes of the stairs again—the ones that creaked, the ones that didn't. This time it was Paula I wanted to see, and not because of weeping but because of silence, something she seemed uneasily wrapped in.

She opened the door right away, as if she'd been expecting me. "I heard you on the stairs," she said. "At least I figured it had to be you, but I had to see for myself. Are you okay?"

"That's what I came to ask you," I said, following Paula inside and into her bright kitchen. "I keep waiting to hear your voice or something."

"Or something?"

I shrugged, felt foolish. "I've missed you singing," I said. "Even the scales, the warming up."

Paula took a seat at the kitchen counter, a stool that lifted her high enough to dangle her feet. She had her hands clenched in her lap, and she was biting her lip.

"It really is gone, Julian. I mean it. I can't make a sound." She didn't look at me directly. I watched her face as it crumpled, her mouth going wide and wavy, tears spilling and squeezing out. I had my hands in my pockets and didn't know what to do with them.

"You haven't," I said. "You haven't lost your voice."

She looked at me with her eyes so wet she seemed to be underwater. I had to look away, down at my feet, at the flowers in the vase. Some were already starting to fade a little, curl at the edges. The tulips were turning themselves inside out and tipping over like drunks.

"What do you mean?" she said. "How do you know?"

"I don't know," I said. "It's just what I've figured out so far, it's a theory. But I think it's your voice that's lost you."

She laughed a little, a small choking sound really, and I hated to hear it, the sound of her disbelief.

"Look," I said, pulling one hand free of a pocket, then the other. "Isn't there a difference between fear of losing your voice and actually losing it? I mean, they say Callas really lost hers, she used it up, broke it somehow, right?"

Paula nodded, wiped at her eyes with a tissue, and watched me. "Callas was never careful," she said. "She never held back, never protected herself. They say even in rehearsals she'd go full voice, even when she had to perform that same night."

"Okay," I said, "and that's something you never did, right? Never do, I mean. You take care, you protect yourself. So I think it's only your courage you've lost, not your voice."

Paula sighed, closed her eyes and opened them again. "Tell me how you are, Jules. I'm tired of thinking about myself so much. How's your dictionary?"

"It's okay, I think, maybe even close to being finished. I'm a steady turtle, that's all."

Paula smiled at me, tipped her head. "Do you feel steady then? Like you really have four slow feet on the ground?"

"With the dictionary you mean?"

She shook her head. "I mean in here," she tapped on her chest. "Or here or here, for that matter." She touched her head, her belly. "Anywhere."

I had to think about it, about the times I felt I might fall over if not for knowing Paula was nearby somewhere, or her voice, something. Even the TV sets were a kind of grounding field for me.

"It depends on the day of the week, or the time of day," I said. "I'm steadiest when I'm on my way someplace, or else on my way back here. When I know what I'm about to do, how many more blocks, how many more minutes. Not because I'm hurrying but because I have a measurement, a gauge."

"Maybe that's my problem, Jules. I've lost my gauge. I thought I knew how many more blocks I had to cover, how many months or years it would take me. And now ... " She lifted her hands and let them drop into her lap.

"Damn," she said. "We ended up talking about me again."

I laughed. "I don't care."

"It's just that I think maybe I want to learn how to be a steady turtle. Maybe I've been trying to do things too fast. Or maybe I need to turn around, or lie on my back. Tuck my head inside for a while. I don't know." She straightened up in her chair, like she really wanted to test how it would feel to stay there without moving.

"Some people aren't meant to be turtles," I said.

She fluttered the ends of her scarf. "I forgot, didn't I. I'm a bird." She smiled at me, a wave breaking into light.

"You got blown off course," I said. "Temporarily."

I wake up in my own bed and ask myself where I am, what day it is? *My apartment. Saturday.* The first morning awake in this place after my mornings in Paula's apartment, her windows and light. This room is dark and small, although my bed is clean and wide. I am remembering a piece of dream, sailing on the water with Warren and Diego and Eduardo. Julian is on the shore, waving in slow motion. I hold out my hands to him and float out of the boat, Eduardo holding me by my foot, keeping me from leaving. But I fly anyway, and then there is music, a tapping sound I think belongs to the engine of the boat. But it is someone knocking, not at my door but a door upstairs, and I wake up. I think of Eduardo holding my foot, and my body floating away from him, letting go. Into the air. If I look down I can see through the water, smooth, colored stones on the bottom of the sea.

In Paula's apartment there are so many mirrors. I see at first how they are placed to catch the light from the windows, and how they make the rooms feel wider, more open with space. But also I am disturbed by seeing myself in every room. I keep getting startled, as if there are people following me, but it is just myself that I see, again and again, looking surprised and sometimes frightened. And sometimes sad. In my own place there is one small mirror over the bathroom sink and that is all, so I walk around there invisible to myself. In Warren's house there is a very long mirror in the bedroom. I remember standing with him there, naked, and he tells me I am beautiful, tells me to look and see for myself when I say to him I do not understand the word. He laughs. "You do understand," he says. "Look." And what I see is my solid brown body, breasts small enough to fit into my own hands, smaller even than before Camucha; I see my dark hair falling straight past my shoulders and the dark nest where my legs meet, my feet turning toward each other a little, my square hands. "I still do not understand beautiful," I say, and Warren touches me with his gentle fingers. "You are," he says. "You are."

N O W   T H A T Sola no longer lived downstairs, I began to wonder if our friendship was something transitional, bound by the time and space of Paula's absence. I didn't think I'd have the courage to dial her number, and yet I knew it was the only way to maintain the fragile thread between us: I needed to reach some gesture in her direction, signal that my doors and windows were open. Because otherwise she'd think I was retreating again to the embrace of my chair and my silences, the ghosts in two-dimensional space that shared or didn't share my world.

Still, I argued with myself, I considered. Maybe she wanted to be left alone, maybe I'd trespassed across the borders of her own silences. I had heard her story, I knew her scars, maybe that meant she had to choose when to open the door to me or not, maybe it was her call not mine that had to come first. Plus, she had that doctor, Warren, and now Diego too. I was the extra piece, the one that didn't quite fit.

"Welcome home Paula!" It was my agent's voice booming over the phone. I was sure he had waited as long as he could, more than a day since my plane touched the ground.

"Thanks, Herman. It's good to be back." I tried to match my false cheer to his.

He chuckled, a jolly uncle. "Good, good, glad to hear it. Jet lag getting to you?"

"A little."

"They say lots of light is good. Fresh air. Been outside yet?"

"Not too much, no."

He breezed past my answers, making me wonder, as I often did, if he truly listened to the other half of his conversations, or if the main idea, for him, was to make sure people heard him. "Listen," he said. "I've been faxing all day, damage control, trying to sort things out. I think we're okay, more or less, but the important thing is to jump right back into the game, sign you up for a few more auditions, closer to home, maybe ..."

"Herman," I interrupted. "I'm taking a break. I'm not singing for a while, I don't know how long." I took a deep breath, released it. "I can't sing."

He surprised me by staying quiet for a full beat, then all he said was "Huh?"

"I don't know what else to say, how to explain it. I just have no voice right now, it's gone—maybe for good...."

"You're not making sense," Herman said. "It didn't just get up and walk away." He forced a laugh. "You had some throat trouble, okay, let's even say you had stage fright. But that kind of thing passes, you know that, it's part of the deal, part of the business. Even the big shots have to cancel every once in a while, right?"

I sighed into the phone. "I know you mean well, Herman, really I do. But I don't have any choice, not right now." I got ready to hang up the phone, I wanted to crawl back into bed. I felt as if I still had days of sleep to catch up on.

"Look," he said, his voice quiet and serious now. "I'm not going to let you drop out of it just like that. You've got real talent, a gift, something you've worked hard for all these years. It's too good to waste." He waited for me to say something, to protest even, but I was too exhausted to try.

"I'm going to call Isaac," he said, his trump card. "He'll know what to say, since it's obvious I've got no weight with you. And I'm not going to ask your permission."

I didn't even have a chance to say good-bye before the click.

THE DEFINITIONS had begun to veer away from me like slippery fish eluding capture; all my nets had holes wide enough for the creatures to swim easily away. I sat at my desk with my fingers on the keyboard, waiting for instructions that never came. Maybe I really had finished it all; maybe it was time to call my editor and say it was time for our last conference. But then what?

I went to the TV screens for relief, watched a program about a blind man who earned his black belt in karate, an idiot savant who could calculate the day of the week for any date in time, past or future, his mind whirring like a computer. Genetically engineered tomatoes now had a shelf life of more than two weeks, but that news didn't make me want to eat one. I went back to my desk, placed my hands on the piles of the letters J and S like a child invoking a magic spell. What did I want? Only this: to know what it would feel like to love a woman and be loved back.

On my computer screen, toasters flapped their improbable wings, surrounded by pieces of flying toast; I could adjust the brownness of the bread and their speed across my screen. Behind me, the ten televisions flickered with activity: talking faces, winning athletes, cars racing, oceans in upheaval. I was the only one sitting still.

"Music isn't more important than air," Isaac said once. I'd been telling him about my going to work with Madame, my father's skepticism. Isaac had his own ideas. "Music *is* air."

He had his hands on my rib cage, holding me in place. "Watch the woodwinds, even the string players for that matter. Breathing is intertwined with the notes, they can't be separated. Ask a bassoon player about air."

I closed my eyes, breathed all the way into my belly.

"Sometimes I think of myself as a conductor of air," he said. "Moving the vibrations so they dance above our heads, through our bodies, our inner ears. When you sing, you're sending your air into me, into the audience, inside them. What could be more intimate than that?"

"And when I'm exhaled, where do I go?"

"Into space," Isaac said. "Forever."

If that was true, then my grandfather's voice, the chanted prayers, were beyond the moon by now, lost to me. Had my father held any of that sound inside his own breath? Had any of it been given to me?

DAYS AFTER Frank's death, the deli still did not reopen. I had to reinvent the part of my routine into which his meals fit so perfectly. I considered and rejected more Chinese because it would mean too many chopsticks and fortune cookies, too much repetition even for me. Berkeley was bursting with options, too many of them, and I didn't want to choose anything. I felt angry at Frank for this desertion, I wanted his wife's soup and the broiled chicken to keep coming somehow, even in the midst of their mourning. But the sign stayed up and the doors stayed locked; darkness hovered inside the shop, and white sheets lay draped across the glass deli cases as if they too were ghosts accompanying the dead.

I walked past Frank's block in the direction of the university, realizing how long it had been since my days of going to the Physics department, wondering briefly if my advisor still kept her same office hours, her same office even. Probably.

There were cafés and restaurants everywhere, beckoning, but there were so many people too, carrying coffee cups and newspapers and books, juggling portable phones and briefcases and backpacks, driving a commotion of baby strollers, bicycles, cars, and trucks. A seductive aroma of fresh bread pulled at me; I saw huge steaming trays of baguettes, rolls, loaves of rye and sourdough. There was a massive display of cheeses from all over the globe. I stood near the doorway, trying to stay clear of the traffic of bodies flowing in and out of the shop, it was busier even than Frank's place. Playing cards were in use as customer service numbers, and voices called out "nine of diamonds" and "jack of spades" and "ace of hearts." My mouth was watering. Next time, I thought. Next time I would brace myself and go inside.

A client cancels my appointment to clean. It is Mrs. Barrett-Jones, and her husband's condition is very bad. "I'll still pay you, of course," she says to me on the answering machine, so I cannot tell her it is all right. I have time to do anything I want. The day is fine: blue sky everywhere, not hot, a small breeze. I even take a book with me, to sit in a small park under a tree.

I think about when the ginkgo tree in front of Julian's house is turning to gold again, and picture myself picking up one of the leaves from the sidewalk. When I hold the small yellow fan up to the sun, the light comes through so I can see all the inside veins, and it is like I am looking through skin.

I D I A L E D Sola's number, using the lemon she'd inscribed with her number. Holding the phone against my ear, I felt as if I were listening for someone's heartbeat. When it rang, I kept watching the street, thinking of the time Sola thought she was being followed, the panic that turned out to be Diego. The connecting click gave me Sola's voice in a recording, her accent familiar and strange all at once. "Please leave me a message," she said, "and I can call you back later. After the beep."

"Thank you for the lemons," I said, my face filling up with heat. I had to remind myself no one could see me, I was talking to the air. "You can call me," I said, hope rising into my lungs and expanding me. Molecules on magnetic tape, saved for the touch of her finger on a button.

"They killed her and not you, and you can't help it."

Isaac was standing in my living room, pacing as he listened to my story. Herman Roth had summoned him, and Isaac arrived without calling first, striding into my apartment in that way he had of claiming every room he entered. I didn't tell him everything, not the part about my father in the camp. But when I told him about my grandfather and my aunt, the names on the gravestones, my voice gone away, he turned on me, his face flushed.

"I've lived with that all my life, the benevolent curse of accidental survival. No reason for it, no logic. It just is. You're alive and she isn't, they aren't."

I backed away from him, pressed myself deeper into the cushions of the couch.

He didn't stop. "And now you've got this voice, this music that wants to rise up in you, and the goddamn murderers aren't going to kill that beauty too because you aren't going to let them. Don't you see? It's the only way to show those bastards that they lost, they couldn't kill us all, they couldn't turn us all into smoke. You see? We're here, we're making music even though they twisted notes into barbed wire, made their victims play Brahms while their own daughters marched past them to the ovens. But the music is still here, in us."

Isaac pounded his chest, gestured with his powerful conductor's arms. His eyes were so bright and fierce, he looked like he wanted to shake me until I could hear him, until I could swallow the rage he was offering me.

"Hate them, if you need to feel something, but don't turn against yourself." He took a deep breath. "Okay, grieve. Be silent for a while. For a while, understand me? Let your voice rest, okay. That's a good thing. But don't give the murderers any more chances to kill. They're finished. And we're still here, singing, making music. And when you decide to sing, you know what? Sing for them, right? What was she, seven, eight years old? She never even got to play a full-sized instrument. So that's what you can do to honor the dead, you can sing for her. You can play all the notes she never got to play. It's your violin now," he tapped me on the breastbone. "Right here."

I sat with my hands twisting together and tried to take it in. Revenge? Was it really possible to sing like that, use my voice to kill the killers?

"They thought they could make us disappear, and every trace of us too, as if we had never existed at all. But somehow we carried art all the way out of the ashes, created our way back into the world. And every time I stand on my podium, every time I lift my baton for the first sound, I'm thinking about how to repay my debt to the dead."

FROM MY living room, I heard Isaac's voice shuddering through the floorboards, not the words but the vibrations, an orchestra of his own making. He had always made me nervous with his bigger-than-life pres-

ence, not to mention his almost-hypnotic power over Paula. Now I worried even more than usual about his volume. Much as I wanted to hold
still and wait for Sola to call me back, I felt that maybe instead of being
rescued by Isaac's anger, Paula needed protection from it.

I'd gotten as far as the foyer when her door opened and Isaac stood
there with his eyes blazing, looking like he'd just finished a performance.

"Julian!" he shouted. "Tell your sister I'm right."

I looked past him at Paula, who sat curled on her couch in the room
that still smelled like Sola.

"We'll see," I told him, echoing what our father had always said.
Nothing was ever entirely hopeful or entirely hopeless. I held open the
front door and waved Isaac through.

Paula had one hand around her throat, a stricken look on her face.
"We'll see," she repeated. "We'll see."

I knew I had to tell Julian something about our father, about what
I'd found out, but I couldn't think of how to begin. I hadn't been
able to say the words to Isaac, focused only on the pieces I could
say aloud. I kept feeling the grip of Huber's hand on my arm, the
intensity of his gaze beneath those remarkable eyebrows.

Did any of us have the right to speak about what my father did
when he himself had chosen to keep silent? Was it his silence that
was choking me now?

ISAAC ROARED off in his silver Jaguar, full of sound and gone.
Paula asked me if I could come back later. Upstairs, I picked up the
phone to call Sola again. I practiced saying hello, speaking toward the
one dark TV screen, imagining Sola's face there, her dark hair shining,
her even white teeth.

"Yes?" she said.

"It's Julian," I said, hearing myself in my own surprised ear. "I'm calling to see how you are." I thought I could feel her smiling, thought I saw
her hands move in the air.

"Oh, it is so nice to have your call," she said. "I am very glad. I think I am all right here, yes, for now, for a little while. And also I am looking for a new place. Remember?"

"I remember." I held the lemon with her phone number on it. "Thank you for the lemons," I said. "For your letter."

"I have your message in my machine," she said. "You are welcome. You can read the words all right?"

"Yes."

"Good."

I held my breath and let it out slowly. Did she really want to be my friend? Did I want her to be?

"Julian, I want to go somewhere for a walk or something, like the day we are climbing up to see the sea. Except I want to get all the way to the water this time. Do you want to come?"

I took several small breaths, in and out, held the bumpy curve of lemon in my hand. I squeezed it, felt the oil of the skin spreading onto my palm. "Okay," I said. I would take one more step outside, just like that.

She told me her schedule, her days for work and her days off. We agreed on a day and a plan, a longer drive this time—to the ocean, not just the bay in the blue distance.

"Okay?" she said. "You can ride in the car for more than one hour? And we can go all the way to the seaside, and put our hands into the water and feel the waves on our toes. Okay?"

I felt like a lemon sliced and floating in a glass of ice water, a signal caught in space by the radio.

"I think so," I said. "Yes."

The present is in the past and the other way around. I am always here, always there. My village lives inside me, when I speak it is my grandmother's voice coming out. My hands are my mother's hands, my baby is still growing in my womb, Eduardo is touching my hair, the murdered ones are crying in my sleep, my dreams are filled with blood, my heart is cracking into pieces, I am washing a kitchen floor,

I am screaming into the earth, I am lying in a hospital bed, sailing under a blue sky.

Opening a window I am burying the dead, slicing a mango, my wrists, a lemon. The juice is my life leaking out of me, I am laughing at a foolish playful dog, I am lost in my grief, the street is wide and familiar, the forest is my refuge and my nightmare, the telephone is ringing, the news is joyful, horrifying, the nuns are washing my hair, praying with their beads, the chair beside my bed is empty, now filled with a stranger, a lover, a friend.

I am rinsing my body in the river, listening to the voice of the river in my sleep.

I WANTED it to rain, wanted to hear it but not feel it, know there was water falling all around me, around my house, but not reaching me. I wanted a skin test for thickness, a measurement for what hurts and what doesn't. If I could talk again with Sola, walk with her one more time in the hills, see the inside of her apartment, maybe I'd discover it was possible to live inside my skin without feeling my nerve endings banging up against the shock wall too many times. Maybe her voice and her hands tapping herself like the blind woman with her cane, maybe mango juice and cilantro and lemons could bring me close enough to touch her.

I stood at the open window, looking out. Everyone in cars seemed to move so fast, hurtling through space in their metal boxes. Sometimes all they used was a casual finger resting on the steering wheel, a foot on the gas pedal randomly lifting and pressing. I could remember my mother driving with a strange music, her hands shaking the wheel as if constantly juggling for equilibrium, her foot on the gas like that of a tap dancer. Her car rocked and jumped down the road, frenetic.

Even as a child, riding in the front seat, I ended up thinking about crashing, about which window I'd climb out of after the impact. On TV they advertised a small hammer to be kept in the car, something to use for smashing out the windshield when you only had seconds to escape, when the car had plunged into water or burst into flames. I used to think everything could be prepared for if you used your head, if you gave yourself over to dreams of disaster.

Now I knew there were things you couldn't predict, experiments you had to figure out as you went along.

Isaac was right about some things, about refusing to let myself be destroyed, refusing to be an accomplice to all those murders. But all I could think about was pressing down, pressing down like my feet were on pedals giving me fortissimo sound, giving me resonance. Madame always urged me to lift my voice into the air, release it like the rising exhalations of every living thing, but maybe what I needed was to plant myself in the soil like Julian's tree. If I could dig deep enough, the dead could hold me upright over their heads, their hands on the soles of my feet. So I could sing from their bones.

I WAS back in Paula's apartment, still surprised to see through her windows the street directly ahead of me, on my level instead of below me, and how that changed everything. The ginkgo tree filled one window entirely, and when a car went by I could see inside to the driver's face, I could see hands on the steering wheel. If someone passed on the sidewalk or went to the playground across the street, I could guess how old the person was, what she might be saying to her child. The world was actual-sized again, vertical and horizontal and amazingly close.

"I brought you something," Paula said, and held out her hand. A small white box. "You're hard to buy for, I have to say. But I hope you like it."

I took the box and shook it gently, hearing what sounded like liquid.

"Open sesame," Paula said.

Inside was a glass snowdome, and inside the dome was a carving of the Little Mermaid, perched on a rock in the sea. The snowflakes glittered on her shoulders and her back, her legs were folded uselessly, her

gaze aimed toward the horizon. She was caught between the impossibility of return and the hopelessness of staying, a prisoner of her own body.

I held the dome in one hand, felt its watery density, put the box down
on the counter so I could cup the glass in both hands. "Thank you, P," I
said. "It's beautiful."

I could still hear Danny Kaye's voice reading the story in my ear, a
record I'd played over and over before I learned how to read the story for
myself, and then to read it for Paula. What was the last line? Something
about the way she spent the remainder of her days looking out to sea for
the life she'd left behind and to which she could never return.

Did we hold on to the places we passed through, or leave some of ourselves behind in them? Accumulation or erosion, or some of both? I
thought about Paula giving so much away when she sang, wondering
how she ever managed to hold on to herself. And my lifelong feeling of
holding on to too much, carrying my father's memories as if instead
of blood I had ether in my veins, tenuous and continuous, filling all of
space.

When I bought the mermaid for my brother, I only thought it
would remind him of our childhood together, the times he read
to me at night. But when he held the dome in his hands, I saw it
was like another kind of TV, a story inside a glass bubble. Julian
turned it upside down, making it snow. I watched his face fill with
pity and realized how heartbreaking it was, the way she was
trapped inside the wrong water, so far from the sea. He must have
understood all that distance.

"I think we needed you to find those pieces," Julian said. "The
story we never knew."

I felt my heart kick, signaling that I had to find a way of telling my brother the things he probably already knew or at least
imagined.

"There's more," I said. "More than the ones that died at
Auschwitz."

Julian glanced toward the door, but I wouldn't let him leave, not until I'd said the words. I found myself picturing a cantor in his white robe on *Kol Nidre*, the holiest night of the year, chanting the ancient dirge. He dropped down to his knees on the beautiful worn carpet of the synagogue, then lowered himself farther until he was lying prone, singing that lament with his face and his belly to the ground and his massive body flat under the gaze of what he hoped was a forgiving and merciful god. I needed to fold myself down to the ground like that, before I could ever soar.

"*Sonderkommando*," I said, and then I told Julian the way the old man had told it to me. I told him all I knew.

F O R A brief irrational moment it occurred to me that the science tapes my father made contained the secrets he never told me, his stories waiting to be unraveled in the voice of a ghost. I imagined finding some reel-to-reel tape recorder and playing them after all these years, discovering for myself at last the truth of his life. But it didn't make sense. The periodic table was the periodic table and nothing more, inert and noble gases just what they said they were. It was Paula who had found out, gathering up some whispered Hungarian puzzle pieces and assembling the picture.

Did knowing his story change anything? I hardly knew what to say to Paula, what to do with the tears on both our faces. I thought of the enormous rock in my dream closet, the door that wouldn't shut. Could I ever find a container large enough to hold my father? Suddenly it was his tattoo that rose up in my mind, the numbers like the scars on Sola's wrists to remind her she was the only one left alive, an inscription of code.

114323. One one four three two three.

None of us could forgive him anymore, or help him rinse the ashes off his skin. It was our story now, my sister's and mine, a fire that would burn all the way through our own lives, and beyond us.

T W E L V E

It was a breezy Wednesday like the one on which I'd left all those weeks ago. At my living room window, I counted the occasional passing car and waited for the mailman. I wanted to believe that somewhere on its way to me was an envelope with a foreign stamp, a miracle from Herman Roth, a letter saying yes to my voice and bringing me back to myself.

Then I saw Sola's car pull up and park in front of the building. Thinking she was coming to collect something she'd forgotten in my apartment, I went to meet her on the sidewalk. She seemed surprised to see me, though she must have known I was back from my trip.

"Welcome home, Paula," she said, pronouncing my name so that it was as rounded as the word *owl*. When she hugged me, I could feel the lean muscles in her arms, the heavy braid down her spine.

We stepped back from one another. "I don't know how to thank you," I said, "for everything."

She shook her head, smiling. "I am full of thanks too."

I saw her face brighten into radiance at the same time as I heard Julian's footsteps behind me. When I turned to see him holding his backpack, amazement washed over me. He'd been expecting her because they were going somewhere together. Sola's beautiful smile was aiming at him.

She glanced at me and back to my brother, whose gaze seemed to open toward her. With one hand Julian held his backpack over his shoulder, and with the other hand he pushed his hair away from his forehead.

"We're going to Point Reyes," he said. "To the ocean."

I took a deep breath and released it, thinking suddenly of the row of lemons on his worktable, Sola's blue message. The changes I'd been noticing in Julian began to make sense. A new scene was unfolding, curtains pulling wide enough to include his own story.

"Are you ready?" she asked him.

I watched them walk together to her car as the wind lifted all the leaves on the ginkgo tree. Julian settled into the passenger seat and cranked open the window to wave at me. Sola climbed in behind the wheel, put on a pair of sunglasses and leaned toward my brother, waving to me through his window. Then she beeped the horn twice as they drove off.

For several moments I stayed where I was on the sidewalk, staring at the empty place where Sola's car had been, listening to the engine sound fade away. I kept seeing Julian's lopsided smile, his hand out the passenger window. They were going to the ocean.

Back inside, the silence from upstairs floated like a blessing. I believed I understood now, more than I ever had, what kind of courage it took for my brother to step past the edges of his safety, what price he had to pay to the chorus of lament in his head. We each had to learn our own songs of bravery. And there was one piece of music that had to come through me before anything else could.

I pulled out my father's old prayer book, the one we had used when Julian and I prayed together during that week of *shivah*. And when I began to chant the Mourner's Kaddish, I understood where Isaac was wrong, the part about grieving in silence and then returning to music afterwards. No, that was the discovery I had to make for myself: the mourning had to be inside the music. The losses belonged to me, to my voice, and the sound had to contain them too.

Maybe it shouldn't have been true but it was: something became wider inside me, the space I hadn't been using because I hadn't ever found it before, the space between my bones and the bones of the dead.

No one could have taught this to me, this resonance. I didn't know what the words meant, I sang in a mysterious and ancient tongue. But for the first time in my life my voice was coming from all that openness inside me, the cavernous chambers of my heart and lungs, and the nameless substance that carries the memories and experiences and wisdom and suffering of the ones who came before us.

I was singing in the voice of that broken violin, the suffocated cantor, the unspoken agony of my father with the weight of those bodies in his arms. I poured the sound waves back into space. Over and over, I was filled.

We drive together toward the coast, Julian's foot tapping on the floor of my car, the windows open. I know he is nervous, but maybe he is not so nervous as the last time, when we are driving up the steep hill. This time we are curving through a forest, trees reaching up higher than any I am seeing in my life. Julian says they are called redwoods, although they do not look red to me. But the light is coming down like some kind of delicate veil, I think it is almost like very fine sand or even like the flour dust shaking out of my hands after pounding tortillas. I am wondering what my grandmother is saying about this forest, what these trees are saying when they speak to her. And already this place is a painting on the inside of my eyes.

Suddenly, we come out of the forest and into the sun again, golden brown hills spreading wide.

Julian says, "It's like a different country in there, under the redwoods. All this light out here, and all that shadow."

Now we are looking at cows, horses, a small white church. I smile, because everything is a new painting. "These are all different countries, to me."

"To me too," he says, and we are laughing.

The waves push up until they cannot help it, they fall over, they have no choice. It is what they are given, this movement, this rising up and falling over, breaking into foam and rolling back under, pulling at the sand and stones, washing the feet of the birds. And I feel as though the stones inside me are a little softer in the path of the river, a little smoother now from letting the words pour out, so the remembering is not only a wall around my heart but is open. A little. Because now there is Diego, who knows a piece, and now there is Julian, who knows how to listen, how to be a witness too. So I do not have to hold it all alone, even if I know I am still the only one to carry the sounds of the children calling out for their mothers to help them, even if I know the blood is still drying in the earth.

No matter what, I still have this world to touch with my hands and memorize with my eyes, the world in all its texture and shape and color, the baskets of my grandmother weaving and weaving in my hands. Egg yolk leaves on a golden tree. Whiteness of teeth and clouds and bones. Ruby blood dripping slowly, slowly. The true green of a new plant pushing up from dark wet earth. *Verde. Verdad.* Indigo salt water stretching to forever.

I T W A S Wednesday all over again. *Miércoles*, the day that sounds like miracles.

Sola stood next to me on a boulder at the edge of the sea, watching the waves rising toward us, and breaking. I took a deep breath, imagining that I could finally be the water instead of the rocks—I could learn to hold on and let go at the same time.

The old man in Budapest had given my father's story to Paula, who had given me the story too; Sola had offered hers to Diego, and to me as well. We needed the stories to tether us to the world; sharing them among ourselves could keep us connected to the dead and to one another.

Voices were filaments in the ether.

We could live in two places at once—carry the past inside the present. We could travel faster than the speed of light.

I reached all the way across the infinity of space, I reached for Sola's hand.

ABOUT THE AUTHOR

Elizabeth Rosner is a graduate of Stanford University and received a master of fine arts in creative writing from the University of California at Irvine. Her poetry and fiction have appeared in *Poetry East, Southern Poetry Review,* and *Another Chicago Magazine,* among other publications. She lives in Berkeley, California.